MW01154048

Upon a
Pale Horse

Russell Blake

First Edition

Copyright © 2013 by Russell Blake. All rights reserved. No part of this book may be used, reproduced or transmitted in any form or by any means, electronic or mechanical, including photocopying, recording, or by any information storage or retrieval system, without the written permission of the publisher, except where permitted by law, or in the case of brief quotations embodied in critical articles and reviews. For information, contact Books@RussellBlake.com.

ISBN: 978-1491066461

Published by

Reprobatio Limited

When he opened the fourth seal, I heard the voice of the fourth living creature say, "Come!" And I looked, and behold, a pale horse! And its rider's name was Death, and Hades followed him. And they were given authority over a fourth of the earth, to kill with sword and with famine and with pestilence and by wild beasts of the earth.

Revelation 6:7-8

ONE

Flight

March 7, New York

Keith stood in line with his fellow passengers, a procession of humanity that shuffled forward with the torpor of a giant multi-legged organism. At the head of the beast, two women checked boarding passes, studiously ignoring any hint of friendly contact as they scanned bar codes with company-issued courtesy smiles.

JFK airport was packed to capacity, in its usual state of chaotic frenzy in the early evening as travelers sought to escape New York, some finishing up their business days and flying back home, others just beginning their journeys. If Keith belonged anywhere in the scheme, it was in the latter group. He was tall, with a leonine head atop broad shoulders, brown hair with flecks of gray just beginning to appear at the temples. His piercing blue eyes scanned the backs of the boarding crowd as the jet that would take them to Rome was fueled and readied. If his fellow travelers had cared enough to evaluate Keith, they would have guessed him to be a tired businessman embarking on yet another trip to cut a deal.

He shifted his weight from foot to foot, clutching his eel-skin briefcase in one hand as he adjusted the shoulder strap of his carry-on bag with the other, regarding the boarding area with casual precision, scanning the faces of the few seated stragglers for any hint of suspicion. His eyes swept the area, but as far as he could tell, nobody was paying the slightest attention to him. He was anonymous, just another in the throng, unremarkable. Just as he'd hoped he would be. He'd gotten away clean.

The icy gray deluge continued from the sullen clouds roiling over the city, occasional gusts of wind slamming sheets against the heavy glass of the

1

terminal. The ground crew wore slickers, loading baggage into the bowels of the plane as they hurried to finish their task and get back under shelter. The squall had blown in unexpectedly – yesterday had been sunny and crisp, as springtime in Manhattan could be. But overnight everything had changed, mirroring Keith's mood, the turbulent front a fitting metaphor for the storm taking place in his brain.

"Good evening sir. Welcome aboard," the gate attendant chirped at him with the sincerity of a well-trained parrot.

Keith didn't reply. Instead, he nodded and hurried forward – only to be stalled by another line at the end of the jetway as passengers waited to board. Hurry up and wait, he mused, but then his thoughts turned to other, less mundane matters.

The flight had been booked online with a one-time use debit card drawn on a bank in Bermuda – an operational account he'd kept off the books from a trip five years ago. He'd been negotiating with a financier who'd been instrumental in laundering funds for the Agency, defining the terms of his disappearance just ahead of federal prosecution for bilking his investors out of billions in a Ponzi scheme that had ensnared the wealthy across the U.S. He'd had an oily charm to him, an ease to his manner and a labile fluidity with veracity that was sociopathic, if highly effective. But as much as he'd been useful for financial errands that couldn't fly by Congress, his flamboyant lifestyle and lavish expenditures had finally caught up with him, and increasing numbers of his trusting investors had been demanding their money back. Keith's job had been to figure out how to make him vanish, and to evaluate whether he could keep his mouth shut and find a new life in Malaysia, or become another notch on a wet team's belt.

The financier hadn't listened to reason, but the problem had ceased to be a concern when his sport-fishing boat had sunk off Panama, taking all hands with it. Keith didn't question how that had been achieved – he'd merely done his job, signing off on the report that had sealed the banker's fate. The details weren't important, and Keith didn't feel a trace of responsibility. He was an analyst, and he was paid to analyze, which is what he'd done, rendering a judgment based on experience and his take on the man's stability, which wasn't good. What the Agency did with the information wasn't his problem. His job was to be right. And he was very good at it.

A stewardess greeted Keith at the jet door and directed him down the closest aisle to his row, just behind the expansive business class section, the exclusive pods roomy and lavish in comparison to his economy slot. He hefted his bags and pushed along, and experienced a momentary sense of unease he shrugged off.

Nobody was in business class – the area was unoccupied.

He stashed his carry-on in the overhead compartment and took his window seat, sliding the briefcase forward in front of his feet. Thankfully the flight looked only half full, if that. The online seating map had shown the spot next to him as being vacant on the Boeing 767, so at least he wouldn't have to contend with a chatty companion for the seven hours it would take to get him to relative safety.

Safety.

He wondered at the innocuous word – how benign it sounded, the promise it offered – and wondered whether he'd ever be safe again. He'd covered his tracks as best he could, erasing any traces of his exploration into forbidden areas of the Agency's database, a tribute to his ability to hack with the best of them – a skill that had been one of the primary reasons he'd been recruited fifteen years earlier. It had only been once his ability to predict had been noted by his superiors that he'd begun his career climb, ultimately becoming a special situations analyst, which was Agency parlance for a troubleshooter, a Jack of all trades. Keith was very smart, able to see things others missed, to assemble seemingly random variables into intelligible patterns, making sense out of the nonsensical. It had served him well, and he'd been a rising star in Langley, his future bright.

Until he'd poked his nose where it didn't belong, and began pulling on a thread that led to a discovery so shattering it challenged his reason, and made him question all the comfortable assumptions he'd made about the world – the constructs that explained why things mattered and what his place in the order was.

Why? Why couldn't he have just left it alone?

The question haunted him, but to no useful end. Once on the path, he could no more ignore the pieces falling into place than he could decide whether to be right- or left handed. It was fundamental to his nature.

But now he was the man who knew too much. He vaguely recalled a film with that title, though he'd never seen it.

The body heat from the passengers combined with the high humidity to make the interior atmosphere muggy, and Keith reached up and twisted the air on, a bead of sweat working its way down his forehead. The nozzle hissed its flow at him, and he wiped the perspiration away with the back of his hand as he looked around the cabin.

Only a few passengers in his section, just in front of the wings. Maybe twenty people, no more, all seated now, in anticipation of what would likely be a rough takeoff. He leaned over and took another glance at business class. Still no passengers. Probably a function of the economy, he mused. For all the statistics, things were still bad and getting worse, and nobody believed the official numbers anymore. Unemployment statistics ignored the legions that had been out of work for over a year, a sizeable number that was growing daily. His back-of-the-napkin calculations put the true number at more like twenty-five plus percent, not the seven or eight touted by the administration. Money was tight and getting tighter, so it didn't surprise him that the much more expensive seats up front were vacant. Everyone was cutting costs, and most could manage a few hours in a chair rather than a mini-bed for that kind of cash.

Keith pulled the in-flight magazine out of the pocket in front of him and absently browsed the entertainment section as his mind raced over his next moves. Italy would be a good base – the infrastructure typically Latin and informal, the attention to detail lackadaisical at best. Nobody would make too much of a big deal out of him checking into hotels without showing his passport, which wasn't the case in most other places.

He had enough money stashed to last him six months, maybe eight or ten if he watched his expenditures carefully, and had a second passport in a different name he could use to disappear. That was cash he had squirreled away outside of the system; his two hundred grand in stocks and bonds and the equity in his house were a write-off for now, until he could get things straightened out and figure out what he was going to do.

Assuming he ever got things straightened out.

Some things weren't fixable. His fear was that this was one of them. So disoriented was he by the revelations of the last weeks that he wasn't sure where he stood anymore. The conspiracy he'd discovered was so vast, so far-reaching, so devastating, that he had a hard time believing anything now. It was all lies. Everything.

He mentally shook himself – that kind of thinking wasn't useful, and it wouldn't get him anywhere but paralyzed with inaction, hiding in a darkened room somewhere. He needed clarity, not confusion.

The woman across from him reclined her seat with a sigh and placed her large purse in the space next to her. Keith's eyes darted from her to the glowing face of his watch. They would push back from the gate soon, and then he'd have the entire trip to ruminate over the mess he was in. A mess of his own devising.

A chime sounded on the public address system, and the fasten seat belt icon illuminated. Screens dropped from the cabin ceiling and a security video played, race-and-gender-diverse actors simulating the smiling calm with which passengers would be expected to suck at precious oxygen or exit the crash-landed sinking aircraft, as they were presumably kept afloat with a plastic life vest or a floating seat cushion in the North Atlantic's freezing seas. Two stewardesses held masks aloft and pointed at their chests, and then demonstrated how to unclip a seatbelt before warning about the potentially devastating consequences of using electronics or a cell phone while in flight.

Keith was pragmatic. He had no illusions about how the world functioned. After fifteen years in the clandestine realm, he understood that few things were as they seemed to the rank and file, and he was okay with that. But there was a line – a limit. There had to be. What he had uncovered wasn't a cynical manipulation the likes of which the Agency specialized in. This was far, far larger; and insane. There was no other word for it. If he was right, which he believed he was, it would make the Cambodian killing fields seem like a summer picnic. "Crimes against humanity" didn't even begin to cover it. Plain and simple, it was diabolical, and amounted to genocide unlike anything the world had never seen.

He fervently hoped for the umpteenth time that he was wrong.

Which wasn't likely. But he needed final confirmation from someone who could look at the data and answer his questions definitively. And all trails led to Rome. He couldn't go to anyone in the U.S. It was too dangerous, and the Agency's reach was too great there, in spite of its prohibition from running any ops on domestic soil. Over the last decade so many protections had been discarded, so many constitutional violations tacitly sanctioned, that notions of safety while in the country were a farce. Plain and simple, the government did what it wanted, due process and

Congress be damned. From personal experience he understood that the NSA could monitor every phone call, every email, every movement he made by tracking cell phones or credit cards and scanning the countless traffic cams and other surveillance gear that had been quietly installed in every American city – for the population's protection, of course. And the group responsible for what he'd discovered had been at it for fifty years at least, so there was no question that its power now was massive and all-encompassing.

Keith watched the stewardess nearest him walk down the aisle with a desultory glance at the female passenger's seat back and purse, and the tingle of anxiety in his stomach blossomed into a full-blown panic attack as she failed to tell her to return it to its upright position or stash her bag. That wasn't the protocol. Something felt wrong. The flight attendant averted her eyes, seeming to be far away as she went through the motions, and also ignored that his seatbelt wasn't fastened.

Maybe she was having a bad day. God, he knew how that was. Maybe a boyfriend had dumped her or she'd gotten news of a layoff, or the biopsy of that lump in her chest had come back with ominous findings. Countless things could explain her lack of diligence. Keith forced himself to take deep breaths and calm down. Not everything was evidence of a threat. He'd made it. He was on his way, and by the time his departure was flagged by the computers he'd have touched down and melted into the crowd.

He'd need to touch base with Becky at some point, obliquely, through some sort of a cutout, to let her know that he was okay. They'd been dating for four years, getting serious, discussions of weddings and children increasingly common, and she knew nothing of his sudden disappearance, which was for the best. If she was questioned, there wasn't much she could tell anyone that would put her at risk – all she really knew was the early part of his saga, where he'd developed a fascination with cattle.

The plane jolted as it rolled back from the gate, and then the turbines kicked up with a whine and they were taxiing in the worsening gloom towards their position, third for takeoff. The woman across the aisle's lips moved slightly as she reclined with closed eyes, and Keith realized with a start that she was praying.

Of course she was. She still believed in a God that would protect her from harm. Keith had long ago discarded those notions in favor of the harsh evidence that this was all there was. Part of him wished that he could escape into the belief of an afterlife where good deeds were rewarded; or barring that, could at least knock back a dozen mini-bottles of hard liquor to numb his soul. But it was no good. Nothing could provide solace at this point but confirmation of the truth.

The engines wound to high pitch and then he was pressed back into his seat as though by an invisible hand. Rain streaked off the wings, leaving white froth as evidence of their passage. He joined his praying cabin mate in closing his eyes, and waited for the lift into the air that would signal the true finality of his escape. The aluminum tube hurtled down the runway until physics took over, the curved upper surface of the wing creating lift at somewhere around a hundred fifty miles per hour, and the jet leapt into the sky, gray as elephant hide, and ascended into the clouds with a roar.

Sixteen minutes later, Flight 418 to Rome disappeared from JFK's radar screens, vaporizing east of Long Island, over the Atlantic.

TWO

Bad Day by the Bay

March 8, San Francisco

Jeffrey Rutherford pedaled hard as he glided between weaving cars, avoiding the cable car tracks as he wound his way through early rush hour traffic to his office in the financial district. Steam drifted from manhole covers as he crested the final rise – it was all downhill from there, the hard part of his thirty-minute commute from his flat in the Marina district done, gravity now his friend.

A foghorn sounded from the distant bay as he broke through the lingering haze on Nob Hill like a wraith on wheels, the street otherworldly under a dense blanket of fog that had yet to burn off. A bike messenger darted from an alley in front of the car he was trailing, nearly causing an accident, and he clenched down on the brakes, narrowly missing the Jaguar's rear bumper as both his tires skidded along the asphalt. The truck behind him blared its horn, as though Jeffrey were to blame for the abrupt stop, and he gave the driver the finger before swinging around and shifting through the gears, the race down the slope akin to flying as the wind whistled in his ears.

Two blocks before he hit Market Street, he rolled up onto the sidewalk and leapt nimbly from the Trek hybrid, pausing in front of the bronze glass office building's entry doors before shouldering the bicycle and carrying it into the lobby. The two security guards eyed him skeptically, as they did every morning he rode to work instead of driving his car, and the younger of the two men offered a wave.

"Top of the morning to you boys," Jeffrey called as he approached them. "You have a place for this in the back room?"

Same question every time, a comforting formality for everyone.

"Sure thing. You know the way by now."

Jeffrey walked past the bank of elevators to a steel door at the rear of the building and twisted the knob, then set his bicycle against the nearest wall and tossed his helmet on the seat. The bicycle thing had started as a concession to the girl he'd been dating a few years back, who had been all about the environment and sustainability and green living. It had seemed like a good idea at the time, and it always made him smile when he thought about how the bike had lasted a lot longer than the relationship.

The trip to the fourteenth floor was fast — there still weren't many workers arriving, it being a good forty minutes before business hours. Jeffrey stepped out of the elevator and strode down the marble-floored hall to the suite of offices leased by his employer of five years: Michelson, Roth, and Loaming, attorneys at law, where he was one of thirty associates working long hours for too little money. He ducked into the bathroom, shrugged his backpack off, and set about making himself presentable. Khaki trousers, a blue oxford button-up shirt, burgundy loafers to match his belt. Gone were the days of gray pinstripes, at least in these offices — most of the clients he met with were either high net worth captains of industry or Silicon Valley entrepreneurs, neither of whom favored formality. The senior partners still trotted out vested suits and somber dispositions, but that was all show, he knew, to give the firm an air of gravitas whenever a new prospect showed up looking for representation.

The firm dealt in intellectual property, contract law, real estate, and Jeffrey's niche, asset protection, which usually amounted to structuring things so obscenely wealthy clients didn't have to pay taxes. It hadn't been his first choice of specialties, but he'd been convinced that it would be a lucrative direction after two years working a contract law desk at another firm, and had dived into the discipline with enthusiasm when he'd gotten a whiff of the money to be made doing it right.

Which he was still waiting to see manifest in any real way. Unfortunately, even with his annual bonus, his hundred-thousand-dollar-a-year income didn't go a long way in San Francisco, and unless he made partner at some point, or went into private practice and risked it all trying to build a book of business, he was just another overworked stiff putting in very long hours to make others rich.

Studying himself in the mirror, he ran a brush through his dark brown hair and then slipped it back into his backpack along with his riding togs. At least he wasn't running to fat – the riding more than ensured that even though he was chained to a desk most of his life, he used up more than he took in. That wasn't the case for the other attorneys in their late twenties he knew. A sedentary lifestyle and no time for exercise had already worked its magic on many of his peers, and the doughy look of the well-fed and soft was the norm, as was a future of heart disease and obesity that he was hoping to avoid. He took another look at his strong cheekbones and hazel eyes and noted the slight discoloration beneath them – it had been an endless month with a heavy workload, and his normal hours now ran twelve per day at the minimum, six days a week.

The bathroom door swung open and another young man stepped in, taking in Jeffrey before he moved to a stall.

"Hey, cowboy, good morning. You trying to save a few bucks on gas again?" the newcomer asked in a mocking tone.

"Bill, you should know better. It's not the gas, it's the frigging parking. Thirty bucks a day. Who's got that kind of mad loot to throw around?" Jeffrey quipped, finishing his inspection.

"One day, my boy, one day," Bill replied. Jeffrey was all of a year younger, but Bill looked to be a decade further down the road, courtesy of too many working dinners with clients. Bill was one of the M&A group, which as far as Jeffrey could tell spent as much of its time eating and drinking with clients on their tab as doing actual work.

The toilet flushed and Bill went to the sinks and rinsed his hands, studying his crisp white shirt and dark gray slacks, then allowed his eyes to drift over to where Jeffrey was finishing with his bag.

"What have you got going for lunch today?" he asked.

"Same as ever. Chinese take-out at my desk. I'm still buried. It never stops."

"Too bad. I've got a meeting with some fat cat clients and you could come along. They could probably use some asset strategies."

"Let me take a rain check. Feel them out, and if they're serious, I'll make time. But if I go with you, I'm just going to have to stay two hours later to make up for the time I lose."

Bill shook his head. "Suit yourself. Shrimp cocktails, lobster Thermidor…Mmm."

UPON A PALE HORSE

"Eat an extra one for me."

Jeffrey made his way to his small office and dropped the backpack into a corner before confronting the heaping mound of documents on his desk. It seemed to grow overnight, papers multiplying like paper bunnies, and he groaned before squaring his shoulders and turning, reluctant to start the day before grabbing a mug of coffee. Work could wait a few more minutes – he needed to rehydrate and get some caffeine in him so he could think clearly.

In the break room, Jeffrey made small talk with one of the paralegals, Samantha, as the coffee brewed. Jeffrey didn't typically mingle with his coworkers – not due to any elitism on his part, but rather because his mind was always on other things, and he just couldn't see the point of being chatty. Samantha prattled on about what a handful her eight-year-old was, and he felt himself tuning out, as if sucked into the depths of a long tunnel where the break room was a dot at the far end. He exhaled with a palpable sense of relief when the machine was done spewing forth its brew, and waited for Samantha to pour herself a cup and leave before attending to his own.

Back in his office he sat behind his generic desk and peered at his flat-screen monitor, checking his messages for anything urgent. The usual invitations to seminars and requests for clarification clogged his inbox, but his attention was drawn to one from Cindy Lower, his ex-girlfriend – another casualty of his long hours, demanding schedule, and the general apathy they created. He clicked it open and read the terse, one-sentence message advising him that she'd slipped his key beneath his apartment door half an hour ago, and wishing him a nice life.

Short and sweet, that was Cindy's way. Another attorney he'd met at one of the neighborhood watering holes, they'd gotten along well enough, but she'd really wanted someone who didn't have as many demands as he did. Attorney-attorney relationships rarely worked, and theirs had been no different. Things had gradually grown more distant over the past four months until it was obvious to them both that it was time to move on. Jeffrey had mixed feelings about that, but when all was said and done he wasn't heartbroken – they'd shared some laughs, given it a try, and discovered that it wasn't meant to be. Their parting last week had been civil – some might say passionless – as only the conclusion of discussions between two lawyers could be, and in his mind he'd already begun to move

11

on. He was quite sure she had; Cindy wasn't one to let time slip by without her agendas being met.

He typed a single word response – *Thanks* – and went through the rest of his mail, pausing to read a few attachments dealing with jurisdictional issues and IRS bulletins on the use of non-grantor trusts. That part of his morning ritual concluded, he was just digging into the pile of contracts in front of him when his intercom buzzed at him like an angry hornet. Jeffrey stabbed the line on and leaned forward.

"Mr. Rutherford, I have a woman on two who is asking to speak to you."

"A woman? Who is it?"

"Rebecca Simms."

Jeffrey racked his brain, the name vaguely familiar, but it elicited no immediate connection with a face. He eyed his three-quarters-empty coffee cup and debated whether he could leave whoever this was on hold for a few minutes while he replenished it, and then thought better of keeping a potential client waiting.

"Sure. Put her through."

He pressed the blinking button for the held call. "Jeffrey Rutherford," he said in his best professional adult voice, always feeling like a fraud when he used it.

"Jeffrey? It's Becky."

He blinked as the name registered. It was his brother's girlfriend of now…was it three years? Could it have been that long? He'd spent a week with them on his last trip to D.C., where they both lived, and an image of a perky woman of diminutive stature with freckles drizzled across her cheeks sprang to mind.

"Becky! Sorry I didn't put two and two together on the Rebecca Simms thing. To what do I owe the pleasure?" he asked with sheepish jocularity.

"I guess nobody got in touch with you…" she said, her voice tight.

"In touch with me? About what?"

"I…I wanted you to hear it from me first, and not see it on the news," she started, and then trailed off.

A tickle of apprehension played in Jeffrey's stomach. "What's wrong, Becky? It's Keith, isn't it? Is he okay? Was he in an accident?" Jeffrey demanded.

"Yes. I mean…no, he's not okay, and yes, he was in an accident…" Becky's voice cracked on the last word, and Jeffrey's anxiety went five-alarm, dreading what was to come.

"What?" he said, standing, suddenly uncomfortable sitting down. "What happened?"

"He…he was on a plane. You probably saw the news already. It was the one that disappeared yesterday. Out of JFK."

His chest felt like someone was tightening a steel band around it, constricting his ability to breathe. "No, I didn't see anything…"

"It blew up minutes after takeoff, Jeff. No survivors. They're all dead, Jeff. Everyone's…dead. Keith's–"

The clatter of the handset against the glass protective desktop was as loud as a rifle shot in the small room.

THREE

The Italian

Rome, Italy

Antonio Carvelli read the paper as he sipped his postprandial espresso at the sidewalk café on the bustling viale Regina Margherita where he religiously retired after his exhausting lunch, taking in the young female students with an appreciative eye over the top of the day's newspaper. Pigeons dodged the hurrying pedestrians with typical Italian fearlessness, much as jaywalkers made a sport of being narrowly missed by racing traffic on the boulevards.

Two stunning brunettes clad in pants as tight as second skins meandered by, their rapid-fire discussion lost to him as a delivery truck ground its gears, the diesel engine roaring as the hapless driver struggled to find third. One of the pair's gaze darted at his position, catching his look, and smiled in a way that clearly indicated that he had not a chance in hell of ever seeing anything more of her.

Carvelli sighed and returned to his reading, his study of the local fauna concluded, at least for a time. He'd read the long article on the jet crash in the United States, noteworthy in Italy primarily because nineteen Italian tourists had been lost, and then moved to lighter fare, skimming over a long editorial parsing the finer points of some proposed immigration legislation as he digested his meal. The stance of the author was clearly anti-Muslim, voicing the popular opinion that immigrants should be free to do as they liked, as long as they conformed to the local norms and didn't try to convert Saint Paul's into a mosque or force everyone to wear veils.

Two more pages, and he was confronted with the bare upper torso of an aspiring starlet rumored to be the companion of a top government minister – not necessarily a scandal, even though he was married, because, well, look at her. It was freely understood that men were only human and could be ensnared every time if tempted with succulent flesh, especially if accompanied by alcohol. The minister had of course denied everything, which was obligatory, but nobody believed him, and the corners of Carvelli's mouth tugged upward into a small smirk as he studied her profile. He knew the man in question, and if he could muster the energy to take that on, more power to him.

The waiter returned, seeing that Carvelli's cup was empty, and placed the check on the table as he cleared it, as was his custom with the professor. Carvelli folded his paper, stood, and fished in the pocket of his immaculately tailored navy gabardine slacks to extract a wad of bills. After leafing through them, he left a generous tip. His time for introspection over, he proceeded down the sidewalk, back to his office on the campus of La Sapienza, *Università di Roma*, where he'd been a professor as well as a research scientist for the last three decades.

A stiff breeze tousled his thinning, graying hair, worn long. He donned a pair of sunglasses as he walked, traffic streaming by, everyone in a hurry, on Roman time, where the lifestyle was to rush madly. But it was a lifestyle he was accustomed to, and which he wouldn't have traded for anything – it kept him alive, feeling young and vital, even as fifty disappeared in his rear view mirror and sixty became an ominous immediacy rather than a distant destination.

Twice divorced, he kept a small apartment near the university where he spent the week before retiring to his family's country estate on weekends, usually with a young conquest in tow. He knew he was a stereotype, the lecherous academic who was only too willing to participate in the experimental phases of his students' educations, but he didn't care. Life was short, and after two failed attempts to understand the insanity of his mates, he was now a confirmed bachelor, and happier for it. His peers could snigger all they liked – he had no complaints, and only wished he'd gone down that road a decade earlier.

Carvelli turned the corner and glanced up at the front gates of the university grounds – his second home, where he'd spent most of his adult life after a brief period in the private sector, which hadn't suited his temperament. He'd inherited a fair amount of money when his parents passed on; he was one of three siblings, all legatees to a dynastic fortune of no small proportions, so he didn't have the innate drive to climb a corporate ladder in pursuit of filthy lucre. The only thing that had ever interested him was the research side of his work, and developing a better arthritis salve hadn't been his cup of tea, no matter what the pay.

As head of his department, most of his time was spent in the lab, which was as it should be. His career was punctuated by frequent publication of his abstracts and periodic books, all in his areas of specialty – epidemiology and virology. His latest had been a local hit, tracing the history of malaria and the more interesting story of the companies that had fought to develop anti-malarial drugs, only to see their innovations squashed by larger competitors who didn't want a cure cutting off their revenue from lucrative treatment patents.

That was another aspect of his work he found redeeming: He wasn't afraid to tackle controversy, and he was somewhat of a celebrity for his maverick nature and colorful condemnations of the status quo. While it was a headache for the university administration, he was now viewed as iconic, and his cynical barbs and willingness to spout off to the press his opinions on public health policy had endeared him to the citizenry, if not always to his fellow faculty members.

The afternoon flew by as he immersed himself in his work – highly speculative research into a possible cure for liver cancer involving stem cells, pioneered in his lab and now being developed by a mirror team in France and another in Germany. If early results were borne out in more comprehensive clinical trials, it could be a breakthrough that would mean an end to the disease during his lifetime, and a crowning achievement in an already noteworthy career. Unlike many of his peers, he wasn't consumed by taking credit for advances – he was confident he would be recognized when the time came, as he had been fourteen years earlier when he'd shared the Nobel Prize for his work on antiviral drug development. He was regularly consulted by large pharmaceutical companies because of his open, curious stance. Ironically, he earned five times his academic salary consulting for them, though it occupied only a scant few minutes of his time every month.

Hours drifted by, and when the daylight that streamed through his window was replaced by the soft glimmer of lamps, he put aside the sheaf of reports and rose from behind his desk. The halls were quiet now, classes long since over, and he looked at his watch with a silent curse. He'd lost track of time again, and it was already seven-thirty – later than he would have liked, given the date he'd agreed to with his latest paramour. It was a fifteen-minute walk to his building, but he wanted to shower and deal with a few errands before meeting her, and he'd be hurried now, a state of affairs he'd hoped to avoid.

He threw on his blazer and wrapped a lightweight white wool scarf around his neck, and stepped out into the hall. He paused to re-lock the door, and started when he heard an echo from down the long corridor, near the stairs – the rustle of clothes, perhaps, or maybe just the stiffening wind blowing through the ill-fitted windows, worn by the eons and as leaky as the Roman treasury. He looked up and peered down the dark passageway, but didn't detect anything troubling – the area was empty, as far as he could tell.

Even with the security provided by the university patrol, it wasn't wise to venture into dark, empty spaces at night in Rome, so he headed towards the main stairs at the other end, near the elevator, which had been out of service for a month. His footsteps reverberated off the ancient plaster walls as he descended to the main floor, where he could expect a few people to be lounging around, waiting near the security station for their rides to arrive. The sense of foreboding lifted as he rounded the banister on the second floor landing, and was forgotten by the time his feet touched the ground floor, sounds of murmured conversation drifting up to him from the front entrance foyer.

"Good night, professor," Max, the head of night security, called to him as he pushed through the tall wooden doors, hundreds of years old and burnished, rounded, and scarred by countless generations of students bustling through them.

"Night, Max," Carvelli replied over his shoulder, hands thrust into his jacket pockets against the spring evening chill.

He traced his way through the streets, past a seemingly endless procession of humanity intent on getting to important destinations as quickly as possible. Garlic and basil drifted in the air, the distinctive pungent perfume like an olfactory advertisement for the small restaurants along the way that were already packed with diners, early birds who had hoped to beat the dinner rush. His mouth flooded at the aroma, the promise of tonight's date tugging at his imagination, hungry for food and then hours of athletic frolicking with a young lady a third his age. He grinned to himself as he walked, and an old woman carrying two faded cloth shopping bags eyed him distrustfully, as though he was some kind of lunatic, which he supposed some would argue he was. Eight blocks from the university he turned the corner onto his street, the apartment only a few hundred yards further. He dodged the refuse bins that his neighbors had put out for collection the following day, holding his breath as he moved past the containers – an automatic response from his childhood, now almost unconscious from years of conditioning.

At his building, he looked around before unlocking the front door, and then mounted the stairs to his third-story *pied-a-terre*, relieved to finally be home.

On the landing, a man in a sharp business suit descended from the floor above him – a visitor, not one of his neighbors – and Carvelli was raising his keys when the man spun and drove a syringe into the back of his neck. He felt a stab of pain and cried out, but the man's black-gloved hand had clamped over his mouth, muffling it, even as another man came running up the stairs from the second floor.

The dark passageway blurred as a sensation like floating weightlessly swept through his limbs, and then everything dimmed before it went dark.

When Carvelli came to, he was sitting in his dining room, his arms bound behind him with some sort of soft fabric – maybe a necktie, he thought, as he fought to regain full awareness. His assailant was standing by the table, arms folded across his chest, studying him impassively, his eyes dead as a shark's.

"My wallet's in my jacket. I don't have anything of value other than the cash and credit cards," Carvelli said, his words sounding slurred to his ear, probably the result of the drug.

"That's fine. Very good. But we're not here to rob you, professor," the man said in a surprisingly feminine voice, the tone soft, his consonants sibilant with a latent lisp. "We're here to discuss your meeting schedule."

Carvelli's eyes darted from the man to his companion by the window, the curtains drawn, the only illumination in the room provided by the overhead lamp. "I…I don't understand."

"Perhaps. But I want you to think. Who were you supposed to meet with this week?"

"Meet? What do you mean, meet? Nobody. I don't know what you're asking."

The two men exchanged a glance that chilled Carvelli's blood, and his pulse quickened as he read the intent in their expressions.

"Really. I don't understand the question. I'm not trying to be difficult," he tried again. This was some sort of mistake. It had to be. Why were two thugs mugging him in his own house, talking in riddles?

"Are you quite sure, professor? Or should I say, doctor? That's right. We know all about you. Now let's try again. Did you receive any calls over the last week? Maybe from a foreigner asking questions, or wanting to meet?"

"A foreigner? I really have no idea what the hell you're talking about. Who are you people? What do you want?"

His interrogator shook his head, a humorless smile playing over his face, a cold thing at home in a graveyard or a slaughterhouse, cruel, no amusement in it.

"I'm afraid it's not quite that easy, professor."

Carvelli's body was found two days later. When the police broke into the apartment it had already begun decomposing, aided by the warm water in the bathtub the professor had decided to make his final resting place. Long slashes on each arm had stained the water red, and a hastily scrawled note on the kitchen table explained his inability to go on anymore in the face of the insurmountable depression he'd been battling for months.

The postmortem was perfunctory, no evidence of foul play apparent. The funeral service filled one of the larger cathedrals, the revered man honored by his friends, co-workers and students, as well as a *Who's Who* of dignitaries from the government and pharmaceutical industries. Everyone agreed that it was a shame such a brilliant mind had decided that the cold embrace of death was preferable to one more day on the planet, but then it was impossible to predict these things, and it was best to remember his notable accomplishments and contributions to the human condition rather than dwell on the manner of his passing.

Two days later an impassioned editorial from the nation's highest medical authority argued for greater investment in mental health, using the professor's last act as a cautionary tale about the risks in ignoring a problem that could affect anyone, at any time.

It was, as were all such editorials, routinely ignored by a populace weary of being taxed to death by an administration as profligate in its waste as it was larcenous in its diversion of funds to cronies and pet causes.

A week later, the incident had been forgotten, and another scandal involving a porn starlet and the president occupied the front page, the passing of an academic lacking the necessary weight to warrant a more than transient position in the news.

FOUR

Flight Redux

Jeffrey's remaining time at the office was a blur of apologies to his coworkers and condolences from the law firm as he scrambled to hand his work off to others in preparation for catching a plane. This was one of the times that his eidetic memory came in handy – he had photographic recall of every document and detail that he had in process, and so was able to delegate the minutiae on the most important projects with digital efficiency. It had been a part of him since birth, and he'd long ago moved from embarrassment over what he viewed as his freakish gift to acceptance. But he still didn't share the fact that he could recall everything he memorized to the tiniest detail, preferring to avoid calling attention to himself – although he'd won his fair share of bar bets during his college days using it to his advantage.

Becky had told him that a memorial service was planned for the following day, graciously organized by Keith's employer, the equivalent of a funeral when there was no body to inter. He'd checked flights and could get an afternoon non-stop if he hustled. She'd offered to postpone the service for another day, but Jeffrey, in a state of shock and operating on automatic pilot, had assured her that he could make it.

He ground to a halt after twenty minutes of triage on his open files. Realizing that he'd done all he could, he opened an internet browser and pulled up the news coverage on the crash. The accounts were interchangeable, long on speculation but bereft of facts. What he learned was that the plane had taken off on time, climbed per the flight plan, that the communications with the tower were routine, and that sixteen miles east of Long Island the plane disappeared, with no warning or hint of anything amiss. A big weather front had been pounding the coast, but the jet had

21

been above the clouds by the time it dropped out of the sky. Theories abounded, but they were nothing more than hurried ad hoc rationalizations for a mystery. The plain truth was that nobody knew why the plane exploded – and that it had exploded was now confirmed by the Coast Guard and search boats, which had found the debris.

He shut down his computer and estimated his timing. He'd have to leave the bike there and take a cab home, spend no more than ten minutes packing an overnight bag, and then haul ass to the airport if he was going to make it onboard. With the security screening procedures, it was an easy two-hour delay once at the airport, and he was quite sure that after a plane had gone down for no good reason the mood wouldn't be relaxed.

Jeffrey threw three fat files into his satchel, usually left in the office on bicycle days, and then pulled on his backpack. With a final glance around his modest space he moved to the door and then stopped, a sudden bout of dizziness throwing him momentarily off-balance. He took several deep breaths and the disequilibrium subsided – probably a combination of shock and a blood sugar crash from the commute; he'd skipped his post-ride breakfast bar, Becky's call having thrown his morning into disarray.

One of the senior partners met him in the hallway, a somber expression on his wizened face, his polka-dotted red bow tie a jaunty nod at what passed for creativity in the stodgy offices, and stopped in front of Jeffrey, managing to block the way with his small, wiry frame.

"Jeffrey. I'm so sorry. I wanted to tell you in person – you have the full support of the firm. Take as much time as you need," he said, his eyes revealing the lie as his lips formed the words. Every day Jeffrey wasn't working, every hour, a client would go unbilled, and money made the legal mare run. It was the lifeblood of all firms. Billable hours. A grieving sibling out of the office for days, or God forbid, a whole week, was cataclysmic. Clients paid through the nose for Jeffrey's expertise because they expected timely results, not excuses for non-performance laced with personal problems.

None of which he said. He didn't have to. Both he and Jeffrey knew the game.

"Thank you," Jeffrey said, glancing at his watch in what he hoped was an obvious manner. "I'm on my way to the airport right now. I appreciate the sentiment."

"Anything you need, you can rely on us for."

"That's comforting, sir. I appreciate it. Now, not to be rude…"

"Go do what you need to do. I just wanted to convey my deepest condolences. I've lost as well, so I know what it's like."

There wasn't anything to say to that, so Jeffrey nodded in what he hoped was a suitably grateful manner and averted his eyes – the bow-tie trembling ever so slightly from the partner's breathing was suddenly irritating beyond belief, and he was afraid to speak in case he fell apart. His older brother was dead, blown to bits over the Atlantic, and this pseudo-academic mouthed shallow aphorisms, expecting him to be appreciative? He was suddenly enraged, but choked the sentiment down. He wasn't thinking clearly. The little man was just trying to show that the firm cared. Obligatory, perhaps, but a kind gesture nonetheless.

The partner stepped out of the way, belatedly realizing that he'd delayed the young associate at an inopportune time, and Jeffrey pushed past him, trying to cover the ground between his office and the elevators without any further interruptions. He could feel the eyes of his coworkers boring into him as he passed, the news having obviously spread on the office tom-toms almost as soon as he'd called his boss. Nothing was quite as fascinating as tragedy, and Jeffrey was as close as you could get without being on the list of victims. He did his best to ignore the scrutiny and muttered a silent thanks to Providence when the elevator pinged and the highly polished stainless steel doors opened to admit him.

After a brief talk with security about his bicycle, he practically ran out the front entrance and waved to one of cabs rushing down the street. The taxi pulled to the curb a few yards past him with an almost comic screech of rubber, and Jeffrey jerked the rear door open and shouted his address as he slid onto the cracked vinyl seat.

Finally immobilized, with no more distractions, the harsh reality of his brother's death slammed into him with the force of a sledgehammer. He and Keith had been close growing up; his older sibling had been his best friend throughout their school years, when he'd guided Jeffrey and acted as a father figure when theirs had died when Jeffrey was nine, the victim of a massive coronary. Over the years they'd grown apart, a casualty of living on different sides of the country as well as both their schedules growing increasingly hectic, with Jeffrey in law school and then pulling long hours paying his dues as a freshly-minted attorney, and Keith busy building a career with the State Department. The trip to D.C. where Jeffrey had met

Becky had been the first time he'd seen his brother in three years, since their mother's funeral. Long years of closeted problem drinking had finally caught up to her in the form of massive hemorrhaging, and she'd died alone, too weak and drunk in her home in Santa Cruz to get to the phone to call for help.

And now Keith was gone. Forever.

He watched as they rolled up Lombard on the way to Van Ness, groups of homeless junkies loitering on the sidewalks only steps from some of the most impressive edifices in the Bay Area, and he shook his head, hoping to clear it. In his mind's eye the same scene kept replaying over and over – his brother's silent scream as he plummeted thousands of feet to his death in the shattered fuselage of the plane, the end of his life a foregone conclusion, but taking endless seconds to drop to the frothing surface of the cold ocean below. It was a hellish image of his own devising, the very worst-case scenario. For all he knew everyone had been killed instantly, no awareness at all that their existences had just reached an abrupt conclusion, one moment alive and fiddling with laptops and pillows, the next simply…no longer of this world.

But the certainty that the lingering horror his imagination had created for his personal viewing enjoyment was the truth wouldn't be banished to the recesses of his mind. The vision of Keith's mouth, forever frozen in a panicked O as he freefell to certain death in the towering waves below, skittered through his consciousness like an errant pinball. He closed his eyes and moaned, then opened them with a start as the driver, a turbaned immigrant who'd seen everything, by the look on his face, glanced at him in the rearview mirror.

"Hey, buddy, you okay?" he called out. The heavy Plexiglas barrier between the front seat and the rear muffled his voice, but his accent still made the second word sound like "body" to Jeffrey.

Jeffrey wondered what film the driver had picked up the seemingly obligatory cabbie phrasing from, but quickly lost interest.

"Yeah, sure. Just a bad day, is all," he said with a look that ended further inquiry.

When they reached his building, he paid the fare and told the driver that he'd want a ride to the airport in ten minutes – with his mind somewhere else, the last thing he needed was to get into an accident on the way, which was a possibility given how his morning had gone. They agreed the taxi would wait for him off the clock, and Jeffrey thanked him as he hopped out of the car and trotted to the front door, keys in hand.

Packing was easy, if morbid – a black suit, an overcoat and some underwear, along with a change of casual clothes. He still had the somber outfit from his mother's funeral, and after a quick trial of the pants to confirm that they fit, he quickly folded the garments and put them into his bag. His loafers clicked on the dull hardwood floor as he moved to the bathroom and retrieved a shaving kit, and when he stepped into the living room, ready to leave, the clock on the coffee machine confirmed he'd only been there for eight minutes.

Traffic to the airport was light, most of the cars headed the opposite direction, and Jeffrey busied himself with answering his email on his phone – mainly expressions of sympathy from his colleagues, with a few instructions from clients peppering the stream. Although he kept drifting back to the image of his brother dropping from the sky, he forced himself to respond to everyone, welcoming any diversion from his nightmarish replay.

A flock of starlings winged by overhead as the car took the airport off-ramp, the sun now out in force, glistening off their ebony feathers as they defied gravity. The driver was mercifully silent, having lost any enthusiasm for interaction, and contented himself with a dissonant tape of atonal music that most closely resembled a phalanx of car horns honking arrhythmically while a woman yowled over the din.

A sea of brake lights greeted them as they rounded a long curve, and they stopped at a hastily erected checkpoint manned by highway patrolmen with long faces and nervous dispositions – no doubt in response to the accident that had taken Keith's life, which struck Jeffrey as simultaneously typical and depressing. Never in the history of air travel had any terrorist event been foiled by police staring into cars and randomly pulling people over to search them, and yet that was unhesitatingly one of the useless responses any state of alert was met with. Because those chartered with protecting the population had to appear to be doing something, even if it was wholly pointless.

Eventually they reached the terminal. Jeffrey pushed a wad of dollars through the Plexiglas receptacle and eased out of the taxi, pulling his bag with him. Inside, a pronounced armed presence announced itself as officers with bomb-sniffing dogs moved through the lines of passengers waiting to check in. A particularly exhausted-looking beagle brushed by him, and for a moment Jeffrey and the animal locked eyes, the dog's baleful gaze resigned to a thankless shift sniffing for something it would likely never find. The sense of futility was palpable, and then the beast was past, moving to the next line, its heavily armed minder scanning the throng like he could spot trouble on looks alone.

Jeffrey swiped his credit card at the automated ticket machine, selected a seat, and collected his boarding pass, and then moved to the counter to have his ID checked. The ticket agent was courteous but mechanical as she tapped at her terminal with the warmth of an animatronic figure at an amusement park, and Jeffrey wondered whether she despised her job or was merely heavily medicated. He had watched her process the person in front of him, the transaction as impersonal as feeding change into a parking machine, and he was struck by how many interactions he had with that same dynamic. What was it that drove people to take jobs they disliked so profoundly that their only recourse was to treat their charges like objects, a subtle but unmistakable slight that was obvious yet completely deniable?

The woman handed back his ID and over-enunciated a gate number, pointing to where it was printed on the pass, lest remembering the number thirty-two overload his cognitive abilities and doom him to wandering the airport aimlessly in search of a flight that had left without him.

Why so negative and judgmental? he wondered to himself, and realized that it was his brain's way of dodging the image of his brother's final moments, combined with a healthy dose of self-loathing for not having tried harder, not having spent more time with him or called more often.

There's no rewind in life. That had been one of his brother's pet sayings, and it sprang to mind as he followed the crowd to the TSA checkpoint on the way to the gates. Indeed not. The problem with reality was that it was for keeps. As his brother knew.

The line was moving at a snail's pace, the passengers coagulated in a clump where a humorless security worker checked ID and boarding passes before the travelers sent their bags, jackets, and shoes through the X-ray machine and waited their turn to be irradiated by scanning systems that a child could defeat. Jeffrey watched as a rotund officer stood by observing one of the security team pulling a sixty-year-old Vietnamese woman aside for a more intrusive search, and bit his tongue rather than ask whether anyone really believed that going through her belongings like honey badgers after grubs would keep the skies safer.

The internal dialogue was unlike him, and once he was through he stopped at the bar and paid twelve dollars for twenty cents' worth of slightly flat draft beer, seeking the relief it would bring with a greedy, bottomless thirst. Ten minutes later he was feeling less anxious, less like he was a spectator at a bad version of the film rendition of his life, and he left a generous tip as he slid off the bar stool and went in search of his flight.

Once on board, he watched as his fellow passengers wedged their belongings in overhead bins and then closed his eyes so he wouldn't have to interact with his seat mate, a nervous-looking man with a bad oily-black comb-over who smelled vaguely of onions and peat.

As the plane gathered speed and launched up into the sky, the vision of his brother's mangled body falling into the Atlantic sprang fresh into his mind's eye, and for the rest of the five-hour flight he gladly paid a small fortune for the slim respite promised by sparkling mini-bottles of vodka, delivered by an unsmiling stewardess who clearly wished she was anywhere on the planet but tending to him.

FIVE

In Memoriam

When Jeffrey arrived at his hotel, ten minutes from the funeral home in Georgetown where the memorial service would take place the following morning, his breath smelled tainted to him, a sticky film of impending hangover coating his mouth like rancid oil. The clerk didn't seem to notice, processing his credit card with one eye on the ball game playing on an oversized flat screen monitor in the bar at the far end of the lobby. Jeffrey declined the offer of assistance with his bags, found his room on his own, and barely got his suit hung up before collapsing on the bed, the alcohol and plastic airplane food having taken their toll.

Two hours later he cracked an eye open and glared at the overhead lamp, and then rolled over and willed himself to his feet, his head pounding from the unaccustomed chemical bludgeoning he'd dealt it on the plane. He checked the time and saw that it was almost midnight, and reconciled himself to ordering room service at nosebleed prices.

After a seemingly endless wait his meal turned up, an omelet that would have been an embarrassment at any fast food restaurant, and he chewed the soggy tasteless mess with sedulous resignation, the fitting end to the worst day of his life. He set the alarm clock for eight before going into the cheerless bathroom and brushing his teeth, and then spent the rest of the night tossing and turning, each dream worse than the last.

The following morning he awoke before the buzzer went off. He took his time showering, hoping that the tepid stream would both revive him and wash his hopelessness away. Coffee in the lobby helped some, but when he caught sight of his reflection in one of the decorative mirrors by the front desk he almost didn't recognize the haunted figure staring back at him. He looked like complete shit, the travel and bad night compounding the grief etched into his young face like war wounds.

He decided to walk to the funeral home, figuring the exercise would do him good. When he stepped out into the crisp spring morning air, the chill pinched at his skin, and he pulled his overcoat tighter around him. He had an hour to get to the service, which would be just about right if he hurried, he thought. More importantly than taking his mind off his grim destination, it would ensure that he didn't have scads of extra time where he'd have to greet his brother's entourage, none of whom he knew, other than Becky.

An occasional gust of wind blew harsh against him, chilling him to the bone, unaccustomed as he was to weather this cold. His breath steamed in front of his nose in curt pants as he pushed himself to move faster, stoking his internal furnace to stave off the creeping dread that flowered at every pause. He was one of the only idiots walking, most preferring to be insulated from the elements by their cars, cocooned in privileged comfort while morning shock jocks bayed mean laughter at their own jokes. As one block became ten, the sense of heightened surrealism he'd felt at the hotel increased. Was he really on his way to his brother's funeral?

Memorial service, a voice in his head reminded. There wasn't so much as a fingernail to bury – a certainty now, judging by the morning TV reports on the search results, or more accurately, non-results. Any vestiges of the unlucky passengers had been consumed by the Atlantic, swallowed up as though they'd never existed. An image of a shark shaking a torso in its clenched jaws flitted through his thoughts and he pushed it aside, preferring a vision of his brother, smiling, sitting by the fireplace in his apartment, cradling Becky from behind, a decent budget-Bordeaux only half-finished in his Costco goblet. A shock of his usually unruly hair hung roguishly across Keith's brow, giving him an air of nonconformity he studiously cultivated – his differentiator in a gray city of cookie-cutter bureaucratic wonks. It had always amazed Jeffrey that Keith had taken a government job. With his skills and brain he could have done virtually anything, gone anywhere.

None of which ultimately mattered. Not now.

He rounded a corner and saw the red brick façade of the funeral home, an unctuous affair with colonial pretensions that was slightly wrong in the neighborhood – the brickwork too even, the wood accents on the windows and above the doors too clean, too precisely milled, too freshly painted, an artifice of antiquity created to lend an air of solemnity to an always-unpleasant farewell. Several tinted-windowed Lincoln sedans were parked nearby. Another pulled up as he approached and disgorged a couple about Keith's age clad in expensive black, the woman's face haughty and pale, the man's puffy with the tell-tale effects of frequent debauchery.

Jeffrey waited until they entered the building and glanced at the time – he was five minutes late, which was close enough. Hopefully he could get in and out with a minimum of fuss, saying his last words and slipping away like a phantom before anyone could smother him with sorrow and pity. He'd come up with a fitting eulogy on the plane and committed it to memory. Short and sweet, and if he garbled any of it, it wasn't like he would ever see any of the attendees again.

An attendant, suitably solemn, greeted him at the door and guided him to the assembly room, where twenty or so people sat on folding chairs staring at a photograph projected on a screen in front of red velvet curtains. It was a recent snapshot of his brother, by the looks of it on a boat, blue water and stainless steel railing in the background. Keith was grinning at the camera, a twinkle in his eye, merriment writ large on his features as the wind tousled his hair. Jeffrey felt his throat constrict and he struggled to swallow at the sight – there Keith was, another moment Jeffrey hadn't shared with him, participant in a life that he knew little about.

He moved to the front, where most of the seats were empty. Becky caught sight of him and stood, then hugged him awkwardly, tears in her eyes as he reciprocated, his arms around a woman who was in truth largely a stranger. She snuffled against his jacket and then pulled away, searching his face for something he couldn't give.

"You made it. I'm…I'm so glad. It would have meant a lot to him," she said in a hushed whisper as she led him by the arm to the chair next to hers.

"Of course I did. Nothing could have kept me away."

"I'm so sorry, Jeff. It's…it just doesn't feel real. Like it's some kind of horrible dream."

Jeffrey nodded. "I know the feeling, Becky. I still can't believe it."

They settled into a silent funk, each lost in their own thoughts as feet shuffled against the granite floor, restlessly waiting for the service to begin. A tall, gaunt man with gray receding hair approached the podium by the side of the raised platform immediately in front of the curtains and tapped the microphone, calling for attention from an already captive audience.

UPON A PALE HORSE

"Ahem. Welcome, everyone, and thank you for coming. We are here today to celebrate and remember the life of…" – he surreptitiously checked a slip of paper with the names of that day's services on it – "…Keith Anthony Rutherford. You here, his friends and family, were precious to him, and it's clear that he was equally precious to you. Without any further ado, I would like to invite you to come forward and speak a few words honoring him." He glanced down at the paper again and read the first name in the column on the right. "Rebecca Simms?"

Becky shivered next to Jeffrey and then exhaled as she stood, pulling her shoulders back as she stepped to the dais, now vacated by the man so that the participants could say their piece.

The orations were predictably depressing, countless anecdotes demonstrating Keith was a prince among men and that he would be forever missed. Jeffrey listened as if from a great distance, the words morphing into one long buzz as he studied the rolling slideshow that had been assembled, presumably by Becky, projected for all to view. Keith as a child. Keith and Jeffrey. Keith and his parents. Keith as an adolescent, as a teen, in college, behind the wheel of his first new car. The dull snick as each photo changed had the finality of a firing squad chambering rounds, and Jeffrey's vision blurred as tears flooded his eyes.

"Jeff. Jeffrey?" Becky was nudging him after one of Keith's co-workers had finished his heartfelt speech.

Jeffrey snapped back into the present and wiped his eyes on his jacket sleeve, then rose and went to the podium, the disorientation still threatening to drop him.

Five minutes later he returned to his seat, his eulogy a mental blank other than a vague recollection of saying he'd miss his brother forever. Two more people Jeffrey had never met spoke, and then the slideshow stopped on the first photograph again and the lights brightened by several shades as classical music was piped in from concealed speakers. Becky took his hand and they stood, waiting until everyone had been able to tell them how sorry they were for their loss, and then they found themselves in an empty room, the ordeal over. She turned to him and released him, looking like she'd aged five years in the last hour.

"That's it, I guess," she said uncertainly, a catch in her voice.

"Looks that way," he agreed.

"I'm going to miss him so much…I loved your brother, Jeffrey. I really did."

Jeffrey wanted to be alone, but his sense of decency and obligation kicked in and he found himself inviting her to have a cup of coffee with him at a nearby café. He half hoped she would decline, but she didn't, and instead merely nodded mutely, waiting for him to lead the way.

When they were seated, their order taken, Becky began talking in a low voice, sounding disjointed and unsure of herself. Time went by and they nursed their coffees as she filled Jeffrey in on their life together, their plans for the future, and then she arrived at the recent past.

"So he'd been acting strange?" Jeffrey said, echoing her words.

"Yes. It was like he was growing apart for no reason. He was working later and later, and didn't want to see me at all for the last ten days or so. I didn't even know he was going to Italy. I mean, he'd just gotten back from Europe…he had to travel for his job, but he'd tell me he was leaving town for a few days when he did. This time, nothing. I had to find out from the airline that he was on the plane to Rome."

Jeffrey wondered how much he didn't know about his brother. Could he have met someone else? He didn't voice the possibility, but it occurred to his attorney's mind that there were two sides to every story. "Did he ever act like that before?"

"Never. It was like he was a different person. At first I thought it had to do with the research he was doing, but then, when he just shut me out…"

"Research? What kind of research?" Jeffrey tried not to sound agitated, but the hair on the back of his neck prickled.

"I don't know. Something about cows."

"Cows? Was it for work?" Jeffrey sounded puzzled.

"I don't know. I mean, I don't think so. He went on and on about it, and then just closed down. It was like he became a different person…"

"Tell me how it happened. What was the project he was working on?"

Becky sighed, and then took a long sip on her coffee before signaling to the server for another one.

"It had to do with the animal mutilations that started appearing in the late sixties and continued through the eighties. Apparently thousands of cows and horses, but mainly cows, were found with their blood drained, their organs missing, and a host of other bizarre stuff. I don't know how

Keith got onto it, but you know how he was. Once he got his teeth into something, he was like a pit bull – relentless."

"And you're *sure* it wasn't work-related? I mean, I only have a sort of cursory idea what the hell he did for the State Department, but maybe it was some sort of side project?"

"No, because at first he would talk about it with me, which he never did with anything from his work. So this was all Keith."

"What did he tell you?"

"That he'd found some inconsistencies in the data and the eyewitness accounts, and was suspicious, looking for patterns."

"Suspicious of what?"

"He never said. Just that something was off."

"Off."

"That's what he said."

"And then he grew distant?"

"Yes. At first I thought it was just moodiness – some kind of midlife thing. Then I decided it was his obsessive streak again. You know how he could be. He'd disappear for days at a time, sometimes a week or more, involved in a project he couldn't talk about due to security clearances. Part of me always suspected that was a convenient cover for his nature. He would stay up all night sometimes when he was on to something. He always insisted it was for work, but I don't know…"

"Don't feel bad. He was like that as a boy, too."

"I know. I didn't take it personally. But then he stopped calling, and the few times I came by to see how he was doing, it was like he couldn't get rid of me fast enough. After years together, suddenly it was the cold shoulder. I was afraid it was another woman or something, but that wasn't Keith. He was a good guy. Quirky, but he wasn't a cheater," she pronounced with certainty.

Jeffrey hesitated, unsure of how to best respond. "No, I don't think so either. But where does that leave us? Can you think of anything else he said?" he asked.

"Well, I didn't tell anyone this, but he was freaking me out the last time I saw him." She paused and her face changed to a look of annoyance. "Damn. I almost forgot. He gave me something to give to you." She fished around in her purse. "Here. This is for you." She handed him a paper stub.

"What…what's this?"

"That's what I mean by he was acting all weird. The last thing he did before he left my place that last time, about a week and a half ago, right after getting back from Europe, was give me that. It was one of the things that made me really uncomfortable. It was like he knew he was going to die." Becky seemed to run out of steam. "Which is crazy. I'm sorry I told you. It sounds completely nuts. Unless you believe in psychic ability or whatever, which I don't. But now I'm not so sure…"

Jeffrey studied the slip of paper. At the top, in green ink, was the name of a pawn shop in Washington, D.C. It was date-stamped two weeks earlier. But the rest was unintelligible to Jeffrey, mainly because it was in Chinese, the characters meaning nothing to him.

"I've never seen a pawn ticket before, but that's what it looks like."

"That's my guess. Anyway, he made a big deal out of making sure you got it, so it was pretty important to him. Which reminds me – I have a box of his stuff at my place that you might want. Odds and ends. And there's his condo that needs to be cleaned out. I have a key to the place, but Jeff…I can't do it. I just don't have it in me. I hate to lay it on you, but there's nobody else."

"No problem, Becky. I completely understand. I don't really want to do it, either, but I'm his brother, and he would have done it for me."

"There might be some insurance from his work, or maybe a will…although he never discussed it. You'd know more about that than I would, being a lawyer and all."

Becky was doing the best she could, he could see, but she was barely holding it together. Keith's death had hit her hard. She meant well, but she wasn't equipped to deal with the details. Neither was he. But ducking it wasn't an option. Becky was the girlfriend, not the wife. Which left him.

Her coffee refill arrived and she sipped at it as he retreated into his thoughts, mentally making a list as he considered what would be involved in arranging his brother's affairs. He leaned back in his chair and eyed the sky.

"I'll have to get a death certificate and then go through his stuff to see where he banked, what broker he used, who holds his mortgage," Jeffrey said, thinking out loud.

"I can help, Jeffrey. Only…not right now. I need some time. This has changed my whole life, and I don't know what I'm going to do…"

"Of course. You've done way more than enough organizing this service, Becky. This has put you through the wringer. Don't worry about anything – I'll deal with whatever needs to be done."

"I wish I could tell you more about those last weeks, Jeff. But there just isn't much to tell. Except…well, how close were you two? Really? He didn't talk about you a lot, and I only met you that one time…"

"We used to be pretty close. It's just that when we both grew up, things got complicated. Between school and work, and him moving across the country, we sort of got wrapped up in our own lives. I guess that's my way of saying that we didn't see each other nearly as much as we should have. But it happens," Jeffrey said in a low voice, and then gazed off at the trees across the street, some of them hundreds of years old, he could tell by their height and girth.

They both sat silently for a few minutes, and then she spoke again, calmer now.

"I have a couple of photo albums too. He left them at my place one night and never bothered to pick them up. About six months ago. I'd been bugging him about his childhood for a while, and one night he showed up with a bottle of wine and the photos. I suppose you're right. He was a little odd…"

"I'll tell you what. I'm going to need some time to deal with his estate. I can't see any way of doing it without flying back out here at least one more time. Hold on to everything until I return, and we can sort things out then. This is going to take a while, so there's no rush."

She nodded and finished her coffee, then looked around as if lost. "I can't believe this is happening…"

"I know, Becky, I know."

He walked her to her car and declined the offer of a ride, preferring to walk back to the hotel. He needed to move, to cover ground, to have some silence after the grim discussion with Becky. There was a lot to mull over. And the logistics of dealing with his brother's affairs weren't going to be simple, he could already see that. He hadn't thought about it until then, but there would be a lot of things to handle, and nobody but him to do it.

Jeffrey watched her little Ford disappear around the corner, and then he set out the way he'd come, back to the hotel, more questions in his mind than answers.

A dark gray sedan pulled away from the curb a block down the street and followed Becky's car, its windows tinted dark, mud obscuring part of the license plate. Jeffrey didn't notice, nor did he register the nondescript man who took up a position a hundred yards behind him, just another working stiff carrying a briefcase and a newspaper, on his way to a tedious day of monotony.

SIX

The Agency

"What did he know?"

George Thorn, the deputy director of the CIA, shook his head and shrugged at the question, deliberately taking his time with his answer. The questioner was not a man to be trifled with – enormously powerful, and one of the richest men in the nation. Thorn had been summoned to New York to meet with him rather than addressing the entire group to which he and the man belonged. It was better if some things were kept away from the others, although the two generals in their clique knew, and in fact had helped orchestrate the latest operation.

"We're not completely sure. We do know he was poking around in areas that were sensitive. Restricted. Top secret, and not in any way related to his work."

"Yes, yes. I'm aware of all that. How he was able to gain access is another troubling matter."

Thorn looked around the room – the sitting room of a penthouse suite in the most exclusive building in Manhattan, the cost per square foot more than if it had been cast in pure gold. Two Picassos adorned the walls, along with a Renoir that belonged in a museum. The questioner, Reginald Barker, was old, old money – the kind of money that had prospered during the Second World War from funding both sides of the conflict, in addition to now owning the largest investment bank on Wall Street and having its tentacles in oil, real estate, military contractors, and Big Pharma. It was the kind of money that would never show up on any *Forbes* list – the sort that ran nations, and Barker had been actively doing just that for at least fifty of his seventy-nine years, after inheriting the mantle from his father, a hard-nosed industrialist who had taken the billion-dollar legacy he'd been handed when Barker's grandfather had died and built it into a mega-empire.

"Indeed. But don't forget that he was a computer expert. With fifteen years of experience with our systems. He ran some of our hacking groups. This was not an ordinary analyst."

"That's precisely what has me worried."

Thorn nodded. "Me too. But we believe we've contained it."

"Yes. Blowing planes out of the sky is akin to using a sledge hammer to kill a fly." Barker reached to the side table and opened an antique humidor, selecting one of the Cohibas he favored. He snipped the tip and touched it to a platinum and diamond lighter. He didn't offer Thorn one, and Thorn didn't expect it. That wasn't their relationship.

"We discussed our options. This had to be stopped immediately. As soon as we understood he was leaving the country, we needed to act. We couldn't take the chance he would escape on the other end," Thorn said.

"I see the media is treating it as another regrettable accident – an unexplained explosion. At least that's going according to plan."

"We're confident that the flight recorder won't show anything unusual."

"Then it's a dead end. Pardon the pun."

"Yes. Although we're still tying up loose ends."

"The Italian."

"No longer an issue," said Thorn with an air of finality. "He was clean."

"Nobody's clean in this," Barker spat. "He was a potential trouble spot. I'm glad he's off the table. Stupid bastard couldn't keep his fool mouth shut. It got him what he deserved."

"Yes, well, at the moment, everything is progressing nicely. Our Defense Department contacts are on board, although they aren't sure for what. Just that everything's going to change soon. Permanently."

"That's putting it mildly," Barker said, studying the fine ash on the end of his cigar, tendrils of smoke drifting to the ceiling where they were discreetly sucked into the air filtration system, to be blown out over Central Park after being run through two different types of carbon filters.

Thorn had been a close friend and confidant of Barker's for forty years, and was part of the innermost sanctum, the true hall of power. Thorn was also wealthy – not nouveau riche billionaire level like some of the members of the last administration, but seriously wealthy, which was a closely guarded secret. To most he was a tireless champion of freedom, working as the number two man in the CIA for decades, his worth unquestioned. He didn't have a private jet, didn't live in a twenty-million-dollar mansion, took reasonable vacations, had been married to a decent woman for most of his adult life, wore a stainless steel Omega watch. Thoroughly unremarkable in most ways. Which was how he liked it.

For as long as he could remember, he'd been part of the plan, which had morphed over time, but was now more urgent than ever before – not only because of Barker's advancing age, but also his own…and other factors outside his control. It had never been more important for there to be no screw-ups. A lifetime of preparation had gone into this, resources that were unimaginable devoted to this new, final phase. Nothing could be allowed to interfere with it or derail it.

Nothing.

"I'm worried that the analyst may have not taken all his secrets with him. Is there any chance that he talked?"

"Not that we can see. We're monitoring his contacts, including his girlfriend, and there hasn't been a peep. No, it looks like he was working this one on his own, which makes sense given his personality profile. It would actually be surprising if he had shared it – he was compartmentalized with his work, and drove that home with his team time and time again. I'd say there's virtually no chance that he passed anything on."

Barker fixed Thorn with a hard stare, his gray eyes cold. "We're down to the finish line. Everything's in place. The WHO program, the manufacturing, the political jockeying, everything. We're long past the point of no return, and we can't have anything interfere. Never mind the money we'll make. That's meaningless at this point. No, we're going to forever re-mold the world, solving a host of its problems in one fell swoop. You can be proud to be a part of it."

Thorn nodded, his assent obligatory. This was ground well covered, and he didn't need to be sold on it or reminded of the stakes. They were taking a bold step that would do what many privately understood was essential to the survival of the species, but were afraid to voice out loud. That was the difference between wolves and sheep. He was one of the few, the chosen, who would do what needed to be done, moral quandaries be damned. He'd devoted his entire life to this cause and didn't need convincing that it was the single most important thing that would happen. The societal, religious, and financial impact would be profound, and out of the change would emerge a new and better order. Of that he was sure.

"What steps are you taking to confirm that there's no further danger?" Barker asked, interrupting Thorn's rumination.

"We're watching the girlfriend and the brother – we're working on having NSA backdoor monitor their cell phones, but that can take weeks absent a warrant. As it is, those are probably dead ends."

"I have some thoughts on that," Barker said, taking another satisfied draw on the cigar.

When Thorn left the penthouse he felt a swell of excitement. They were so damned close to changing the course of civilization. Perhaps one day he would be remembered in the history books, but he doubted it – his contribution would be silent and unacknowledged, which was as it had to be. The world wasn't capable of grasping what they were about to do. Better to allow events to unfold, to play the part of silent spectator than catalyst. The end would justify the means, and the outcome would be its own reward.

SEVEN

Break In

Jeffrey took his time returning to the hotel, the walk helping to clear his head only a little. Once back in the lobby, he walked to the bar, which was just opening, and sat on a stool and ordered a single malt scotch, neat. The bartender nodded and rattled off the possibilities, and Jeffrey selected Glenfiddich.

The burn of the potent nectar seared his esophagus and then spread warmth from his stomach outward, numbing the worst of the anxiety that had been afflicting him all morning. The scene in the funeral home had been innocuous but painful, and the discussion with Becky puzzling. He frankly didn't know what to make of her revelations. Rather than bringing closure to his brother's death, all she had succeeded in doing was raising questions.

He ordered a second drink and mulled over his next steps: He'd need to get into Keith's place and look around, throw away anything perishable in the refrigerator, and see what files he had for clues about his brother's financial affairs. But he wasn't up to the task just yet. He felt like crap; the ceremony had sapped his energy and brought up a heaping serving of guilt large enough to bury him. And from his experience dealing with his mother's passing, he knew that he would be spending considerable time sorting through Keith's belongings and making arrangements to liquidate his condo and deal with his possessions. Death might have been final for the victim, but it created considerable work for those surviving, and once again, the burden would fall on him.

The bartender returned with a raised eyebrow, silently inquiring whether Jeffrey wanted another, and Jeffrey shook his head, ordering a beer instead. He wanted to get drunk, really drunk, pie-eyed to the point where he couldn't think, but that wasn't a solution to anything. And the lingering ache in his head from the flight's vodka-fest was still there, only partially banished by the amber elixir that sat atop the bar's middle shelf, promising blessed oblivion.

He finished his Samuel Adams and signed for the tab, a princely number that was as close to robbery you could get without brandishing a gun, and then made his unsteady way to the elevator, suddenly drained from the morning, tired in spite of the caffeine he'd ingested and wanting nothing more than to crawl under the covers and hide from the world. A few hours of napping wouldn't hurt, he reasoned as he stepped into the elevator. His face was sallow in the conveyance's mirrored back wall, and he selected his floor with a noisy exhalation while waiting for the doors to close.

In his room, he debated getting online and dealing with any incoming emails but then rejected the idea. He stripped off his suit and draped it over a chair, and then padded into the bathroom for a shower. Once done, he considered ordering room service for lunch but opted instead to throw himself onto the bed, face down, his body shuddering as he sobbed into the pillow, eventually growing still before the room was filled with the drone of his snoring.

Four hours later Jeffrey awoke, groggy and hungry. He donned his casual clothes and hefted his coat, and after a cursory glance in the mirror and a token running of a brush through his hair, he went down to the hotel restaurant and ordered a late lunch, opting for caffeinated soda rather than more booze. His head pounded like drills were boring their way through his visual cortex and into his frontal lobes, and he silently rued his decision to down the two double Scotches – a move that was unlike him, as was all his drinking in the last twenty-four hours.

But perfectly understandable, he thought, gulping a glass of water with a twist of lemon floating in it. It's not every day your only brother vaporizes in a front-page disaster. Part of him was still tugged towards getting obliterated so he wouldn't have to confront the grim errands awaiting him, but he wrestled that impulse back into the dark recesses of his mind from whence it had come. There was no point delaying the inevitable.

Jeffrey chewed his twenty-five dollar steak sandwich slowly, determined to wring every ounce of pleasure out of it as he mulled over his next move. As unappealing as it was, he'd need to go to his brother's place and deal with things there. Even as he reconciled himself to doing so, he realized that he wasn't entirely sure where it was – Keith had bought it since the last time he'd been there, taking advantage of the abrupt drop in values as the economy had nosedived.

He fished his cell out of his pocket, navigated to his address book, and punched in Becky's number. She had the key and knew the location. Maybe she'd even have a change of heart and want to give him a hand – a long shot, and way above the call of duty, he knew. The phone rang four times before she answered, sounding out of breath.

"Becky?"

"Who is this?" she snapped.

"It's me. Jeffrey. Keith's brother?" he responded, wondering if he hadn't been the only one to hit the bottle after the service.

"Oh…Jeffrey. I'm sorry. I didn't recognize your voice…"

"Is everything all right? You sound–"

"No, Jeff, it's not. I…somebody broke in while I was at the funeral home this morning. I've been burglarized. The police are here right now, taking a report…"

"Jesus. Are you okay?"

"Yeah, sure. I'm fine. It looks like they only got a few things. My laptop, the stereo…it's not like I stored diamonds here. Still…it's an invasion."

"I'm sure. Good Lord, I don't even know what to say…"

"I don't think there is anything. Don't take this the wrong way, but I'm kind of tied up right now…what did you need?"

"I wanted to see if I could stop by and get the key to my brother's place, and then I realized that I have no idea where you live, or where he did," Jeffrey admitted sheepishly.

"Oh, the key. Of course. I'll give you my address and you can come by. I think it's safe to say I'll be here for the duration."

Becky lived nine blocks north of the hotel, and Jeffrey was able to pull up a map on his phone to see the best way to get there. He debated taking a taxi but decided to walk, hopefully burning off the last of the toxic residue from his brief flirtation with alcohol poisoning. He paid the bill and used the bathroom, then pulled his coat on and exited onto the main street, striding purposefully, the sun's rays warming him in spite of the frigid air. When he reached the building he saw a squad car parked in the red zone to one side of the doors, and hurried up the four steps to the intercom panel with Becky's name neatly handwritten in blue ink on a glass-protected tab to the right of a black button. Twenty seconds later the door buzzed in response to his call. He pushed it open and climbed the stairs to the third floor, as instructed.

Becky was standing in the hall by the first door on the left, speaking in a hushed voice to a uniformed officer taking notes, his radio squawking intermittently as he completed a form. His face was slack, his eyes revealing nothing as they shifted to give Jeffrey the once over before returning to his pad and checking off another box. Jeffrey waited until he was done and had handed Becky a pen and the clipboard to sign before he approached.

Becky's eyes glistened as she looked up at him and smiled wistfully. "You found the place," she said.

"Yes. Exactly where you said it would be." Jeffrey returned the smile.

"I guess I should have said to look for the building with the cop cars in front. Nice neighborhood we have here…"

Jeffrey stepped closer and tipped his head in the direction of her door. "How bad is it?"

"See for yourself. They're about done. But there's not a lot they can do, according to Officer Klutsky here and his twin. Everyone's just going through the motions. Best they can offer is that my computer or stereo might show up on a hot sheet if the thieves try to sell them."

Jeffrey followed her a few yards to the door. She pushed it open and motioned with an open hand for him to take a look.

The room was in shambles, drawers dumped out on the floor, papers everywhere.

"Damn. Looks like it's been hit by a tornado."

"Now you know how I'll be spending my evening. The cops think it was junkies. Apparently there've been a host of robberies in the last week. The only thing that's weird to them is that it looks like the lock was picked. There's no sign of a forced entry, so they're not sure it's the same gang. The others were obvious break-ins where they jammed the lock or broke a window to get inside."

Her voice cracked as she finished and her shoulders sagged, and a small part of Jeffrey's heart broke. After all she'd been through, the timing couldn't have been worse. Before either knew what was happening, she was in his arms, sobbing against his chest as he held her tentatively, unsure what to do next. The moment only lasted a few heartbeats and then she pulled away, wiping her tears from her face with the back of her hand. He looked at the two officers conferring by the bedroom door, giving her a chance to compose herself.

"I'm…I'm sorry, Jeff. Some days really suck, you know?"

"Yeah. I do."

The two uniforms walked towards them, as unenthusiastic as any humans Jeffrey had ever seen, and offered a few insincere platitudes before excusing themselves and leaving, their work done. Becky's eyes swept around the room. She sighed, went into the kitchen, and returned holding a shiny brass ring with two keys dangling from it.

"The keys to Keith's kingdom. You're lucky — at least they didn't steal them. Oh, and here, I wrote down his address. It's about fifteen to twenty minutes away, over by Logan Circle." She checked her watch. "Unless you try it during rush hour, in which case you can double or triple that."

"Are you going to be okay here?" he asked, eyeing the mess on the floor.

"Sure. It looks worse than it is. It'll actually give me something to do besides sit here and cry, so maybe they did me a favor…"

"You're taking it way better than I would."

"What's the alternative? If I stop to consider how much bad has happened in just the last few days, I'd probably wind up in a padded room."

He nodded. "Then I'm going to get going. Let me know if you need anything."

"Do you want to take your brother's stuff? I have it in a box over there…Had. Had it in a box. Now it's that pile over by the window."

"Can I ask you to hold onto it for now? I don't know what I'm walking into at his place, and I don't want to bite off more than I can chew. Unless you want it out of here…"

"No, that's not it at all. I'll keep it until you get things under control. Don't worry about it. It's all just odds and ends, anyway. Nothing super important," she said.

They walked back to the door and he stepped across the threshold into the hallway, then gave her another hug, realizing as he did so just how little he knew her or about his brother's life. Time had a way of racing by, especially if you were busy, but that seemed like a facile, inadequate excuse now that Keith was gone forever. He made his way back down the stairs and set out for the larger street two blocks away, where with any luck he could find a taxi.

The man tailing him moved from between two buildings on the far corner and settled in a comfortable distance behind Jeffrey, who was oblivious to his shadow, his head spinning from the events of the day as he hurried to get a cab before traffic came to a standstill.

EIGHT

Legacy

"What do you mean, you lost him?" Thorn growled, his voice slightly distorted by the cell phone signal.

"He rounded the corner, and by the time I caught up he was gone. The car was paralleling him up a block, but couldn't swing around in time."

"Do you think he spotted you?"

"No. The guy's a boy scout. I think it was just unlucky timing. Besides, based on what we heard at the girl's apartment, he's headed for his brother's condo, so we can pick up the surveillance there. We've got it wired; we'll know if he so much as farts. I just wish we could get the tracking going on his cell – this is doing it the hard way."

Three seconds of silence went by, the emptiness on the line hanging heavily in the air.

"I'm working on it. Should be any minute. In the meantime, get over to the condo. And no more screw-ups. Do I make myself clear?"

"Perfectly. And if I can make a suggestion, until we have his phone live, let's get a three-man team on him. Obviously two aren't enough."

"Whatever you need. I'll make the call."

The field operative switched the line off, slipped the cell back into his pocket, and glared at his partner, sitting to his left behind the wheel of the sedan they'd been assigned, stopped at a red light.

"Get over to the condo. We know he's going there."

"Crap. Traffic's going to be a bitch headed that direction."

"Tell me something I don't already know. The big guy wasn't happy, by the way."

"No, I don't expect he was. But as you pointed out, it's not a catastrophe. We'll pick him up on that end."

"Besides which, we're probably wasting our time. You heard him. He doesn't sound like he knows anything."

"Agreed. But that's why we get paid the big bucks."

"Remind me again when that starts?"

"Soon. Really soon."

"Tell me the one about the three bears next."

The light turned green and the car in front of them surged forward, the German import's powerful engine catapulting it down the street like a heat-seeking missile. The driver stepped on the gas and their Dodge sedan lunged after it before the driver eased up with a grin.

"Wish they'd give us one of those high-roller-mobiles every now and then. Big Benz. Zero to sixty in, what, five something? This thing's lucky to get out of its own way with a tailwind."

The passenger murmured assent and reached over to stab the radio on, then settled back into his seat for another shift of waiting for the brother to do something besides go for walks and sleep.

"That's it, over there. Pull into that space. I'll only be a couple of minutes," Jeffrey said, pointing to the glowing red sign over the display window, nothing but Chinese characters advertising the shop on a blue fabric awning that provided shade from the afternoon glare.

"It's your money. But I gotta run the meter. You sure about this?" the taxi driver grumbled.

"Yeah. No problem. Like I said, it'll be quick."

The driver twisted the wheel and glided to a stop by the curb. "Suit yourself."

They were in Chinatown, having pulled beneath an ornate entrance arch with three pagoda roofs that bridged the street as they made their way to the address on the pawn slip. The sidewalks teemed with pedestrians, a sea of black hair bobbing with the steps of the locals as they rushed to whatever destinations called to them. Jeffrey swung the door open and stepped out, narrowly missing colliding with a paunchy Asian man texting intently on his phone. The man grunted and threw him a dark glare and then continued with his errand, melting back into the crowd as Jeffrey got his bearings.

The shop was nothing special from the outside, televisions, stereos, and other treasures dust-covered in the window, and Jeffrey wondered what he was doing there as he ambled through the entryway. A chime sounded in the back as he made his way to the glass display case that held watches and rings and also served as the counter. An ancient gray-haired Chinese man who resembled nothing so much as a praying mantis with a Fu Manchu mustache emerged from the rear of the shop, thick coils of cigarette smoke following him out, the city's business non-smoking ban clearly not rigidly adhered to in this neighborhood. He studied Jeffrey as if evaluating the condition of a boom box and nodded.

"What can I help you with?" he asked in surprisingly good English. Jeffrey wasn't sure what he'd been expecting, but a part of him was prepared to negotiate whatever transaction took place with sign language or in pidgin.

"I'm here to pick up an item," Jeffrey said, offering the man the ticket.

"Number two seventy. It's in the lockup. I'll get it. Wait here," the man said, then spun with surprising agility and ducked behind the beaded curtain that led into the shop's bowels.

Jeffrey's gaze skimmed the collection of odds and ends in the cases, a palpable air of desperation tainting the atmosphere – at least that part had lived up to his expectations. The items were evidence of a last resort, the financial end of the road for their owners, willing to hock them for pennies on the dollar. Jeffrey knew these places existed, but thankfully he'd never had to set foot in one until today – a day of firsts, as it turned out.

The proprietor returned carrying a guitar with a yellow tag hanging from the headstock and set it carefully on the counter before removing the paper rectangle and squinting at the numbers.

"This was one I was hoping would go into default. 1969 Fender Stratocaster. I don't need to tell you what it's worth."

Jeffrey looked the cream-colored electric guitar over, the finish faded and nicked, and nodded. He had a rough idea – both he and Keith played guitar, and this was a collector's item, no question.

"Does it have a case?" Jeffrey asked, picking the instrument up and strumming a few chords.

"No. What you see is what it came in like. That'll be three hundred sixty dollars."

"Three hundred? That's all?" Jeffrey gawped, surprised at the nominal figure.

"That's all the owner wanted. Three hundred, plus interest and my fee."

"No wonder you were hoping to never see him again," Jeffrey said, and opened his wallet. He extracted the two hundred-dollar bills he kept folded behind his driver's license in case of an emergency, and counted out the rest from the twenties he had. It left him with only sixty dollars, but he could stop at an ATM later or get money at the hotel's machine.

The owner rang up the deal and asked Jeffrey to sign the receipt. "Where's the guy who brought it in?" he asked as Jeffrey scrawled a signature.

"My brother. He had an accident."

"Ah." The single syllable contained a universe of possible meanings, like a hologram, where the smallest element encapsulated all other information within it. Jeffrey set the pen down and hoisted the guitar by the neck, careful not to bang it against anything.

"That's it?"

"Unless you wanna sell a Strat," the man shot back, his eyes half hoping that Jeffrey would take him up on it.

"Not today. Thanks…" Jeffrey said, then ducked out the door, mindful of the passers-by as he moved to the waiting taxi.

The driver didn't comment when Jeffrey arrived with a Jimi Hendrix guitar in tow. He looked at Jeffrey uninterestedly in the rearview mirror and then edged into traffic, anxious to make it to their final destination so he could finish his long shift, which had started at six that morning.

Jeffrey watched the sidewalk streak past him as the taxi wove in and out of the stream of cars, heading north towards Keith's condo, and wondered why his brother would have pawned one of his instruments – especially one that valuable, an easy twelve- to fifteen-thousand-dollar rarity. He supposed he would never know, but could understand why his brother wanted him to have it if anything happened to him. They'd both been rabid Stevie Ray Vaughn fans growing up, and had aspired to emulate the bluesy virtuoso's talent as teens, before adulthood moved them away from their dreams and into the mundane world of grownups. A 1969 Stratocaster in the right hands sounded like nothing else in the world, and Jeffrey could remember playing it when he'd come to visit, along with several other guitars Keith had acquired over the years.

The thought of jamming with his brother caused a lump to form in his throat, and he closed his eyes for the remainder of the ride, Keith's ghost visiting him in his memories as the cab bumped its way north along the shabby streets.

NINE

Memory Lane

"He's in the flat," the driver reported, listening to the feed from the condo over his ear bud.

"We'll be there in two or three minutes," his partner said. "Then it's back to hurry up and wait."

"At least he showed up, as predicted. The old man would have gone ballistic if he'd just disappeared and we'd lost him."

"Nah. Like I said, the guy's a civilian. He's got no idea we're on him."

"Probably true. Which is nothing but good for us."

"Roger that."

Jeffrey twisted the knob and inched the door open, hesitant to enter his brother's abode. Even though he knew Keith was dead, it still felt like a violation of his privacy. He drew a deep breath and peered inside the gloomy foyer, then bit the bullet and stepped across the threshold, taking care to lock the door behind him.

He glanced around, eyes roaming over the gleaming hardwood floor and contemporary furniture in the living room directly in front of him. A few pieces of Ikea art hung on the walls for color, framing the large flat screen monitor mounted above a stereo, with an adjacent cabinet containing at least two hundred CDs. Jeffrey walked over to where three guitars stood on stands in a corner and returned the Strat to its vacant stand, then slowly gazed around the room. Nothing surprising – typical Keith, a bachelor who prized music and minimalism. A few magazines sat on the coffee table in

UPON A PALE HORSE

front of the inexpensive couch – a *Guitar Player* and a *PC Weekly*. Keith's tastes obviously hadn't changed much once in D.C., right down to steadfastly refusing to buy a car.

Jeffrey moved into the bedroom and was struck by how neat and organized everything was; then reasoned that if someone had gone into his apartment back in the Bay Area they would have walked away with the same impression. Old habits died hard.

The refrigerator contained a carton of milk that didn't expire for another week, and Jeffrey found a glass and poured it full, more out of looking for something to do than thirst. He drank as he took a mental inventory of the condo's contents, then when he was finished, carefully rinsed the glass and placed it in the sink, where several others sat – also rinsed, he noted.

Jeffrey ferreted under the sink and found a box of dark green garbage bags, whipped one open, and proceeded to empty out the refrigerator. He wasn't sure when he'd be able to make it back, given his work schedule, but it could be a while. No point in letting the place turn into a science experiment in his absence.

A computer station caught his attention in the spare bedroom, which was set up as an office, and once he was done with the kitchen he walked in and slid open the file cabinet next to it. The computer was gone, which would make sense if Keith still toted a laptop everywhere, as he had as long as he'd been working. That was another habit Jeffrey and Keith shared. Of many.

Bank statements, a brokerage account, bills, mortgage payment receipts – all were neatly organized in clearly marked folders. The sense of spying on Keith again swept over Jeffrey, and he almost closed the file cabinet before shaking the feeling off and plodding forward. He looked at the mortgage – three hundred and six thousand owed. Jeffrey scanned the room again with appreciation. Keith had been an astute property buyer. He would have estimated based on the building and the neighborhood that the place was worth at least half a mil, even in the worst economy since the Great Depression. So old Keith had some equity built in, no question – the only one being, how much. That would be a subject for a real estate agent.

He opened the brokerage statements and did a quick tally. Another almost two hundred thousand in holdings as of the last summary. Jeffrey wasn't sure how much Keith earned per year, but it couldn't have been enough to sock away that sort of nest egg. But he recalled his brother telling him that he was doing well in the market, mostly with options on commodities like gold and silver. He just hadn't hinted at how well, obviously. That was ten times the money Jeffrey would have guessed he'd accumulated.

Jeffrey turned on the lights as dusk arrived and continued his investigation, Papa Chubby crooning the blues from the stereo as he moved from the office and into the master bedroom closet, where there was a safe bolted to the floor. He'd need to get that opened by a locksmith, but he didn't have the heart right then, and decided to leave it for his return. Whatever was in it could wait. It wasn't like he didn't have all the time in the world.

When his stomach rumbled, he checked the time and was surprised to see that it was already nine o'clock. Hours had raced by, and he'd been completely oblivious to their passage. Jeffrey sped up his inventory, and after another ten minutes returned to the living room, ready to call it a night. He powered the stereo down and did one final slow turn around the room.

His eye caught the shape of the Fender guitar his brother had pawned, and he stepped over to it before looking behind the couch – the natural place for a case to be stashed. Sure enough, a battered old rectangular case was wedged behind it along with the others. He freed the Fender's and popped it open, sliding the guitar home, nestled safely in the orange interior. He reached over and retrieved the paperwork he'd found and placed it inside next to the instrument then closed the latches as he felt in his pants pocket for the house keys.

Jeffrey toted the garbage and the case out into the hall, then flipped off the light and locked the door, his project completed, at least for the moment. His chest was tight with grief as he walked slowly to the garbage chute and dropped the bag into the abyss, a part of his brother going down the slide with it. He knew it made no sense, but the feeling was undeniable, and his vision blurred as he made his way to the elevator that would take him back to the lobby, away from the shadows that seemed redolent with Keith, his essence in every nook, every object. It seemed sacrilegious to have gone through his things, like raiding a cursed tomb, but Jeffrey understood the necessity. The world kept on turning, even if Keith was no longer a part of it.

The thought depressed him more than he could have described, and when he exited the building, carrying his brother's final legacy, his shoulders were hunched and he looked beaten, his steps uncertain and heavy on the cold concrete sidewalk.

The watchers exchanged glances and then the passenger got out of the car, determined not to lose him this time. He leaned forward and whispered to the driver.

"What's he got there?"

"Guitar. His brother had a bunch of them. Probably a keepsake. We've already been through everything with a fine-toothed comb. It's all clean, so it doesn't matter."

"All right. He's probably going to get another cab, so stay close. I'll call for you when he does. My money's on him returning to the hotel and getting wasted again."

"I won't take that bet," the driver said, then the door closed and he was left to the muted drone of the engine as his partner walked unhurriedly behind Jeffrey, an innocuous figure out for an evening stroll.

TEN

Hit and Run

When Jeffrey arrived at the airport at ten the following morning, on the ticketing agent's advice he paid extra to be in the first boarding group, preferring to carry the guitar onboard and stow it in the overhead bins rather than trusting it to the baggage handlers – if he was first on, he was guaranteed to have room for it.

Once on the plane, he naturally thought about his brother and the enigma he'd become. Becky's misgivings aside, it did seem odd that he hadn't told her he was taking an international trip, unless there was a good reason. And what about his unusual behavior those final days? Keith, skulking around, consumed with forty-year-old animal mutilations? What did that have to do with anything? He took Becky's agitation with a grain of salt – she wasn't necessarily firing on all cylinders with the stress, and perhaps she was seeing conspiracies where none existed.

No matter how hard he tried to make the fragments add up, though, he couldn't; and as the plane took off and ascended through the scattered clouds, he decided that he might never know what his brother had been thinking or doing. Besides which, none of that would bring him back, so it was pointless to dwell on it. Now Jeffrey needed to figure out how to move forward, not try to recreate the last weeks of his brother's existence.

When the stewardess came around, he decided to ignore his commitment to sobriety and ordered two mini-bottles of vodka, silently limiting himself to only those two, and possibly another in an hour. Just enough to stay comfortably numb and maybe doze – his night had been restless, disrupted by nightmares he couldn't remember on waking but which left him feeling like a piano had fallen on him.

He began reading a book he'd bought at the airport, a treasure hunt theme of pure escapism, and found himself nodding off before he'd made it thirty pages. The next thing he knew the plane was descending on approach to SFO, twenty-five minutes out from the airport.

On the ground, he opted to take the BART train into the city, foregoing the taxi in favor of frugality, and after a half hour ride, he disembarked at the Embarcadero station and caught a cab to his apartment. Relieved to be home after the whirlwind of travel, he set his new guitar on a stand next to his Gibson Hummingbird acoustic and unpacked his clothes, briefly debating whether to dry clean his suit before he shrugged and hung it back up in the closet – with any luck at all, it would be decades before he'd need a funeral suit again, by which time hopefully the damned thing would have rotted into nothingness, taking with it the cursed memories that were an indelible part of its fabric.

It took him an hour to clear his email inbox and get organized for work the following day, and after responding to a few of the most urgent requests, he sat down with the financial file he'd brought and began making a list of action points he would need to pursue in order to handle his brother's estate.

Becky had taken the day off from work. Cleaning her apartment more than occupied her time between long periods of staring off into space, Keith's absence like a throbbing hole in her heart that would never heal. She hadn't wanted to tell his brother, but part of what made Keith's recent distance from her so disturbing was that they'd been just about ready to set a wedding date, the time for starting a family overdue. And then he'd shut down, slowly at first, and then abruptly just before his European trip two weeks earlier. At least he'd told her about that one; not like Rome, which had taken her completely by surprise.

She placed a photograph that had been torn from its silver frame back into the protective metal rectangle and set it on the bookcase, a happy memory of better days, taken at the Washington Monument on a weekend early in their courtship: Keith grinned infectiously at the camera and Becky leaned against him, beaming like a supernova. His eyes seemed to glitter in the photo, and Becky suddenly couldn't draw breath. She looked away, crying softly, and chastised herself for her weakness. She cursed Keith: *Damn you. Damn you for leaving me alone, never to hold you again.*

The tears continued, Becky powerless to stop them, her stomach in knots as she shuddered with boundless grief. She collapsed onto the sofa and lay there, helpless, unable to do anything but mourn the loss of her soul mate – the best man she'd ever known. Why had he been on the plane? *Why, God, why?*

Eventually the emotional storm faded, replaced by a cold numbness, nothing more left in her. The reality of Keith's death came and went, and sometimes, in the quiet moments like now, it overwhelmed her.

She struggled to her feet, gazing around as if surprised that she was still in her living room, and then blew her nose into a paper towel she'd been clutching to clean the photos. This was no good. She couldn't do it. She just couldn't. It was still too fresh.

Becky returned to her cleaning, and by late afternoon she was done, the glass shards all gone, the damage hidden. Her phone rang but she ignored it, staring dully at the handset as it screeched, its strident tone filling the apartment with sound. She didn't want to talk to anyone. Not now. Maybe tomorrow, when she had to go back to work, assuming she could make it without breaking down. But not today.

Relieved to finally be finished, she went into the bathroom and twisted the shower handles on, then stripped and stood under the stream of water, letting it calm her, wash away the grit and dust, and maybe a little of the sorrow. She remained like that for half an hour, and then when her fingers resembled oblong prunes she shut it off and grabbed a thick towel from the nearby rack, taking her time drying herself before taking her measure in the vanity mirror.

She looked like shit. No surprises there. Haggard, miserable, none of the healthy glow that had been her norm as recently as a few days ago.

She opened the cabinet and retrieved her makeup, then applied a light base, evening out the discoloration beneath her eyes before dusting her cheeks with a hint of rouge. Studying the result, she shook her head. It was no use. But necessary if she was going to get something to eat – she hadn't gone shopping in days, and there was nothing left in the refrigerator but some celery and yogurt.

From her dresser, she selected a long-sleeved sweater and a pair of jeans and then grabbed a down jacket with a hood from the hall closet on her way out. Outside the building, she debated taking her car but opted to walk the three blocks to the little corner market where she could get necessities, enough to tide her over for at least a few days. It was getting dark, but her neighborhood was one of the better, relatively speaking, in a city with a deservedly bad reputation. Until yesterday's break-in, she'd never felt unsafe. How quickly everything could change.

The big delivery truck, its lights off, roared down the street and slammed into her as she crossed the intersection. Moving at over fifty miles per hour, its massive grill and heavy bumper were as deadly to a hapless pedestrian as a lethal injection. Becky was dead before her body hit the ground like a rag doll, bouncing twice and then rolling to a halt in a heap.

The truck continued on without slowing, then rounded the corner and disappeared. There would be no witnesses to come forth, no images from a conveniently located traffic camera – the one at the next intersection had gone dark earlier that day, leaving the area effectively blind.

Becky's form lay motionless in a crimson puddle, her head crushed against the hard asphalt. By the time the EMT van arrived she was already cool to the touch, another regrettable victim of the hit and runs that plagued the city in even the most upscale neighborhoods.

ELEVEN

An Offer

Jeffrey's first day back at the office was surreal, the everyday tedium punctuated by bouts of apathy that washed over him like emotional tsunamis. He found himself staring out his window for long stretches, doing nothing, as if transported elsewhere, and by the end of the work day he'd accomplished no more than fifty percent of what he'd set out to do.

As he was closing down his computer, an email from a headhunting firm hit his inbox, asking him to call one of their account executives as soon as possible about a unique opportunity. Jeffrey had never gotten one of those before, and his curiosity was piqued. He was relatively happy at his firm, but it never hurt to listen, and he found himself dialing the 800 number on his cell phone so it wouldn't show up on the company bill.

A deep voice boomed from the phone when the call connected. "Roger Anton. Can I help you?"

"Yes, Roger. My name's Jeffrey Rutherford. I got an email from your firm asking to contact you as soon as possible about an opportunity?"

"Jeffrey Rutherford. Hmm. Just a second. Let me check my files." Roger rustled some papers on his end and then returned. "Ah, here it is. Yes, something's come up, and you were identified as a perfect candidate for the position. Specialist in international asset strategies for corporations, some mergers and acquisition background, young, but suitably experienced..."

"If you don't mind my asking, who's the opening with?"

"I'm afraid that's confidential at this juncture, Mr. Rutherford. We would need to have an interview with you in order to divulge the details beyond generalities."

"Well, thanks for thinking of me, but I'm not interested in jumping through a bunch of hoops only to discover that it's someone I wouldn't want a job with," Jeffrey said. "I'm very happy with my present employer, if it's all the same to you."

"Yes, well, I can see your point. Perhaps I can share a few details with you that would sway your decision making. First, it would require relocation to the East Coast. Second, it would require signing confidentiality agreements over and above attorney-client privilege. And third, it would boast a substantial increase in pay over whatever you're making now."

"I don't really have any interest in relocation."

"Perhaps you could be persuaded." He named a figure that was more than double Jeffrey's current salary. "Bonuses have been running twenty to fifty percent of salary with this firm."

Jeffrey quickly did the math. He sat up, his attention now fully focused on the headhunter.

"And your fee?"

"Paid by the client."

Jeffrey digested that. "What's the mechanism for interviewing? I can't miss work. I recently had a death in the family and I'm already running behind."

"I'm sorry to hear that. We can do this two ways – I can fly out and meet with you tomorrow after work, or you can fly to my office the following day, on Saturday, and be back in time for cocktails Sunday."

"That's aggressive."

"They want the position filled by next week. You're on a short list we culled by surveying our contacts. The firm is prepared to make a decision by the end of the weekend, and would like the new hire to start as soon as possible. Which brings up a delicate question – how much notice would you need to give your present employer?"

Jeffrey considered the question, his heart rate increasing as the discussion became more serious. "Probably two weeks. But I could see about cutting it shorter. As long as I offered some sort of a transition plan where I could offer guidance to the team, they might let me go sooner."

"We have considerable sway, Mr. Rutherford. If you're selected as the candidate, I'll make a phone call. I know your senior partners very well. That likely wouldn't be a deal killer."

Jeffrey hesitated. "I think it would make more sense for me to fly out on Friday night or Saturday morning, so that if this proceeded to consummation, we could knock it out over the weekend. If you fly out here, I'd still need to meet the group you represent before they hired me, correct?" Jeffrey asked.

"True. Very well, then. I'll make travel arrangements for you and email them. Figure on a very early flight on Saturday, which would put you here by two, and meeting with me by three. If all goes well, we can do a dinner meeting Saturday evening, and have you back in San Francisco by mid-day Sunday."

Jeffrey thought about the proposition. That was insane money as a guaranteed salary, given his age and experience, and the bonus made it even better. His throat clenched as he imagined the increase – no more riding a bike to work and trying to nurse his ten-year-old Honda Accord along for a few more years. The car had been a gift from his mother and Keith when Jeffrey had passed the bar, but even then it had been three years old when they'd bought it, with forty thousand miles. Now, with a hundred and twenty, it was limping more than running.

He looked out at the skyline, the sun sinking below the tops of the neighboring buildings, and made a snap decision.

"Sounds like a plan. By the way, where's the firm located?"

"I'm sorry. I thought I mentioned that. It's in Washington, D.C."

TWELVE

The Interview

Saturday morning, Jeffrey was at the private jet terminal at San Francisco International Airport, walking across the tarmac to a waiting Citation X, still trying to get over the surprise of being told he was going to be flown cross country in a private jet chartered by the law firm that was interested in him. It was 5:45 a.m., and the first hesitant glimmers of dawn streaked the sky with watercolor hues as he approached the stairs. A uniformed stewardess next to it, perky as if she'd been up for hours, greeted him with a warm smile and motioned to the stairway.

"Good morning, sir. We're ready for takeoff. There's hot coffee, juice, and a variety of breakfast items on board. My name's Jennifer, and I'll be your attendant for the flight. May I take that?" she asked, gesturing to his carry-on bag.

"No, I'm fine. If we can find someplace to stow it in the cabin, that'll be good."

"Of course. Watch your step."

Jeffrey mounted the stairs, pausing to nod to the two pilots in the cockpit who were completing their pre-flight checklists.

"Good morning," the older one said, turning to him. "Ready to get going?"

"Absolutely."

Jennifer directed him to a chocolate leather seat and indicated the recliner across from him for his bag. He placed it on the seat and she ran the seatbelt through the handle before buckling it.

"Just in case we hit some bumpy air. Which is unlikely. We'll be well above the weather. Our flight plan has us at forty-three thousand feet most of the way, so it should be smooth sailing," she assured him. "Can I get you something to drink while we're waiting to taxi?"

"No thanks. Maybe some coffee once we're airborne."

"Very good, sir," she said, and moved back to close the exterior door.

Jeffrey sank into the plush leather in wonder. He'd never flown in a private plane before, and this one oozed expensive refinement, with heavy burled walnut paneling lacquered to a high gloss, leather everything, and a state-of-the-art monitor mounted forward with a U.S. map and an icon of the plane blinking on the screen.

Ten minutes later they were in first position for takeoff, and he was pushed back into his seat by the thrust of the powerful engines as they launched down the runway and then streaked up into the sky, climbing at a seemingly impossible angle before banking over the fogbank that cloaked the bay and heading east.

The trip was everything he imagined it would be, Jennifer waiting on him as if he were a visiting dignitary, anticipating his every need. He declined the offer of a cocktail, preferring to stay sharp for his meeting that afternoon, and instead focused on catching up on work, still badly behind after his three-day sabbatical. And now, here he was, winging his way back to Washington, a city he'd only been to twice before in his life.

He'd chosen a navy blue blazer and white oxford broadcloth shirt with a conservative burgundy tie that matched his belt and shoes, which nicely complemented his khaki slacks. Once they reached their cruising altitude he took off the jacket, and Jennifer hung it in a small closet at the front of the jet. As they sliced through the sky at six hundred miles per hour he wondered silently at how much the trip cost, and figured it at somewhere around fifteen grand each way, minimum. Whoever the firm was, money was obviously the least of its concerns, which boded well for his pay scheme if he got the job.

That he was interested was a given. It would be years before he would make anything like the figures bouncing around in his head, and even with the crappy East Coast weather, it was worth relocating. And it wasn't like he was married to San Francisco. Other than a few friends, more weekend drinking buddies than anything, he was footloose and fancy free, most of his college chums having moved away to careers either in New York or Los Angeles. And his romantic life was a shambles, so it wasn't like he would be making a huge sacrifice.

When they landed the sky was gray. Pregnant clouds lolled over the city, threatening an imminent downpour, which matched his mood from the last time he had been there only three days before. When he negotiated the stairs to terra firma he was assaulted by a gust of icy wind that sliced through him like he was naked. He had a brief vision of nearly nude old men running to dive into a partially frozen lake, an image from a TV commercial long forgotten, and he shivered involuntarily as he walked to the terminal.

A tall, dignified Hispanic man in a black driver's suit, replete with peaked cap, stood by the building's double doorway, a laminated red sign with his last name on it lest Mr. Rutherford somehow miss him in the crowd of one. Jeffrey followed him to a black sedan and ensconced himself in the back seat, marveling at the white glove treatment he'd received so far. If the intention had been to impress him, it was working.

The car negotiated the weekend roads with the precision of a guided missile, and in forty-five minutes it glided to a halt in the underground parking garage of a modern building only a few minutes from the White House. The driver, who hadn't said a word during the entire trip, shut off the engine, slid from behind the wheel, and rounded the vehicle to hold Jeffrey's door open for him. Jeffrey shouldered his overnight bag and followed him to an elevator, studying the man's profile as they waited for it to arrive: lean, fit, probably mid-forties, the small puckers of adolescent acne scars the only visible imperfection.

When the elevator arrived at the fourth floor, Jeffrey found himself in the granite-floored reception area of the executive search firm. A ravishing Asian woman wearing a severe business suit gave him a hundred-dollar smile from behind the reception desk.

"Mr. Rutherford? I hope your trip was pleasant?"

"Yes, thanks. Everything's been perfect so far."

"Good. Let me ring Mr. Anton and let him know you've arrived. Have a seat. Can I get you anything while you're waiting?"

"No, I'm good. Thanks, though," Jeffrey said, sitting on one of the tan leather couches.

The woman pressed something on an unseen console and murmured into her headset, then returned her gaze to Jeffrey, who was looking around the offices with polite interest. The furnishings looked expensive, as did the receptionist.

"Mr. Rutherford, please come this way. Mr. Anton will see you now."

Jeffrey followed her back into a labyrinth of offices – considerably more than he would have guessed an executive placement agency needed; but then again, he had about as much experience with that animal as he did with private jets. They arrived at a koa wood door that was partially open, and the woman gave a courtesy knock and motioned for Jeffrey to enter.

A heavyset man with thick, obviously dyed hair the color of wet straw, wearing a gray pinstripe suit that cost more than Jeffrey's car, stepped out from behind the desk, hand extended in greeting.

"Jeffrey Rutherford. The man of the hour. Welcome. Roger Anton. You can call me Roger," he said, eyeing Jeffrey the way an eagle eyes a rabbit.

Jeffrey took his hand and shook it, noting the perfectly manicured nails and the strong but not overwhelming grip. "Pleased to meet you, Roger."

"Sit," Roger invited, tapping a heavy leather upholstered chair in front of his desk. "Throw your bag by the couch and take a load off."

Jeffrey did as instructed and sat, waiting for whatever this was to begin in earnest. Roger made a token offer of a beverage, and then dived straight in, reciting the high points of Jeffrey's mundane legal career from a file on his otherwise immaculate desk, beginning with his grade point average and finishing with his last two major assignments.

"That's impressive. You really do your homework," Jeffrey conceded when he'd finished.

"Yes, we do. My company specializes in well-researched assignments, and we pride ourselves on having a stellar track record of satisfied clients. We don't invite candidates for an in-person interview unless we're already convinced they're what the doctor ordered. Fortunately for us both, you fit the bill to a tee. At least on paper. But there's a lot that a file doesn't convey, which is why I've moved mountains to get you here and give you the once-over before I introduce you to the client – one of the top law firms in this city."

"Well, fire away. I'm a captive audience," Jeffrey said with a slightly nervous smile.

The grilling lasted an hour, and Jeffrey was surprised at how well-versed on the intricacies of international corporate and banking structuring Roger was, venturing into arcane areas normally the province of highly specialized attorneys, making a few mistakes Jeffrey was sure were deliberate to test his acumen. At the end, Roger sat back, seemingly satisfied, and then fixed Jeffrey with an intense gaze, the whites of his eyes almost glowing.

"You probably have questions of your own, young man," Roger invited in a more collegial tone than the rapid-fire questioning to which Jeffrey had been subjected.

"How did you hear about me?"

Roger peered up at the ceiling and frowned. "The corporate world is a small one once you travel in exalted enough circles. Your reputation precedes you. You've done work for several clients who are known to me, and they gave you a glowing recommendation. I'm not at liberty to divulge which ones – confidentiality being my stock in trade – but suffice to say their input was impressive enough to warrant considering you when this opening came up."

"There have to be countless lawyers who specialize in this area."

"Ah. There are. But most are too old, or have their own practices, or have baggage my client would rather not deal with. As you'll see this evening, the senior partner of the firm is somewhat of a character, and has very set opinions about what sorts of personnel he takes on. One of his criteria is age – he's of the opinion that a man's best years are between the age of thirty and fifty, so he won't hire anyone over thirty-two. You're twenty-nine. You're already in charge of your own, admittedly small, staff. You're single, so you don't have two whining newborns and a wife berating you for staying late at the office. And you're still hungry – I know it when I see it. It's a given that you're very smart. All the candidates are. But honestly, you're the last interview, and in my opinion, the perfect fit."

"Fair enough. Who's the law firm?"

"Before we get too far down that road, I need you to sign a confidentiality agreement along with a boilerplate non-disclosure. Purely a formality, but an essential one."

Roger leaned forward, lifted his handset, and barked a terse instruction. Moments later another woman, this one a brunette in her thirties wearing slacks and a green silk blouse, appeared with a file and handed it to Roger before slipping out wordlessly.

"Take as long as you need to look it over," Roger said, pushing it toward Jeffrey.

It was a standard blanket NDA, no surprises, and after giving it a careful perusal Jeffrey signed it and sat back expectantly.

"My client is Garfield, Fairbanks, and Lereaux."

Jeffrey's face didn't betray his disappointment. He'd never heard of them.

"They're not a household name, but I can assure you that their client roster reads like the *Forbes* list. They're a specialized firm that augments the in-house legal departments of some of the largest corporations in the country. Banks, manufacturers, pharmaceutical giants, conglomerates, you name it. As you might have intuited, money isn't in scarce supply. Their support role in class action suits alone runs into the eight figures each year, as does their lobbying arm, and that's not their largest area of expertise. It's a relatively small group, but frankly, the pay can't be beaten, and if you do well, within a short period of time you'll be a seven-figure man."

Jeffrey swallowed, trying to remain calm at the mention of his future and undreamt-of levels of wealth in the same breath. "It sounds like a great opportunity."

"That's the understatement of the year. Look, Jeffrey, I know your firm. It's a good, solid outfit, but it's a mill, like going to work at a factory. Tell me you don't clock sixty to eighty billable hours per week. I know the drill. You've got no chance of making serious money there until you're older than I am."

"It's not that bad."

"Don't bullshit a bullshitter. Of course it is. And this is your ticket out. Look, you seem like a decent chap, so I'll lay this on the line. Whether Garfield takes you or one of the others is immaterial to me – I still get paid no matter who they hire. But you've impressed me the most, and if I recommend you, you'll get the job. So I need to know that you're onboard, and will give notice as soon as possible, and do whatever is required to move here within a matter of days. If you won't, any of the others will, so this is your moment of truth. Figure out what you want, and if you have any reservations about this, tell me now, in this room. Because once you're sitting across from Joseph Garfield, you're a shoe-in, and I don't want to waste my ammo bringing a non-starter to that table."

"I…frankly, this is extremely attractive. What you've described, running my own team, working with high-profile clients, being more than adequately rewarded…if I seem uncertain, it's because I'm just taken aback by how fast all this is happening. I mean, we only first talked a day or so ago, and now you're telling me I'm at the head of the line for a career-changer."

"Welcome to the game, Jeffrey. Don't you think you've spent enough time in the bullpen? You can't warm up for the rest of your life. Fate's smiled on you. I'd grab this with both hands and never let go."

Jeffrey nodded. It was everything any young attorney could hope for. But in spite of all of that, something was making him uneasy. Probably the pace – they were moving at Mach ten, and Jeffrey was used to driving in the slow lane. "You make a compelling argument."

Roger smiled wolfishly. "That's part of the gig, Jeffrey. Let's not beat around the bush. You want this, or not?"

Jeffrey paused, the conflicting emotions within him battling for supremacy, and then logic took over.

"Of course I do. When do I meet my new boss?"

THIRTEEN

Dinner and a Date

The driver took Jeffrey to the hotel Roger had booked for him – the Four Seasons in Georgetown. When he disembarked at the lobby entrance his sense of disbelief intensified at the sheer opulence. They were sparing no expense, and that feeling was underscored when the bellman opened his room door for him and gave him an orientation tour. Jeffrey tipped him ten dollars, reconsidering the five he was going to hand him, and when the man left Jeffrey shrugged his jacket off and plopped down on the bed, groping for the TV remote as he breathed the hotel's rarified atmosphere, a hint of something exotic, perhaps jasmine, in the air.

Dinner would be at the hotel's premier restaurant at seven, with Roger and Joseph Garfield. If there was going to be anyone else there, Roger hadn't told him, and he presumed if there were they wouldn't matter for the purposes of his evaluation. The television news was filled with the latest atrocity in the Middle East, angry mobs chanting unintelligibly for the cameras as an American flag smoldered in the background, a professionally concerned newscaster trying to flog the slim details of a bombing into a half hour of interest.

Jeffrey considered the whirlwind of unusual activity that had become his life over the last week, and wondered where this latest chapter would lead. Maybe it was time for a change. When he took all the emotion out of the decision, getting the position with Garfield would be the best thing that could ever happen to him, even if it meant suffering through some unpleasant Washington winters. As the minutes ticked away and his dinner grew near, he became more convinced that he'd made the right choice in telling Roger he wanted the job.

Downstairs, he approached the restaurant maître d' at exactly seven and was shown to a table in a secluded corner. Roger was already there, chatting with an older man dressed much like Jeffrey in a blazer and semi-casual slacks.

"Jeffrey Rutherford, meet Joseph Garfield," Roger said as they stood, and Garfield reached to shake Jeffrey's hand with an iron grip. Jeffrey did a quick scan of Garfield's face, the skin taut and smooth, a network of fine wrinkles in all the right places, his complexion glowing with prosperity, his gaze clear and hawk-like, his steel-gray eyes those of a predator at the top of the food chain.

Garfield returned the scrutiny, and after an uncomfortable few seconds he offered a professional grin, the expression as practiced and genuine as a politician's. He released Jeffrey's hand, as though he'd taken Jeffrey's measure through some sort of osmosis, and then motioned with his head at the table, where a bottle of Rioja waited on the white linen tablecloth, two Riedel goblets filled with several ruby inches, the third still empty, awaiting Jeffrey's arrival.

Jeffrey sat, taking in Garfield's lean jaw line, not an ounce of the soft-living flab that many attorneys sported as they approached the ends of their careers. Quite the opposite; Garfield seemed to project vitality and a glow almost like an aura, as if his presence had altered the physics of the atmosphere around him, imbuing it with confident energy by virtue of his moving effortlessly through it.

"A pleasure," Garfield said easily, his voice modulated, the slightest trace of a southern accent playing at the edges of the syllables. "Thank you for agreeing to fly out to meet with us. Roger here assures me it was time well spent."

"I hope so, Mr. Garfield."

"I grilled him most of the afternoon, and he still showed up for dinner, so you have to give him that," Roger said, picking up the bottle and pouring Jeffrey a generous measure. "This is excellent. I hope you like reds. One of Spain's best," he explained.

Jeffrey raised the glass to his nose, savoring the bouquet before holding it out in a toast. "Again, thanks for the hospitality."

Roger and Garfield clinked their glasses against his and took appreciative swallows, and then returned their attention to Jeffrey, who suddenly felt like something on a laboratory slide. Garfield began speaking quietly, the voice of a man accustomed to his audience paying attention to what he was saying, and described the opening Jeffrey was interviewing for, stressing the attributes he prized the most, which mirrored what Roger had already told him. The entire speech took five minutes and was as well-crafted as a Shakespearian sonnet, building at the end to the point where Jeffrey almost felt as though he should applaud.

The questioning followed. Roger sat quietly, contributing as much as a stuffed boar head while Garfield expertly raked Jeffrey over the coals, probing every aspect of his professional and private life. The interrogation was civilized but laser-focused, and after a half hour of it, interrupted only by ordering their meals, Jeffrey felt like he'd been cross-examined by an A-team prosecutor, and was clearly guilty as charged – only of what, he had no idea. Then, as abruptly and intensely as it had begun, it stopped, and Garfield returned to making small talk with Roger, seemingly having made a decision, and now focused on extracting maximum enjoyment from his filet, which he attacked with the gusto of a shipwrecked sailor.

Over coffee, Garfield reclined against his seat back and checked his cell phone for messages, then set the little device on the table and leaned forward.

"I like you, young man. Roger assured me I would, but you never know until you're in the clinch. He also indicated to me that you want the position, so it seems as though we've got a match. Welcome aboard. He'll draw up the particulars of the offer and get them to you within twenty-four hours. I've got a good feeling about this, and frankly, one of my larger clients could use your expertise sooner rather than later, which is why there's a rush. If you could start on Monday it wouldn't be soon enough, but I understand that's not feasible. As it is, I'd like you to commit to getting back here as soon as humanly possible – within a week would be best. Are you okay with picking up and leaving everything behind in San Francisco? I realize this is abrupt," Garfield asked, not really in doubt about what the answer would be, Jeffrey could tell.

"One city's pretty much like the other when you're spending most of your time in the office, sir, so I don't have any misgivings. As I told Roger, if the opportunity is substantial enough, I'll move mountains."

That was the right answer, because both men nodded, another successful deal concluded. Garfield rose, extending his hand again.

"I'm sorry. I committed to spending tonight with my wife at the opera, and it started half an hour ago. For that brief respite, I thank you, but I can't miss the entire thing or I'll never hear the end of it. Roger, you know what to do. Jeffrey, safe travels, and see you soon," he said, and then sauntered out of the restaurant, looking neither left nor right, the room seeming to shrink when he left, as though he'd taken a substantial portion of the oxygen with him.

"You weren't kidding. He's impressive," Jeffrey said to Roger, the last of the second bottle of wine all that remained in their glasses.

"You don't know the half of it. I'd say you're one lucky bastard right now. Let me pay the bill and we can get out of here; have a drink at the bar to celebrate. I'll have everything ready for you by the time you land in S.F. The plane won't be available for departure until tomorrow at one, so you can afford one nightcap," Roger said, waving off any objection with a practiced hand.

The check could have bought a timeshare, and once it was settled Roger led Jeffrey to the lounge, a contemporary affair that reeked of prosperity, and ordered two glasses of Glenlivet after taking a seat at the half-full bar. The Scotch tasted like liquid gold, and Roger ran down a checklist of items that would be in the package as they toasted and then nursed the drinks, Roger's eyes twinkling as the alcohol hit home.

Jeffrey was preparing to call it an early night when Roger nudged him and squinted over Jeffrey's right shoulder at the other end of the bar. He followed Roger's stare, and found himself looking into the dark eyes of a striking young woman – a brunette with alabaster skin, high Slavic cheekbones, and luxuriant shoulder-length hair, mid-twenties, who was just getting comfortable as she waited for her drink to arrive. His breath caught in his throat as her gaze shifted briefly to Roger, then returned to Jeffrey, a blink of merriment in it, as though they'd been caught enjoying a joke that only they were privy to.

Roger's elbow dug into his side and he leaned in, his high-octane whisper practically singeing Jeffrey's ear.

"Holy shit. What I wouldn't do to be young again. Here's some cash for the drinks – I'll leave you to this. We old dogs need our beauty rest, and if you play your cards right, you may need the flight to catch up on the sleep you miss…" Roger slipped a hundred dollar bill under Jeffrey's glass, finished his Scotch with a gulp, and dismounted from the bar stool. Jeffrey thanked him and watched him teeter off somewhat unsteadily, the potent cocktail having apparently rushed straight to his head.

The woman's drink arrived – a Cosmopolitan, one of the lounge's specialties, per the menu – and she took a grateful sip, downing a third of it before closing her eyes as if offering a silent prayer of thanks. When she opened them again, Jeffrey realized he was gawking. She smiled and the room tilted, and suddenly there was only her, everything else consigned to meaningless background noise, her teeth sparkling as a darting pink tongue flicked an errant drop from the corner of her mouth. She took another sip, this one smaller, and Jeffrey felt the liquid courage flush his face as he stood and moved to the barstool next to her.

"Excuse me. Is this seat taken?" he asked, imagining himself sounding like a modern Cary Grant in the refined environment. At least he hoped so, because the faint whiff of perfume he got was as powerful an aphrodisiac as if she'd offered him a lap dance, and at that moment he wanted to hear her voice more than anything in the universe.

"It is now, I guess," she said, the words musical, like the tinkling of exotic wind chimes on the steppes of Central Asia.

Jeffrey sat and held up his almost-empty tumbler in a cheer, and she raised her martini glass in kind, the smile returning as her eyes devoured him, a willing sacrifice to the goddess before him.

"You're almost dry," she observed, draining another third of her drink with elegant relish.

"I plan to fix that right now. Cosmo?" he asked, and she nodded. He held up two fingers to the bartender and the man nodded before busying himself with their order. Jeffrey turned back to his new friend. "Rough day?"

"You don't know the half of it," she agreed with a small shrug.

"I'll bet mine could top it," Jeffrey tried, and she gave him a skeptical look.

"I doubt it. I've just spent the last nine hours in a closed-door negotiation with some of the most tedious clods in Washington. Toward the end I wanted to stab myself in the eye with my pen just to get out of sitting there one more second."

"Ouch. Sounds horrible. Are you staying at the hotel?"

"No. I live in town. But I needed a drink after that before I go home."

"What do you do?"

She gave him an appraising glance and smiled mischievously again, raising one eyebrow in the process. "Is that a personal question?"

He blushed. Thankfully, the bartender arrived with two fresh drinks, saving him further embarrassment.

"No, no. I meant, what were you doing in the meeting? Are you an attorney or something?" he tried again.

"I wish. I'm the personal assistant to one of the bigwigs. Which means the same long hours the shiftless lawyers work for a fraction of the pay." She held her new drink up to the light, as if distrustful of it, then tasted it before nodding in approval. "What about you? What's your story?"

"I'm here for a job interview. Looks like I aced it, so I'm going to be moving to Washington soon."

"Really! Congratulations. That sounds like as good a reason as any to celebrate on a Saturday night…" She clinked the base of her glass against his. "What kind of job?" she asked, sounding genuinely interested.

Jeffrey grimaced. "I almost hate to tell you. I'm one of those shiftless lawyers who gets paid way too much for doing very little."

Her eyes widened and it was her turn to look embarrassed. "I totally didn't mean it like that…"

"No offense taken. Besides, after a day like today, drinking with a beautiful woman at the Four Seasons qualifies as one of the best things that could happen to me. Even if she hates lawyers."

"I don't hate lawyers. It was just an expression. A figure of speech."

"Oh, come on. Everyone hates lawyers. It's the American way. I know. And we mostly deserve it," he said, and she reappraised him, her eyebrow rising again in a way that he found extremely sexy. Then again, there wasn't much about her he didn't find arousing, and it wasn't just the booze talking.

"So seriously. What are you doing to celebrate your big day?" she asked.

"I was thinking about problem drinking and then passing out to TV news."

"Wow. You go, wild man. By the way, I'm Monica. What's your name?" she asked, offering a slim hand to him.

"Jeff. Jeffrey Rutherford."

"And where are you from, Jeffrey Rutherford, esquire?" she asked, a slight mocking tone in her voice.

"San Francisco. The city by the bay."

"Don't tell me you're going to sing that Journey song next."

"Only if they start karaoke early in this joint."

They enjoyed their drinks, bantering back and forth, and Jeffrey learned that Monica was born and raised in D.C., had attended Georgetown and gotten a degree in Liberal Arts, and had been working for the same corporation straight out of college for the last four years.

"I hate it, but it pays the bills."

"A familiar story. Kind of why I show up for work every day instead of going sailing."

"Really? Do you sail?"

"Not nearly enough. So tell me. What's a beautiful, intelligent young lady like you doing hanging in a place like this on a weekend night? Don't you have a date or something?"

She pouted. "Not likely in this town. The ratio of women to men is sick. Basically if it's male and has a pulse, much less a job, it's in high demand. You'll see when you move here. When is that, by the way?"

"Next week."

"Really? And have you ever been here before?"

Jeffrey decided not to mention his brother's service last Tuesday. "Once or twice. But always for short visits."

"Well, there are some pretty happening places if you know where to go. If you're with a local, I mean. In fact, I could probably be convinced to show you a few spots if you're game. I don't know what your schedule's like…"

Jeffrey's heart fluttered. "I have nothing planned. But I don't have a car."

"I do."

She slammed the rest of her drink and pushed it away, and he followed suit and waved the bartender over, paying for the drinks with the hundred Roger had left.

"Well, Jeffrey, I guess you're now my captive audience. I don't normally troll high-end hotels for out-of-town lawyers, but you're a cute one, so what the hell, you only live once," she said, the smile still in her voice, the alcohol giving her a welcome lift. "Promise you won't cut me up and bury me in a shallow grave, and we should get along fine."

"I could break a nail or strain something, so I gave that up years ago. I promise," Jeffrey intoned gravely.

She stood, and he was happy to note that her body was in keeping with her face. She filled out her outfit in all the right places, and he felt like pinching himself when she took his arm and led him out of the bar.

"All right, Jeffrey. I hope you've got some stamina, because I like to dance, and it's Saturday night. Get ready to do your best John Travolta."

"Call me Baryshnikov," he said, and they weaved into the lobby, where Monica presented her valet stub and took up position by the front entrance. A red Alfa Romeo convertible pulled up in a few minutes, and the valet held her door open as she handed him a few bills. Jeffrey squeezed himself into the passenger seat and she wedged her briefcase behind the backrest, and then she was revving the engine as they flew off the grounds and into traffic, the engine straining as she pointed the car at the flickering lights of the nation's capital, Jeffrey smiling ear to ear next to her as she raced through the gears like they were running from the law.

FOURTEEN

Monica

Between the second club and the third, Jeffrey learned that Monica lived with two roommates near Foggy Bottom – female friends from college who had banded together to make ends meet and live in a nicer district than any of them could have afforded on their own. After leaving the hotel she'd stopped outside one of dozens of buildings and disappeared, returning after a few minutes wearing jeans and a colorful top with a long overcoat protecting her svelte form from the cold. Jeffrey felt like a nerd in his business casual, but she shushed him, and by the time they'd hit the third disco they were dancing together like they'd been a couple forever, her body melding to his in a way he'd never experienced.

She explained over the music that she'd taken dance lessons for years, and at one point, when she'd been fourteen, had wanted to be a ballerina in the worst way, but competition was fierce and she'd been passed over for the scholarships that would have been necessary to do it in earnest. Not so the academic scholarship that had gotten her into Georgetown, although she'd also amassed a daunting pile of student loans that she was paying down, and would be for the foreseeable future.

Jeffrey learned Monica was single, had dumped her longtime boyfriend a year before, and was focusing on climbing the corporate ladder rather than doing the dating thing much – and frankly, she hadn't met anyone that had struck her fancy, which was understandable, based on the looks of the crowd at the dance clubs.

A slower song came on, and she emptied her drink in two swallows and grabbed his hand, pulling him onto the dance floor as the lights roved over the throng. The throbbing bass vibrated the floor as she put her arms around him, and when halfway through the song they kissed, it felt as natural as anything he'd ever done in his life.

They stayed like that for a long time, swaying back and forth as they explored each other, and when the music transitioned to another slow song they continued, moving together as one to the languorous reggaeton beat. His pulse pounded in his ears, the alcohol fueling his desire, her full lips every bit as eager as his, judging by her response.

When the music segued into an up-tempo number she moved away, and after favoring him with a long look, took his hand and led him off the floor and towards the exit. Once they were outside, she pressed up against the building's rough brick wall and pulled him towards her. This time their kiss was more urgent, the swell of his interest obvious to them both by the time they parted to breathe. She gazed up at him; then nodded and took a few steps toward the car.

"Come on. Let's find someplace quieter so you can tell me all about why you're still single," she said, and he put his arm around her protectively as they made their way into the night.

The hotel bar was still open, but as they arrived it was last call. They both ordered Cosmopolitans and settled down at a darkened corner table. Only a few die-hard patrons were still drinking, all older businessmen staying at the hotel, and the room appraised Monica as they waited for their drinks. The bartender came over with his final blending of the night, and they again toasted, having lost count of the number of cocktails they'd consumed over the last five hours.

"This has been one of the best nights ever," Jeffrey said, connecting with her glass as she giggled. "To new friends."

"Yes indeed. New friends who are great kissers."

They were both beyond tipsy, the exertion of dancing no match for the deluge of vodka they'd consumed, and she made soft cooing noises as she snuggled closer to him, her head on his shoulder, her hair a soft miracle of herbal fragrance and desirable femininity.

"This is so much better than the last time I was here," he said, and then caught himself. Nothing would kill the mood faster than him going down the morose road bemoaning his brother's death. As he thought it, he felt guilty, and she sensed that something had changed.

"What happened?" she asked, her question innocent.

Jeffrey tried to think of a way out, but he'd put his foot in it now, so he tried his best to duck the question. "Oh, it was just really depressing. A death in the family. It sucked."

She nodded and reached for her glass, moving away from him. "I'll bet it did. I'm sorry to hear it." And then the question he'd been dreading. "Who passed away?"

He killed half his drink, feeling suddenly unfocused, and then shook the feeling off. "My brother."

Time seemed to morph into atemporal sludge, and he was creeping along through viscous mud, his words like the dull rapping of a judge's gavel. Grief washed over him in slow motion, as inexorable as a falling building, and for a moment he couldn't speak. Any words he was going to try lodged in his throat with him unable to clear it. He realized even as his awareness dimmed that he'd put off dealing with his feelings about Keith's death, preferring to immerse himself first in work and now his quest for a dream job. And that dam had to break – it was just a matter of time. That he'd drunk enough to knock a prize fighter comatose hadn't helped, and he silently willed himself back into the present as he registered the shocked expression on Monica's face.

"Oh, my God, Jeff. I'm so sorry. That's…I couldn't imagine what that's like. When did it happen?"

"Not long ago. I don't think I want to talk about it tonight, though, if you don't mind. I shouldn't have said anything. I'm a crappy drunk."

She touched his face with her hand and stared deep into his eyes. "No, you aren't, Jeffrey. You may be a lot of things, but crappy isn't one of them."

And then she was kissing him, and he was lost in her again, reality condensed into a singularity encompassing only them, bright as a flash of solar radiation, their hunger a living thing that wouldn't be denied.

In the room, he barely got the door closed before she was tearing at him, tugging his shirt out of his pants, pulling at the buttons as they maintained their connection, a kiss that went on forever. She moaned into his ear as he cupped a perfect buttock with one hand and removed her top with the other, and then they were on the bed, their clothes frantically shed as they rushed to satisfy their craving. His senses flooded with her smell, and the intensity of their coupling threatened to overwhelm him. They reveled in the small miracle of their bodies' responses as they coaxed and nibbled and thrust at each other. Their rhythm began slowly and built to a crescendo. Monica cried out when she climaxed and bit his shoulder, her eyes scrunched shut as she shuddered with pleasure; and then Jeffrey came as well, spent, and collapsed against her, showering her face with kisses as they breathed together as one.

A few minutes later her gentle moaning had transformed into steady breathing, and soon Jeffrey was asleep as well, spooned against her back, her skin still slick with a sheen of passion as they dreamed together, his arm around her waist as her chest rose and fell rhythmically, two strangers now no longer alone.

FIFTEEN

Doors

"Well, good morning," Monica said, leaning on one elbow as Jeffrey's eyelids fluttered open. Bright sunlight streamed through the gauze curtains, and the glare caused him to wince, his visual reflex a nanosecond ahead of the pounding headache that assaulted him like a jilted bride.

"Good morning," he croaked back, his voice betraying him, and he struggled to sit up, the metallic film in his mouth ample evidence of the prior night's excesses. "What time is it?" he asked, glancing around for his watch.

"Ten-fifteen," she replied, reaching to the bedside table next to her and then handing him his Tag Heuer. "Why, you got a hot date with someone else?"

He jolted and hit his head against the headboard, and the pain from his hangover instantly doubled. "Shit. No, but I have a plane to catch. I've got to be at Dulles by noon – probably earlier, to get through security." He groaned as vindictive devils banged on an evil timpani inside his skull. "I have to take a shower and check out. Damn it."

"Love 'em and leave 'em, huh?" Monica teased, sliding up against him, and in spite of his misery he found his body responding. "I thought you were in a hurry," she whispered as her hand enfolded him, stroking softly.

"Priorities," he said as he turned to her.

Half an hour later he kissed her a final time and then moved to the bathroom, keenly aware that he was running unpardonably late. Monica joined him in the oversized marble stall, the warm water rinsing away the worst of the alcohol residue, and Jeffrey realized that his day was going to get much worse – he was still slightly buzzed.

God. How much had he drunk, anyway? He couldn't remember, losing track of his silent count somewhere around the middle of his time at club number two, as Monica lathered her mane next to him. Even as he berated himself for his recklessness, he marveled at her body, a thing of beauty covered in soap suds.

No time for shaving, he hurriedly pulled on a light sweater and jeans and threw his clothes into his bag as Monica dressed, her wet hair gleaming in the sunlight. He was torn, and if he'd had a choice, would have stayed the rest of the day and caught a red-eye that night. But with a private jet waiting on the runway, he didn't have that latitude. Unfortunately.

Monica inspected herself in the mirror and then pirouetted to face him. She stood on her bare tiptoes to kiss him. "You're coming back, right?" she asked when they disengaged.

"If I hadn't been planning to before, now you couldn't keep me away. Screw the Bay Area. I'm all about D.C." Jeffrey attempted to throw a gang sign, but realized halfway through that he didn't actually know any. The resultant effort looked more like he was suffering a seizure than representing his homies. Monica giggled, a lilting sound that made his heart skip. He couldn't believe how fresh she looked, like she'd slept for twelve solid hours and sipped mineral water all night.

She reached into her pocket and retrieved a business card, then moved to the table and scribbled her home number on the back with the hotel pen.

"In case you get lonely when you return. You know, if you need someone to show you around, maybe take you sightseeing," she said as she slipped it into his hand. He hesitated, and then scooped up his jacket and put it on, felt for one of his cards, and gave it to her. "My cell's on that. I won't have a home phone for more than a few more days, so it's a moot point." He paused, searching for the right words. "Monica, this has been…it's been incredible. Never in my–"

"Shhh." She held her finger to his lips and kissed him again. "Me too. Just call me, that's all I ask. Now, do you want a ride? Or do you have someone picking you up?"

He studied her. "I was going to take a taxi…"

"Not while you're in my town, you aren't. Come on. Let's get moving. I can break some land speed records and get you to the airport on time if we're lucky."

Monica wasn't exaggerating, and when she rolled to a stop at the private charter building her dashboard clock read eleven fifty-four. Jeffrey burned another three minutes kissing her, and then reluctantly swung the door open and stepped out as she popped the tiny trunk so he could retrieve his bag. He hugged her close and gave her a final kiss, and then nodded and walked briskly toward the airport, hoping he could get to the plane on time.

He needn't have been concerned – the pilots didn't seem to notice that he was late, and Jennifer was all smiles as he climbed shakily up the stairs to the plane, apparently not registering that it was all he could do to keep from vomiting.

This time, when she offered him a beverage before they took off, he opted for a Finlandia and soda, and noted with approval that she had a very heavy pour. Once the drink had hit his system he felt a little better, and at cruising altitude, after a feeble explanation that it had been a rough night, the second and third almost had him feeling human.

Roger was true to his word, and when Jeffrey got home and powered on his computer there was a large attachment in his private mail inbox with the formal terms of the offer. $200,000 annual salary, a bonus, $25,000 for relocation costs, a company car, and up to two weeks of hotel while he was looking for a place. Jeffrey read through the fine print and there was nothing unexpected or onerous, but he wanted to talk to his current employer before signing it and returning it the next day. With luck he would be headed east sooner rather than later; and now with Monica, he actually had something promising in his personal life to look forward to in addition to the job.

He ordered a pizza and scarfed down most of it before going to bed early, the three hours of sleep on the plane inadequate to relieve the worst of the pain he'd brought on himself. As he drifted off to sleep, a smile played over his face, visions of Monica filling his imagination as the soporific embrace of slumber welcomed him.

The next day, he requested a meeting first thing in the morning with the managing partners, and tendered his resignation, effective immediately.

Collier Phillip, his boss, recoiled like Jeffrey had set a live snake on his desk when he placed the single page document on his blotter.

"Jeffrey. I thought you were happy here. Tell me what's gone wrong and I'll try to make it right."

"It's not you, or the firm. I was made an offer I literally couldn't refuse."

"Well, tell us what the offer was, and perhaps there's some elasticity in your arrangement here."

Jeffrey did, and Phillip's eyes narrowed, first with a flitting look of disbelief and then the guile that Jeffrey was accustomed to.

"You're kidding, right?"

"No. That's why I took it."

"Well, I'll talk to the other partners, but that's completely out of the realm that an attorney with your limited experience could command."

"Apparently not everywhere."

Phillip grunted noncommittally. "We'll need at least a month's notice so that you can close up your files and we can find a replacement."

"I was hoping for more like a week."

"Out of the question."

The rest of the meeting didn't go well, as Phillip became increasingly adversarial. The final piece of information he wanted to know was the name of the firm that had made Jeffrey the offer. His poker face didn't slip when Jeffrey told him, but he thought Phillip's complexion flushed a few shades.

The timing issue was still a big one, so Jeffrey did as Roger had suggested and contacted him, explaining the resistance he'd encountered.

"Huh. That's not unexpected, I suppose."

"Can you help? You said that you knew some of the senior partners."

"Let me make a few calls. Don't worry about anything. I'll be back to you shortly."

Jeffrey was checking over a contract with Phillip barged into his office, a look of fury on his face.

"I don't know what kind of game you're playing, but that was the most underhanded tactic I've ever seen," he seethed.

"What are you talking about?"

Phillip made a visible effort to rein in his anger, and when he spoke again, it was with glacial calm. "You know damned well. You've got your one week. But the partners would like you to be available to consult on any open issues."

"Not a problem. I trust you won't have a problem if I bill at my new rate."

Phillip turned on his heel and stalked out. Jeffrey smiled to himself at the pompous tyrant's frustration at not being able to ride roughshod over him. The truth was that Jeffrey barely knew the man, who outside his sudden display of concern that morning treated all the associates like indentured servants chartered with doing his laundry. He had a reputation for being high-handed and arrogant, and Jeffrey had been the recipient of it more than once. Turnabout was strangely satisfying, even though Jeffrey had larger fish to fry.

His cell phone rang, and Roger's voice boomed over the line. "I took care of it."

"What did you say?"

"I merely explained how beneficial it would be to do the right thing. You'd be surprised how reasonable people can be if you just take the time to speak to them with love."

"I'll have the agreement back to you in an hour. That was the only sticking point."

"Perfect. Congratulations. Let me know when you're going to be in town, and I'll arrange for a hotel. It won't be the Four Seasons, but I trust it will be to your liking."

"Will do. I'll contact you a few days before I leave. Probably Sunday – I'll need to arrange for a moving and cleaning crew."

"You know my number. Send me an email when you want to travel, and I'll book a ticket for you. It isn't going to be on your own jet, but hopefully you can slum it some."

"I'll be in touch shortly."

He printed out the offer and signed it, initialing each page, then scanned it and emailed it back to Roger, sighing as he pressed the send button. The rest of the day flew by as he hunkered down and worked his way through the ever-present pile of agreements he needed to proof – complex licensing agreements and opinions on IRS code pertaining to their usefulness as tax avoidance vehicles. It seemed like he was just getting started when his two subordinates said goodnight at his door. He hadn't told them he was leaving, and figured he would wait until mid-week to break the news so as to avoid any ill will that might be generated by what might be construed as jumping ship.

Jeffrey had put off any serious consideration about tackling Keith's estate until he got to Washington. Being on the ground there would make things far easier, from securing a death certificate to dealing with a real estate agent. He'd considered keeping Keith's condo, but felt conflicted. It seemed most reasonable to get there and then decide – in another couple of weeks he might feel differently, but for right now all he could remember was the sense of Keith's ghost watching him as he'd cleaned out the refrigerator, and he wasn't anxious for a repeat performance any time soon. The idea of living there, sleeping in Keith's bed and using his space, seemed morbid to him and just, well, wrong. He knew it was silly, but still, he couldn't shake it.

Once home, he thought about Monica, and impulsively dialed her number on his cell, almost hanging up with the first ring. She answered ten seconds later, and after an initial bit of awkwardness, they talked for an hour, the emotions he'd been grappling with clearly mutual.

He told her that he would be flying there on Sunday, and she sounded delighted. He could practically see her smile and flashing dark eyes as she laughed easily with him, and she insisted on picking him up at the airport no matter when his flight arrived.

As he prepared for bed, he caught himself grinning more than once, and realized that he was looking forward to seeing Monica again more than any other aspect of his move east – more than the money, the career boost, the thought of a new city and a new beginning. Whatever they had experienced in their short time together had been exceptional, and he couldn't wait to be with her again in less than a week.

Jeffrey, old boy, he thought, you're already falling, and you don't really know anything about her.

Which was true, but even with the realization, the reality of his emotional response didn't change, and he thanked Providence again that his career and romantic life had taken such an abrupt and fortuitous turn. He just wished that his brother had lived to see it. Having someone to share your triumphs with made all the difference, and now he was alone in the world.

Except for Monica.

A door closed, another opened.

For now, that was the best he could do.

SIXTEEN

Getting Settled

Jeffrey hustled from the lobby of the Washington, D.C. Renaissance Hotel to where the valet waited by his new polar white BMW 550i sedan, courtesy of the firm. He'd been in Washington for seven days, and he'd been so busy with his new job he'd barely had time to think about his living situation. The hotel was covered for another week, but he had a sense of time running out, and he knew he needed to face finding a permanent place now that his meager furnishings were sitting at the moving company depot, awaiting delivery instructions.

He handed the waiting valet a five-dollar bill and slipped behind the wheel, already dialing the office, his phone synched for hands-free operation so he could focus on driving. When his secretary answered he told her he was on his way and to have his group waiting in the conference room when he arrived in ten minutes. He'd alerted her that he would be running late already, having gotten tied up on an early conference call with a client, and he didn't want to waste a breath once he was in the office.

He'd jumped right in on Monday, and after a brief orientation had been assigned a plum corporate client looking to minimize its taxes from several of its U.S. subsidiaries – exactly the sort of thing Jeffrey specialized in. He'd met with its in-house counsel and listened patiently as the three attorneys representing its interests took him through their thinking, and then gently proposed that there might be some better strategies than the outmoded ones they were considering. That had launched a flurry of activity on both their ends, which was only now coming to a head, and there was another meeting with his new firm's lawyers that afternoon to look at the alternatives he intended to propose.

Jeffrey twisted the wheel at the next light and made a left, gunning the powerful engine with satisfaction as he wound down his call. His right hand moved unconsciously to his neck and rubbed it where Monica had nipped him a little aggressively the prior night. She'd spent five of the seven nights he'd been in Washington with him, and they were growing inseparable. He'd won the romance lottery, and his horizons were now limitless – his only regret that he didn't have more time to share. Still, he would take what he could get, which was more than ample, even given his appetite for her, which was ravenous.

A uniformed attendant met him at the underground parking area of the firm's building and Jeffrey hopped out of the car, leaving it for him to park, as was the custom in the crowded area. He moved purposefully to the bank of elevators and straightened his tie as he waited for the door to open. Appearances were important to his new employer, especially when clients were expected, and he'd selected a conservative gray pinstripe suit, pastel blue shirt, and yellow paisley tie for the day, a look he hoped inspired trust and denoted aggressive thinking.

"Good morning, Sarah. Is everyone in there?" he asked once at the firm's floor, breezing by his secretary's desk.

"Yes. They're waiting for you. Can I get you some coffee?"

"Absolutely. Thank you," he called from his office, where he hung up his jacket and quickly checked his computer before heading down the hall to the conference room.

Four men and a woman, all about Jeffrey's age, sat at an oval meeting table, thick piles of contracts in front of each, and Jeffrey cut right to the chase as he took a seat.

"Good morning. Sorry, I got hung up. As you know, the client will be here at two. Where are we with the licensing deal?"

The morning ground on, the minutiae of international tax treaties the topic, and when his stomach growled, signaling lunch time, he was satisfied that they were ready for the presentation. He was in his element: five extremely smart attorneys at his beck and call, hundreds of millions of dollars on the line, with his job to create a defendable strategy so convoluted the revenue agents would never know what they were looking at – not that the conglomerate for whom he was structuring the proposal would be audited anytime soon. When you had a phalanx of lawyers and a top accounting firm working for you, the Service tended to believe that you'd done everything right.

The meeting broke up and he retreated to his office – easily three times the size of his old one. He slid open his desk drawer and extracted a breakfast bar and then grabbed his jacket on the way back out. He had an appointment with a real estate agent to look at his brother's condo, and he'd timed it for the lunch hour, trying to fit it in between his staff meeting and his client's arrival.

It took him fifteen minutes to navigate to the building, where the agent, a middle-aged woman named Jodie, stood by the front entrance, talking at a rapid-fire clip on her cell phone. She held up a finger, tendered a wan smile, and turned away from Jeffrey, walking a few paces down the block, lowering her voice so she wouldn't be overheard. Jeffrey played along, studying his messages on his phone while he waited, and then she finished the call and returned, a no-nonsense expression on her paunchy face.

"Jeffrey Rutherford. A pleasure, I'm sure. We talked on the phone. I'm Jodie," she said in a voice that had been abraded by countless cigarettes and a fair amount of hard liquor, judging by the network of ruptured veins on her nose.

"Yes. Thanks for coming. Let's go up and take a look. I only have a few minutes, and I know your time's valuable…" Jeffrey said.

"Time is money. Lead the way."

Once upstairs, Jeffrey hesitated at Keith's door, his hand betraying an almost imperceptible tremor, and then he inserted the key and pushed it open. He hadn't been back since the single visit he'd made to clean out the files, and when he stepped inside, he was relieved to find that it was just a place, nothing more – no sense of invading his brother's space or violating his memory as he and Jodie did a walkthrough.

"Well, it's in nice shape. Why are you selling it?" she asked, noting the features with a practiced eye, tapping the details into her phone as she took photos of the view, the bathroom, and the kitchen.

"I…I'm not a hundred percent sure I'm going to. But I want to understand the market. If it's the right number…" Jeffrey hadn't told her the full story and wanted to keep his options open. He'd looked at a few places, but now that he was standing in the condo again, he realized that none of them had been as nice or as centrally located. He was surprised by the direction his thinking was headed, but he gave no indication, preferring to study the view.

"I'll have to run some more comps, but my gut says six to six-fifty. This area's white hot again. It's almost completely recovered from the slump a few years back. The positives are that it's a great building, nice neighborhood, good size, modern appliances, and it eyeballs nicely. Negatives are parking, no doorman, and only two bedrooms. A lot of buyers these days have families and are looking for three, so that narrows your pool some. If it had three bedrooms, I think it would be an easy low-sevens sale." She peered at him suspiciously. "When are you going to make your decision? I might have several people who would be interested."

"Soon, Jodie. In the next week or so. Listen, I really appreciate your stopping in and looking at the place. I promise that if I list it, it'll be with you."

"You're starting to sound like a guy who isn't going to sell his place, Jeffrey. Different from on the phone," she said, calling him on what she was sensing.

"No, not at all. It's just that I want to know where I stand. I'm really leaning towards selling it. I didn't haul you out here to waste your time. I promise," he said. To his ear the assurance seemed worth about as much as a gambler's IOU.

She nodded, the exchange all part of the frog-kissing game. "I'll keep the photos in my phone, then. A week, you say?"

"Yes. I just need to do some soul searching and confirm it's really the right step. I inherited it, so it's all kind of sudden."

"I see. Did someone die in here?" she asked suspiciously.

"No. Nothing like that. No murders or suicides."

"It would be disclosable, you know."

"Sure. But nothing bad happened here. You have my word."

"All right. Whatever you say. I hope you don't think me rude, but if we're not going to list this immediately, I'd just as soon get going…"

"Of course. I'll be with you in a second," he said, taking a final glance around the living room.

"No need. I can find my own way out. Call me when you reach a decision."

The door closed behind her and Jeffrey was left to his thoughts. He wandered absently through the condo again, noting the elements he liked about it, probing like a tracking hound for any hint of his brother's aura. Nothing. Just a collection of rooms with his brother's stuff in it.

Back in the car, he cranked the engine over and pulled away from the curb, calculating what to do next. The reality was that the condo was fine – more than fine – and he could decide to sell it whenever he liked. If he took over the mortgage, his payment would be more than affordable, especially with his new prosperity, and the equity he would be inheriting would simply increase over time. From a logical standpoint, it solved a host of problems, and he didn't need to make any permanent decisions – if things didn't work out, he could move and be rid of it in no time.

Damn. He'd completely forgotten about Becky since getting caught up in his move. She still had some of Keith's stuff, and he'd promised to call. So much for honoring his commitments.

He went through his phone book until he found her number, and listened as the phone rang and then went to voice mail. At the beep, he left a brief message.

"Becky. It's Jeff. Jeffrey Rutherford. Listen, I'm in town, and I wanted to see if you could get together, or if I could stop by and pick up that box. Give me a call," he said, and then left his cell number. He debated as he drove, and then placed another call. Monica answered, her voice a welcome sound.

"Hey. I just wanted to let you know I won't be staying at the hotel much longer."

"Congratulations! You found a place. Whereabouts is it?"

"It's complicated, but the location is awesome."

He told her the story as he drove, and by the time he arrived back at the office he'd made up his mind.

Jodie wouldn't be getting the listing. At least, not yet.

The clients arrived and one of his subordinates showed them to the conference room while Jeffrey put the final touches on his proposal. He was just walking towards his office door when his cell rang, and he stopped in and scooped it up, then answered impatiently as he glanced at the time.

"Hello?" The woman's voice was unfamiliar. Tentative.

"Yes, how may I help you?" he asked.

"You called and left a message on Becky's phone."

"Yeah. I'm a friend. Who is this?" he asked, hoping that she'd get to the point before the sun set.

"Her sister. She had an accident. I don't know how well you knew her…"

Knew her?

"Not that well. What happened? Is it serious?" Jeffrey asked, his attention now fully devoted to the call.

"About as serious as it gets. She was run down by a hit-and-run driver last week. I'm afraid she's dead."

SEVENTEEN

Random Chance

That evening Jeffrey and Monica ate dinner at one of her favorite restaurants and then went over to the condo to look it over. Monica declared it perfect, and it seemed like the matter was settled – he'd spend a few days putting Keith's stuff into storage, keep most of the furniture, and then have the moving company deliver his things, leaving the bulk of his furniture to be stored with them. There were only a few items he really cared about, anyway – his clothes, his bed, his books, some personal effects. The rest could stay in storage. The condo was fully outfitted, so other than one long day boxing up everything he wanted gone, it would be painless.

Jeffrey hadn't shared with Monica the bad news about Becky, but he seemed preoccupied, and she eventually dug it out of him on the ride back to the hotel.

"It's just so…terrible. I mean, her whole world gets turned upside down when my brother dies, and then some drunk mows her down only a few days later. I don't know. It just seems so…such a waste. So cruel," he said.

"I'm so sorry, Jeffrey. Were you close?"

"No. I just saw her at the service, and had met her once before. That's it. But she was so…so vital and immediate. So alive, even distraught over my brother. And then, just like that, she's dead. None of it makes any sense. It's just so random. I think that's the part that drives me a little crazy. You cross the wrong street, or get on the wrong plane, and poof. Game over, just like that. We spend our lives thinking if we do the right things, exercise, eat right, whatever, that we have some control, but reality is that it's all completely up to chance."

"Yes, it is. Which is why we have to enjoy things while they last. There's no telling when the ride's over."

"I know. It's just that I live in a world where everything's orderly, and chaos is…it's like a personal insult."

"I don't know, Jeffrey. I mean, sometimes good things can happen out of disorder, too. Like us."

They drove in silence for a few blocks, and then she slid her hand over his. "I'm sorry about your friend. And your brother. It completely sucks, and you have every right to be angry at the universe."

"I'm not angry. Okay, that's a lie. Maybe I am. Just a little."

"If you'd hurry up and get to the hotel, I may have just what the doctor ordered to take your mind off that, mister angry man." She squeezed his fingers, and suddenly the tension seemed to seep out of him.

"Thank God I met you. I guess I can thank serendipity for that."

"No, you can thank the Four Seasons and Absolut vodka." She gave him a sly smile. "Hey, doesn't this thing go any faster?"

Jeffrey made it back to the hotel in record time.

He cleaned out the condo over that weekend, and by Sunday night his boxes had been delivered and the last of Keith's hauled off. Jeffrey and Monica ate pizza and drank Chianti while he finished arranging his possessions to his liking, and after dinner they settled on the couch with a second bottle, the stereo playing in the background as he cuddled with her. When the CD finished, she touched one of the three guitars he kept in the living room with a bare foot and leaned her head back, kissing his neck.

"So do you play those?"

"I've been known to. Although not recently."

"And you're not going to serenade me? What kind of gyp is that?"

"You really want to hear me play? It sounds more like a cat in heat than music…"

"I don't believe you. I bet you're great."

"Wow. And here I thought I was out of ways I could disappoint you."

She swatted at him playfully. "Come on. Play something."

He groaned, and then reached over and grabbed the Stratocaster. It was hopelessly out of tune, so he took a few moments to get it close, and then began picking a melody, the unamplified strings sounding twangy and hollow.

"That's not as impressive as it would be if it was plugged in," he admitted.

"Don't you have an amplifier? Or can you hook it up through the stereo?"

"My brother had one. It's in one of the closets. Are you feeling masochistic or something?"

"No more than usual. What – are you afraid you'll wake the neighbors?"

"Not really. It's just that playing an electric guitar alone, without a band or anything, is a lonely kind of thing. More for doing when nobody's around."

"Hogwash. Look at the White Stripes. Just a guitar and a female drummer. Hey, I can keep a beat."

"Don't I know it."

"I'm serious. I think guitar players are super sexy. Rowrrr."

"Let me get the amp."

He returned a minute later toting a small Marshall combo tube amplifier and a cord. After plugging it in and connecting the guitar, he slipped a pick from the plastic holder Keith had affixed to the top of the amp and fiddled with the guitar knobs.

"Damn. It isn't cooperating."

"Are you sure you know how to play it?"

"Mockery will get you nowhere, my dear," he declared, then unplugged the Strat and set it back on the stand, and grabbed the other guitar – a Les Paul junior.

A burst of distorted static flooded the room and he quickly turned down the amp's master volume, then repeated his tuning experiment and turned the guitar up.

"Remember. You asked for it. I play for free, but I charge big bucks to stop."

He strummed a few chords, and then began playing, working through a few minutes of Hendrix's "Little Wing" before turning the guitar down and setting it aside.

"Wow, you really are good. At guitar, too…" she said, and then threw her arms around him and kissed him long and hard.

He came out of the bedroom later and shut down the amp, carried what remained of the wine into the kitchen, and turned off the lights, tired and content to be home at long last.

The next day was light, his big project put to bed except for some detail work, and he was able to get out of the office at a decent hour. Monica begged off coming over so she could do laundry, having spent every night with Jeffrey that week.

He changed into sweats and considered going to the gym he'd spied three blocks away, but managed to find some computer work to do instead, dealing with some of the remaining loose ends from his old firm. As the evening wore on, he began to get hungry, and he decided to try dinner at a small pub he'd passed one street over. The burger was passable and the draft beer convincingly semi-flat as only British pubs could serve it. After an hour watching soccer he didn't care about, he made his way back to the condo for an early night by himself.

Once inside, his eye moved to the Strat, resting proudly on its stand in the corner, and he repeated his experiment with the amp. Nothing – none of the pickups seemed to work. He jiggled the jack, but all he got for his trouble was crackling.

Frustrated, he went to the kitchen and returned a few moments later with a small tool box. Grateful to have a project to occupy his time, he carefully loosened the strings, pulled the volume and tone knobs off the pots, and then set to work on the faceplate with a Phillips head screwdriver, careful not to strip the screws as he removed them.

When the last one was free, he slowly raised the plastic cover to see what the problem was – likely a broken connection by the pickup selector switch. He peered into the tangle of wires and immediately spotted the issue: The selector switch wires had been cut.

And there was a piece of paper folded up and stuffed into the wiring.

Jeffrey pulled it from the tangle and set the guitar down, and then unfolded the note. His eyes widened when he saw his brother's handwriting – a message from the dead. It was short and to the point, and as he read it his pulse accelerated by twenty beats per minute.

Jeffrey. If you're reading this, it means they got me. Sorry to lay this on you, but you're the only one I can turn to. <u>Do not trust anyone</u> – this is deep shit, and the people who killed me are serious. Assume your phone, computer, car are bugged, as well as your apartment and your work. Again – do not trust anyone. Your life is at risk if you do. Go see Professor Samuel Norton in Virginia – Google him, but always use a public computer. Then get to Zurich. Everything's in a box there at Soderbergh Bank on Bahnhoffstrasse. Box 291, Acct #42-1844. You're on the account. Password is the account number followed by our first dog's name. Good luck, and be careful, Jeffrey. You have to stop them – it's literally the end of the world. Burn this after you read it – don't write anything down, or you're a dead man. Take this seriously – I don't know how they got me, but my death should be all the proof you need. Good luck. You're going to need it.

EIGHTEEN

Them

In spite of it being a moderate sixty-nine degrees in the condo, Jeffrey's forehead broke into a sweat as he reread the missive, a deep sense of dread creeping through him at the obvious – that his brother had known he might be killed, that he knew who was trying to kill him. Part of him rejected the notion that Keith had been murdered, and then his world tilted when he recalled how his brother had died – with an entire jet full of people.

If someone had really killed him, they'd blown a jetliner out of the sky.

Jeffrey closed his eyes and confirmed that the account number, bank name, and the professor's name appeared clearly in his memory. He stood, shifting the guitar onto the cushion next to him, and headed into the kitchen. He opened a drawer and found a lighter next to some black-out candles and woodenly lit the note as instructed, then dropped the flaming paper into the sink and watched it crinkle into gray ash. After running the water and rinsing the evidence down the garbage disposal, he returned to the guitar and spliced the wires back together with a twist of each one, not bothering to solder them, but instead reassembling the faceplate and securing it with the screws, his mind racing.

What Keith had suggested was impossible; and yet he was dead. In a time of heightened security and rampant paranoia, a plane had been incinerated as easily as Keith's note, and nobody was the wiser. He'd followed the news on the investigation as recently as that morning at work, and the prevailing official theory was that a fuel tank had somehow received a stray electric charge and ignited, causing an instantaneous chain reaction and a massive explosion.

Except that he now had an assertion that the explanation was a farce. That the destruction was apparently deliberate, targeted, and that whoever had engineered it had seen no problem with killing hundreds in order to get one man.

His brother.

Who apparently either knew about, or had stumbled across, some kind of scheme that was so big it would change the world.

A chill ran up his spine as he processed the rest of the information – which implied that whoever had killed his brother not only had the power to mount a successful cover-up of the true cause of the plane explosion, but could apparently also mount surveillance on him – simply because he was Keith's brother.

There weren't too many organizations that could blow a jet to dust and get away with it, and that had the capacity to bug everything in Jeffrey's universe. He could only think of one. The government. Which was unbelievable. The U.S. didn't go around blowing up its citizens.

Did it?

If that speculation was correct, Jeffrey was being asked from the grave to take on the most powerful entity in the world. To stop…what, he didn't even know. How he was expected to do it, he also didn't know. But his brother had written the note, which meant that he'd believed it was possible – Keith was no idiot, and had been a strategic thinker in the purest sense of the word. So he'd seen some way to avert this supposed catastrophe, and had died trying. And had now passed the burden to Jeffrey.

He reattached the strings while he teetered on the brink of full-scale panic, outwardly calm but in reality skittering along a razor's edge of delirium. In a blinding instant, he'd gone from being the luckiest man in the world to one of the damned, burdened with knowledge that was impossible…and yet which had to be true.

Jeffrey tried to slow his thoughts. Mechanically he tuned the guitar, mainly to occupy his hands so he wouldn't run screaming from the room. He strummed a series of chords and then put the guitar back on the stand, the message's implications still slamming into him as he tried to cope.

If he assumed it was actually true, he was screwed. Worse than screwed. His brother's death was all the proof of that conclusion he needed. If they, whoever they specifically were, had been willing to kill Keith and the rest of the innocents, why would they stop at killing him too? Why hadn't they already killed him, just to be safe?

The answer popped into his head with a certitude that rocked him. Because he didn't know anything, and they didn't want to arouse any more suspicion. Or alternatively, because they thought he might know something, but had no idea how much, or who else he might have told.

His brother's words seemed like a taunt. Trust no one. Everything is bugged.

Which was insane. A lunatic's conspiracy theory seeped in paranoia and delusion.

Except for the plane.

And…Becky?

Someone seemingly unconnected to anything, but who was the most intimately connected in Keith's life. The most likely to know something, to have been told something.

Also dead within days of the crash.

Coincidence?

The news of the hit-and-run was suddenly more ominous than a simple accident, one of countless that occurred around the country every week.

Had she been killed to silence her? To end any trail?

If that was even possibly true, then it had likely been Jeffrey's own distance from Keith, his lack of communication with him, that had spared his life so far. He was the brother out on the coast, who barely talked to Keith once every six months, and then invariably by email, the minimum contact possible for two very busy young men.

Jeffrey's rational mind grappled with the possibilities the note had raised. A part of him calmed down and looked at things logically. His brother had been acting increasingly erratically. His behavior had changed, and he'd been obsessing over dead cows.

A far more likely explanation than one where the government was blowing up planes was that his brother had been losing his mind. As unpleasant as it was to contemplate, that made more sense. Maybe he'd been doing drugs. Jeffrey knew so little about Keith's life in the past few years, anything was possible.

And that note had been written by someone extremely paranoid. The big question was whether the paranoia was justified, or was that of a mind slowly coming apart, slipping into delusion.

It was obvious that Jeffrey had only two choices: to reject the notions and assume it was the disturbed ramblings of a man losing touch with reality, or to assume that it was the truth, and be suddenly plunged into a world that he didn't want to believe existed. One where a ruthless, shadowy government killed at will, butchering as many as it took, and then contrived explanations and railroaded their captive experts and the compliant media into parroting whatever party line it contrived, no matter how implausible.

He'd never been much for conspiracies. He'd ignored the ongoing speculation about damning questions from prior disasters, attributing it to the disturbed inventions of unbalanced minds. Years ago, when Pan Am flight 103, en route from London to New York, blew up over Lockerbie, Scotland, killing all 259 people aboard as well as people on the ground, he vaguely remembered some chatter about a group of CIA agents returning to the U.S. on the flight with evidence of a drug trafficking ring in the agency. And hadn't there been numerous reports when that plane went down out of New York of something that resembled a missile streaking towards it? The crash investigators themselves had claimed a cover-up, although they'd waited until retirement to say anything. And how about Building Seven of the World Trade Center collapsing at the speed of gravity even though it had never been hit by anything?

Could there really be that big a disconnect between what he wanted to believe because it was in the papers, and what had actually happened? Was he really so blind and apathetic that he'd ignore data he didn't like because it hinted at a reality he didn't want to think possible?

If so, one thing was becoming evident by the second. He couldn't go back. He couldn't un-see the note, or pretend the words his dead brother had written didn't exist. He'd have to treat it as genuine, even if he had doubts about his brother's sanity. The only prudent course was to behave as though he was being watched, and find time to track down the professor and see what he had to say. There was surely no harm in that – play it safe, but not go off the deep end and buy into his brother's delusion hook, line, and sinker.

Yes, that was the best course – trust, but verify. Don't jump to conclusions, but also don't ignore a message from the dead. Because there was still the plane crash to contend with in the alternative theory Jeffrey was forming: one where his brother had been losing his grip. But the plane crash couldn't be easily dismissed. That was a major sticking point in the "Keith was a loon" hypothesis.

One thing was clear: If Keith really had been involved in something worth killing over, he clearly hadn't envisioned how extreme the danger was. Would he have ever gotten onto the plane to Rome if he'd suspected it would be the end of his life? Obviously not. Which meant that he'd misjudged his adversaries. A mistake that had cost him everything.

As his thoughts turned increasingly dark, Jeffrey had a sudden impulse to move, to get out of the condo, to run away and never look back.

Except that given what his brother had warned about, that wouldn't do any good. You couldn't outrun what you didn't understand. As Keith had ultimately learned.

Fine. I'll play along. So think. What can you do? What are the first steps?

If everything was bugged, he was hosed. It would be impossible to do anything.

No. That wasn't correct. It would be harder, but nothing was impossible.

A sudden ugly idea popped into Jeffrey's consciousness as he paced in front of the couch. His brother had assumed he was still in San Francisco. And so he had been – until the job offer had come.

The job that had seemed too good to be true. The one that had resulted in him cutting off all his personal contacts back home and moving abruptly to the same city Keith had lived in. Where, presumably, it would be easier to keep an eye on him.

Was that what all this had been about?

Viewed in the light cast by the note, the offer suddenly seemed implausible. Why pay a small fortune for him to move? To offer advice any of hundreds of other experts could have at a fraction of the price? And he'd followed along unquestioningly. Believed the transparent flattery, that he was special and different. They'd played to his vanity and he'd bought it.

He shook his head as if to clear it. Was he going down roads of his own invention now, connecting something that was innocent and unrelated? Becoming paranoid about things that didn't warrant a nefarious explanation? Following his brother down a rabbit hole where the walls had ears and everyone was out to get him?

Maybe so. Or maybe he was just beginning to see the outline of the truth. Maybe that sinking, anxious feeling in the pit of his stomach was the recognition of veracity.

Whatever the case, he had a problem. The first practical hurdle was that if the warning was accurate, his phone and computer were compromised, as was his car. And if it was the government that Keith had gone up against, Jeffrey could assume that his credit cards and passport were also being used to track him.

The only good news was that up until a few minutes ago, he hadn't known anything, so he couldn't slip up or do anything that would alert them.

Them.

The bad guys.

But now he knew. And the only defense he had was to act exactly as he had before. Any deviation, any hint of subterfuge, would alert them, and then he could expect the same fate that had awaited his brother.

So what was he going to do? If his every movement was being monitored?

The answer came to him as he put on his coat and walked through his front door to have another beer – liquid courage to calm his frazzled nerves and help him think.

He would have to hide in plain sight.

Because it would be the last thing that anyone would expect.

NINETEEN

A Feint

The following day, Jeffrey went to work and slogged through his morning, meeting with his staff, responding to emails. At lunchtime he deliberately forgot his phone at the office – he would begin establishing a pattern of being forgetful, starting now. He left his car in the garage and walked to get lunch, trying to detect any surveillance without success. Perhaps after weeks of nothing, he was only being passively watched. After all, he couldn't have displayed any awareness or suspicion so far, and they were probably convinced that he was exactly what he seemed – Keith's clueless younger brother, self-involved and self-important, strutting like an ignorant peacock, inflated by his recent success and overblown sense of self-worth.

He bought a sandwich at one of the packed delis a few blocks from the office and quickly ate it, then ducked into an office supply store that had internet access and paid for half an hour of time. His first errand was to do a search on the mysterious professor. It didn't take long to find mentions of him, but it was more involved to find a physical address or phone number. Eventually he got lucky, and he committed the information to memory before going back to the articles the man had authored decades before.

The professor was principally associated with cattle mutilations from the seventies a very odd period when thousands of animals had turned up drained of blood, many with their organs missing, and with surgically precise incisions that had been lavishly documented. They'd caused a furor, with public speculation about UFO experimentation and the FBI investigating the possible involvement of Satanic cults. Like most mass hysteria media events, the story had died over time and eventually faded from the public consciousness.

He thought back to the discussion with Becky, about Keith researching the cattle mutilations and becoming obsessed. He'd left the professor's name, and that was the man's only claim to fame, so whatever it was that he'd been involved in must have been related. Jeffrey did a quick internet search on relevant sites and found himself swimming in crazyland – every possible variation of conspiracy theory on the planet seemed to have found a home for a while in the savaging of livestock.

Jeffrey browsed through a few, and then navigated to the FBI's site and read the documents that had been archived, which were exclusively newspaper articles from the period, and of no help other than historical perspective. The investigation had gone nowhere and been quietly closed in the early eighties, when the unusual rash of mutilations ended just as abruptly as it had begun. Apparently the little green men with enough sophistication to build intergalactic spacecraft grew tired of dissecting cows and sheep after a decade, and presumably moved on to abducting trailer park residents.

Try as he might, he couldn't see any smoking gun, but he was out of time for the day – he didn't want to raise any eyebrows by deviating from his normal behavior. He stopped at a pay phone on his way back to the office and called the professor's number, unsure what he was going to say when the man answered, but found himself listening to a message announcing that the number he'd dialed was no longer in service. A part of him wondered whether the professor had also been killed, but he put it aside. It was unlikely that the government was killing retired academics with an interest in cattle. Then again, he mused as he returned to the office, it was also unlikely that it was shooting planes out of the sky and covering it up.

Was that what was happening with Keith's flight? A cover-up? It certainly seemed so. Already the machine was in gear, spinning theories that the mid-air disappearance was a mechanical failure of some sort, a freak accident whose cause might never be known.

His footsteps pounded on the sidewalk as he approached the office, and he realized that he would have to visit the professor in person if he was going to get any answers. But he would need to do it without leaving any traces, which meant no cell and no car. Hopefully the man was still alive and could bring some clarity to a murky situation.

And he would have to get to Zurich, sooner rather than later, and see what was in the box. Without triggering any alarms, which meant that the trip needed to appear to be for plausible, innocent reasons – for Jeffrey, who had only been to Europe once, seven years before, for a week following his graduation.

Back behind his desk, he searched online for an hour and then saw exactly what he needed: a two-day symposium on the changing tax and reporting rules for the European Union, taking place the following Thursday and Friday in Zurich. It would be well within his job description to put in a request to attend it, and with nothing on his plate now other than tying up a few loose ends for the conglomerate's attorneys, he certainly had abundant free time.

He drafted a memo requesting permission to sign up for the conference and book travel, and sent it to his immediate superior – Eric Fairbanks, one of the partners. Other than a welcoming handshake on his first day, he hadn't had any interaction with Garfield, and he'd been relegated to Fairbanks' pool; he was the one who handled the financial end of things, leaving the others to attend to the lobbying and class action support business.

Twenty minutes later his internal line rang, and Fairbanks asked to see him. Jeffrey suited up and walked down the long hall to the partner offices and nodded to the receptionist, who waved him through.

"Jeffrey. Have a seat. What's this all about a conference in Zurich? Are you tired of working here already?" Fairbanks asked.

"Hardly. The situation in the EU is changing literally week to week, and as we saw on the first deal I handled here, our clients are global entities who need cutting-edge counsel. Informed advice. If you looked at the link I sent you, the speakers are heavy hitters in Euro Zone banking and taxation. I normally don't go in for attending conferences, but this is a worthwhile exception. I think we'd get a hundred times the value of the travel and attendance costs. It would take weeks or months of research to get everything they're covering in the two days. Besides which, since I closed the deal last week I've got nothing on the board at the moment, so it comes at an opportune time."

"We're not in the habit of sending our staff on paid European vacations, young man," Fairbanks countered sternly.

"Sir, with all due respect, I wouldn't call sitting in sessions from eight to five for two days a vacation. One of the reasons I try to avoid these is because they're typically like having un-anesthetized oral surgery. But with the fluid situation in the EU, I'm willing to make an exception. I wouldn't have suggested it if I didn't think it was a good use of my time. And if anything comes up between now and then, I can take files with me and work on them on the plane and in the evenings, so my effective usefulness wouldn't be affected in my absence, nor would my ability to bill." Jeffrey figured he would mention the magic words – 'billable hours.' "And of course, the whole thing's a write off…"

"And you really believe this is an essential conference?"

"I wouldn't have suggested it otherwise. I'll only lose two days of office time – I can take a red-eye over the night before. I think it would be a mistake not to go. My understanding is that every major player in the field is sending personnel there."

"I see," Fairbanks said, studying him over the rims of his reading glasses. He took a few seconds to think and then leaned forward. "Let me take it up with Garfield and confirm that he doesn't have anything pressing he intends to assign you. I'll get back to you as soon as I hear from him," he said, bringing the matter to a close and lowering his eyes back to the paperwork he'd been working on. Jeffrey got the hint and returned to his office, confident that he'd be allowed to take the time off.

Two hours later he got a terse email from Fairbanks okaying the trip.

He went to the men's room and splashed water on his face, then dried it and looked at his reflection in the mirror. At least that part of his plan had gone off without a hitch. The symposium had been a brilliant feint, a completely reasonable distraction for anyone watching his movements. He could slip out and get to the bank in the late afternoon, and then would have the weekend there if he needed it. And all under the guise of work-related travel.

In a little over a week, he'd know what his brother had paid his life to discover.

From there, he had absolutely no idea what he would do.

But it was a start.

In the meantime, he wanted to spend some time researching cattle mutilations, and figure out how to get to rural Virginia to see about tracking down the professor. All without raising any red flags.

A tall order, but now that he was committed, there was no way he would turn back.

TWENTY

Suspicions

"Europe! Take me with you!" said Monica, as she pushed her Chinese dinner around her plate at Jeffrey's dining room table.

"I wish I could. It's not like that. It's a conference. I'm going to be in meetings all day, and knowing how these go, probably side meetings after. It's work, not pleasure, unfortunately."

"That's what they all say," she pouted.

"Except this time it's true. With what happened in Cyprus, the rules are changing really fast, and I need to be up on what the current thinking is. It's what I do. My job. Besides which, I'm just getting on a plane, landing and going to the meeting, spending the night, and then flying back after the conference on Friday night. It's actually sort of hellish."

"Put that way, it doesn't sound like that much fun," Monica conceded. "Hey, maybe you can get me some chocolate while you're there!"

"One order of Swiss chocolate, coming up," Jeffrey assured her in his most serious tone.

"Do you have to do many of these?"

"No. Thank God. There's nothing more boring than a symposium with five hundred other attorneys. Usually I'd figure out how to weasel out of it and send someone else, but this is kind of the Super Bowl of Euro Zone structuring, so it's best that I go. Anyway, it's a done deal, and it's only for two days, so I'll be back before you know it."

"What am I going to do to keep myself occupied when you're gone? I've gotten used to having you as my boy toy…"

"Hold that thought," he said, moving his plate aside and standing.

She gave him a flirtatious look. "Our food will get cold."

"That's why man invented microwaves. Or at least one of the reasons, I'm pretty sure."

Jeffrey lay staring at the ceiling as Monica nuzzled his chest, basking in the lingering afterglow of passion, their lovemaking as enthusiastic as always. His heart was torn at not being able to confide in her, but he didn't want to endanger her in any way – and he kept revisiting Becky's death, perhaps an accident, but more likely not. As much as he would have liked to share his internal drama, he wouldn't put Monica in harm's way. It was better that she knew nothing.

He disengaged and went out into the front room, then got online and checked his email, hoping to see something from the brokerage firm or the banks he'd contacted after receiving Keith's death certificate. He had no idea what he was going to discover when he opened the Swiss box, but having a boatload of ready cash wouldn't be a bad idea, and his brother's accounts were just sitting there, engorged with dollars. Only the usual work-related messages had come in, though, and he put off reading them until he was on the clock and could bill for his time. It was company policy to bill for every second spent on a client's behalf, and Jeffrey could see the wisdom in that – otherwise half the day could be eaten up with uncompensated queries that would "just take a second" from clients who didn't comprehend how attorneys earned their keep.

A part of him itched to go on the web and do some research, but he knew better, and had resigned himself to behaving as though every move was being tracked. Which had made his private life difficult, to say the least. Now that he suspected that the condo was compromised, he'd had issues with making love, knowing that someone might be listening in, but it would have seemed strange if he'd suddenly lost interest, and truthfully one look at Monica generally solved that problem. Any reticence he attributed to thoughts about his brother, and she'd seemed sympathetic. It had to be a little weird living in your dead brother's condo, after all.

He pushed the thought from his mind and instead focused on his errands for tomorrow – to stop in at the office supply store and research the best way to get to Virginia without a tail, and to see what else he could glean about the cattle mutilations. He wished he could spend his evenings out somewhere he could get online, but it was foolhardy, and it would have seemed odd if he'd suddenly become uninterested in spending his free time with Monica. For all he knew, that was what had tipped them off about Keith. Again, he couldn't take the chance, so he had to keep to his normal habits, seeming dumb and happy.

There was only one niggling problem, and it had come to him as he'd grown increasingly paranoid since his discovery. Monica. His good fortune with the woman of his dreams had begun at the same time his career had taken off. And she had cinched the deal on him moving to Washington. But how much did he really know about her, other than what she'd told him? He hated the feeling of suspicion that had colored his feelings, but Keith's revelation had changed everything, and he was now no longer unquestioning.

Which brought him to his next agenda item, which he felt rotten about. He needed to know whether Monica was what she seemed.

He'd agonized over it for the last few days, and the only plan he'd been able to come up with had been to hire a private investigator to verify her story. But that was harder than it sounded, given the constraints. It wasn't like he could just call one on his cell or office phone. Even something as simple as that required planning and subterfuge, and he'd mapped out his lunch time and the few evenings of the week that Monica wasn't with him to deal with hiring a PI and making his way to Virginia.

"Honey? Are you coming to bed?" Monica called sleepily from the bedroom, and a pang of guilt stabbed through his heart at the sound of her voice. How low had he sunk to suspect everyone around him – even a woman he was crazy about?

"Yeah. Be there in a second."

He closed his mental list of pseudo-errands and shook his head. It would be a long week. Tomorrow would be the first day he "forgot" his phone at home for the day, continuing to establish the pattern of absent-mindedness he was cultivating for his watchers. Part of him felt like he was going slowly mad, seeing ghosts everywhere, but the rational part of his mind told him that he was being prudent in light of the evidence.

Whatever the case, he felt like a complete shit sneaking around behind Monica's back and going so far as to hire someone to spy on her.

But there was no other way.

And he had to know.

TWENTY-ONE

Boys' Night Out

The next day at lunch he looked up several private detectives and spoke with two, outlining in general terms what he was looking for – a discreet background check and possibly some surveillance. The first couldn't take a job for a week and wanted him to come into the office, but the second was hungrier and agreed to meet him that evening at seven at the British pub.

Monica had already told him that she needed the evening to run errands she'd been putting off and do laundry again, so he was in the clear, a bachelor for the night. He left his phone at home and walked briskly down the empty street, glad there were no other pedestrians out because it would be easier to spot anyone following him. When he entered the bar, he looked around and saw his investigator – heavyset and ruddy-complexioned, wearing a tweed jacket, sitting at one of the booths in the back, as agreed. Jeffrey walked to the bar and ordered a black and tan, watching the entrance as he waited, and when he was confident that nobody had followed him in, he took the seat opposite the man, one eye on the door.

"Owen Jakes. Please to meet you," the investigator said, holding out a hand the size of a bear paw. Jeffrey shook it and introduced himself, then took a sip of his beer, marveling at how good it tasted.

"I don't know how to say this, so I'm just going to spill it and you can figure out whether it's something you can do. I met a woman a few weeks ago, and we've become inseparable. But I don't really know anything about her. And I want to. I'm thinking a check on her work and living situation, and maybe a little light surveillance. Shouldn't take much," Jeffrey explained.

Jakes' face was impassive, unreadable. "Hundred and fifty an hour, plus expenses, minimum ten hours. If we find a rat, then figure another twenty-four to forty-eight."

The numbers hung in the air like a curse, and Jeffrey did a quick mental calculation. It could get expensive quickly. Then again, he was earning a fortune, so what was a few grand if it assured him that Monica was the genuine article?

"When can you start?"

"I can run the trace tomorrow, and any surveillance after that – maybe Thursday. What do you have on her?"

"I…I have a business card, and a photo I printed out."

"What about home address?"

"She lives with a couple of roommates somewhere around Foggy Bottom. I've never been up to her apartment, just outside her building. But frankly, I wasn't paying attention, and it was night, and I didn't know anything about the town…"

"I see. And home phone?"

"Just a cell and her office. Oh, and her car's license number." He'd memorized it – part of the mixed blessing of a photographic memory.

"If she had a home phone it would be easy to skip trace her."

"I know. She doesn't."

"I'll need a grand downstroke as a retainer."

"Do you accept cash?"

Jakes smiled for the first time. "I like you already. Where's the card and the photo?"

Jeffrey extracted Monica's card from his wallet and handed it to him, then unfolded a piece of paper he'd printed that afternoon at the copy center. It was a photo from a few days before of Monica wearing shorts and a T-shirt at his house, beaming mega-wattage at the camera while pouring them wine. He pushed it across the table.

The big man whistled. "Wow. Congratulations. What do you do for a living, Jeffrey?" he asked as he studied the printout.

"Lawyer. But don't hold that against me."

Jeffrey took another pull on his drink and then took out a wad of hundred dollar bills – part of the money he'd gotten out of the bank in San Francisco to cover surprises once in Washington. With a thousand to Jakes, he was left with five, which was more than enough to cover anything except a protracted surveillance he hoped wouldn't be necessary. If it was, he would hit his new bank and pull whatever else he needed under the guise of wanting cash for the trip. He carefully counted out the thousand dollars and slipped it to the detective, who was drinking what looked like a soda. Jakes counted it again and grunted.

"How do I get hold of you when I know something?" he asked.

"I'll call you. How long for the background check?"

"We'll run the plate and check on the company she works for first. That will take a day or so. I'd say give me a call day after tomorrow – Thursday – and I should have something for you."

A man wearing a windbreaker entered and looked around, causing Jeffrey's heart to flutter. The newcomer spotted his friend and walked over, then pulled out a stool and sat down at the bar, his back to Jeffrey. Jakes' eyes watched Jeffrey's reaction without comment, although his eyes narrowed slightly.

"Anything else I should know, Jeffrey? Any pieces of information you might have left out?"

"No. That's it."

"You sure? You look pretty spooked right now."

"It's nothing. I thought I knew that guy. Turns out I don't."

Jakes finished his drink and stood. "If you say so. Call me in a couple days. I'm always in the office during business hours, and if not, my girl can patch the call through to wherever I am."

Jeffrey nodded, and Jakes eyed him one final time before he rose, leaving Jeffrey to pay for the drinks. The bartender came over and took Jeffrey's burger order and asked him if he wanted another beer, to which Jeffrey gave a thumbs up. It would help him sleep, he reasoned, and was completely consistent with what he now thought of as his cover.

Jakes seemed crusty but competent, and hadn't batted an eye over Jeffrey wanting to contact him instead of giving the PI a phone number to reach him. His burger arrived a few minutes later as he was watching yet more soccer, or maybe it was rugby, on the television, and as he bit into the mouthwatering sandwich he congratulated himself for having done as well as he had so far with the whole clandestine thing. The second beer was relaxing him and he was just starting to feel decent when he reminded himself that this wasn't a game, and that the consequence for a slip was a trip to the morgue.

The beer tasted rancid and metallic from that point on, and he declined a third, preferring to make his way back home and spend another night wondering how the hell all this would end, a vision of Monica seared into his retinas from the photo, her smile as innocent and loving as a baby's.

TWENTY-TWO

In the Clear

When two days had gone by with excruciating slowness, Jeffrey practically ran from the office at lunch time, the now-daily walk part of his attempt at exercise, he'd told his secretary, who hadn't given the remotest sign of caring. He was getting better at checking his reflection in shop windows, looking for a tail, and didn't see anything ominous as he ordered his sandwich and stood in line to pay, a predictable creature of habit who would hopefully lull any watchers into somnolent boredom.

He rushed to eat and then made his way to the pay phone to call Jakes.

The gruff PI's voice was matter-of-fact when he came on the line. "The car's not in her name. It's actually owned by a company out of Virginia. Evendale Industries. Ever heard of it?"

"No. Doesn't ring any bells."

"Name doesn't come up on any lists, which is neither good nor bad. Means she has no criminal record. We're waiting for a more thorough search, though. Should be in by the end of the day."

"Where does that put us?"

"Nowhere good. I also did a reverse on the business number, and it comes up as unlisted. Which doesn't necessarily mean anything. Lots of businesses have unlisted numbers. Depends on what they do, of course."

"Of course."

"I took a drive over to the address that was listed on the card, and there's an office building there, so it's not a vacant lot."

"Then it sounds like she's clean, right? I mean, the car could have any number of explanations, correct?"

"Anything's possible. Why don't we wait to see what else comes up before we throw a party, though, okay? All we've got right now is that she

118

has no criminal record and is driving a company-owned car. I'm doing some research on what Evendale is, and that should be in around the same time as the in-depth search. So how do you want to play this? Call me again tomorrow?"

"That seems best. How much have you burned so far?"

"You're almost through your grand. The in-depth search will cost me a few hun. Figure we'll eat fifteen hundred by the time we're done."

Jeffrey paused, digesting the number without comment. "Listen. If I needed to hire a reliable car for a day, without any paperwork, you know anybody who could handle that?"

"Depends. You going to rob a bank?"

"No. I just want to run an errand and not use my car. It's pretty high-profile."

"An errand, huh? Well...I have a Ford Taurus that's not being used. I suppose I could let you have it for the day for a hundred bucks. When do you want it?"

"A hundred bucks!"

"Or you can rent one from any of the agencies for thirty or forty."

Jeffrey thought fast. "No, rental cars are going to look too new. Fine. I'll pay the hundred. I'll need it on Saturday. First thing in the morning."

"I'll drive it into work. You know where my office is?"

"I remember the address. I can find it."

"Suit yourself."

"Thanks for the good work. I'll call you tomorrow, same time."

"I'll be here."

Jeffrey was walking on air as he returned to the office. It looked like Monica was the real thing. Nothing could have made him happier, and as a sea of gray-skinned clerk and low-level bureaucrat faces surged towards him, he questioned just how far out of touch with reality his brother's note had pushed him. Not everything was some plot, and not everyone was bad.

Now he had to figure out how to get away on Saturday so he could get to Virginia and hunt down the professor. The car solved the biggest problem – how to make it a hundred and fifty miles into the wilds without being tracked or going on record as renting something – but he still had to figure out how to lose Monica for the day.

As he waited for the elevator, he was confident he would think of something.

After all, he had so far.

That night their lovemaking was especially tender, their connection even deeper than usual, probably because he was more at ease now that Monica had been vetted. He'd taken her to an Italian restaurant in Georgetown for dinner, and the conversation had been easy, the wine flowing like water as they savored their meals. Upon their return to the condo they'd turned the lights low and Jeffrey had made them each his version of a Cosmo, and they'd bantered about his upcoming trip and the weather finally turning warmer.

He shifted on the bed and stroked her bare stomach, the skin twitching at his gentle touch as he ran his fingers along the slight rise of her abdomen, and she squirmed and moved closer to him, purring like a contented jungle cat. He pulled away and closed his eyes, reveling in their mutual joy, and felt as close to love as he'd ever experienced. Which made it all the harder to deceive her, but he had no choice.

"That was incredible. As usual. You're amazing, Monica. Truly."

"About time you realized it," she said playfully, her eyes closed.

"I do. I'm glad I met you. It's the best thing that ever happened to me."

"So far so good."

He hesitated. "I'm going to have to abandon you on Saturday, so if you need some 'me' time to yourself, that would be your big chance."

Her eyes popped open in surprise. "Why? What's up on Saturday?"

He put his arm over his forehead and stared at the ceiling, unable to meet her gaze. "Just a bunch of BS I've been putting off. I need to spend most of the day rooting around in my crap that's in storage, and look through Keith's, too – I've put it off long enough. I've been so busy I haven't had time to think since I got here, but I have to do it sometime. I need some of my stuff, and I wasn't really thinking when I told the movers to keep it all."

"But we'll still hook up Saturday night, right? I don't have that many more shots at you before you run off to Switzerland."

"Absolutely. I just need the day to go through my stuff and sort it for long-term storage, and maybe look around for a cheaper place. It's costing me a king's ransom to keep it there."

Monica seemed mollified by his explanation, and he pulled her closer, the lie now told, his deception an ugly necessity. She leaned her head back and invited him with a glance, and then he was consumed by her again. Their bodies joined in concert, a harmonious rhythm that was as effortless as it was by now familiar.

TWENTY-THREE

The World According To Sam

"I want to do a day's surveillance, Jeffrey." Jakes' voice was flat over the pay phone, and Jeffrey could practically see the man's face scowling as he spoke the words Jeffrey had been hoping not to hear.

"Why? I thought you said she was clean."

"I don't want to go off half-cocked. You need to trust me on this. When are you going to see her again?"

"Tonight. It's Friday. She'll spend the night at my place, and then take off tomorrow morning. I'm going to pick up the car at your office, remember?"

"Yeah. It's already parked on the street. I drove it in today, filled it with gas, checked the tires. If it's all the same to you, I'll have someone meet you at the office, and I'll tail her from your place."

"Is this really necessary?"

"Yes." The single word had the finality of a jail door slamming shut, and Jeffrey swallowed hard at Jakes' tone.

"Fine. She'll be leaving at around nine a.m." Jeffrey gave him the address. "You have her license number. Red Alfa convertible."

"I know the car."

"Can't you tell me anything more?"

"Not until I have more information. Look, you hired me to do a job. Let me do it. I'll get you a full report by Monday, okay?"

Jeffrey felt panicky, but bit it back. This wasn't going anything like he'd expected after the preliminary report the day before.

"Okay. Do what you have to do. Just be certain. That's all I ask."

"That's what you're paying me for."

The line went dead, and Jeffrey found himself staring at the phone in frustrated puzzlement. Jakes' voice had given nothing away, and he'd refused to even hint at why he wanted to do the physical surveillance. Perhaps it was a gambit to get another day's wages? Which, of course, Jeffrey would be happy to pay, especially when relieved to hear that she'd passed with flying colors. If so, it was a good strategy, and the man knew his human nature. There was no way Jeffrey could refuse to have absolute confirmation. He absently wondered whether he was being scammed, and then banished the thought. Jakes hadn't struck him as shifty or artificial. And Jeffrey considered himself a good judge of human nature, even if he was now questioning the woman he was in love with.

The realization that he was in love stopped him.

But it didn't surprise him. They'd only been together for a few weeks, but they had a powerful chemistry, and he was sure Monica felt the same way – which made it all the more critical for him to be certain about her. There was too much on the line for them both. If he made it out the other end of the nightmare he was involved in, he needed to know she would be there for him, and that what they had was something honest, not an artifice.

Jakes probably sensed all that. Which made his tactic a very smart one, if somewhat underhanded.

Whatever. Jeffrey would play along. It was only money, and he would gladly pay another grand or two to hear the truth, which in his heart he was already convinced of.

Saturday was there before he knew it, and when he parted from Monica it was bittersweet, for reasons only he understood. Once she was gone, he quickly got ready to hit the road. Fifteen minutes after she left he was behind the wheel of his car, driving to the moving company's storage facility where he'd leave the BMW and grab a cab. He'd checked with them and confirmed that they would be open until eight that evening, and he could get access to his storage compartment all day.

Jeffrey parked in the lot and made his way into the cavernous building, pausing to use the bathroom and confirm the hours again with the sleepy desk clerk before slipping back out on the street. Looking around to ensure he was alone, he walked to the main boulevard to flag down a taxi, his cell phone in the car where he'd forgotten it again so he couldn't be easily tracked. Luck was with him, and after a few tries a cab pulled to a stop. Jeffrey gave the driver Jakes' office address and sat back, his thoughts on Monica.

As the car approached the office, he forced his focus back to the job at hand – his drive south to Roanoke and then into the wilds to see if his quarry was still living at the last known address on record, outside a small town called Boones Mill. Part of him hoped so, while another dreaded the meeting because of what it might uncover.

At the office, a desultory, unshaved young man sporting a Marlins baseball cap and a burgundy hoodie stood smoking by the entry. When Jeffrey approached him he looked up with a skeptical expression.

"You Rutherford?" he asked, making it sound like a slight.

"That's me. Got the car?"

The man flicked the butt into the gutter and nodded, then walked down the block to where a black sedan hulked, its clear coat and much of its paint eaten away, looking every one of its at least fifteen hard years, the Keith Richards of cars.

The sullen man held out a key dangling from a chrome fob with a keyless entry remote and a Tecate bottle opener. "You got the money?"

Jeffrey exchanged the cash for the keys and took another appraising look at the dubious wreck, wondering if it would make it out of the city limits, much less hundreds of miles into rural Virginia. "I'll be back by eight or so. Maybe earlier. Where should I leave the keys?"

"Drop them through the building mail slot with a note about where you parked it. I'm pretty sure nobody's going to steal it."

"Yeah. It's got that going for it."

The driver's side door opened with a creak, and Jeffrey was assailed by a musty odor of mold mixed with stale cigarettes and vomit. He lowered all four windows before twisting the ignition, and the engine sputtered to life with a belch of white smoke. His host grinned crookedly and shook his head, and then turned with a wave and made his way down the street.

Jeffrey put the transmission into gear, two warning lights on the dashboard vying for his attention as he gave the car gas. To his surprise, it sprang forward with unexpected agility, and his concern about the vehicle's reliability eased a few notches. After driving his BMW it felt as sluggish as a riding mower, but all he had to do was recall his Honda to readjust his attitude.

And of course, it had the benefit of not being bugged or tracked.

Hard to put that on the sales literature, but it was a feature that Jeffrey was grateful for.

He felt even more comfortable about his new steed once on the freeway headed southwest through rolling farmland, the car purring along at sixty-five, and he turned on the radio and tuned in a talk radio station where a right-wing commentator was lambasting the administration for some real or imagined offense. He quickly tired of the man's strident rhetoric and angry delivery and scanned the dial until coming to a classic rock station where ZZ Top was burning up the frets.

Four hours later, he stopped at a fast food restaurant on the outskirts of Roanoke and got a shake and a hamburger crafted from hormonally augmented mystery meat. He sat outside at a white molded plastic table, enjoying the blustery mid-afternoon as he consumed his questionable meal. By his figuring, he was forty-five minutes away from the professor's last known address, so he should have plenty of time to discover whatever there was to learn – assuming the man was still alive and living there.

The hamlet of Boones Mill was little more than a dusting of homes nestled among rolling hills, with a string of industrial buildings and stores fronting along the highway, and it was so unassuming that Jeffrey almost missed the turn north on Boones Mill Road, a two-lane ribbon of dark asphalt winding through the trees. He stomped on the brakes and the car pulled hard left as he twisted the wheel, and he silently prayed that the tires were in better shape than the rest of the sedan.

He kept his speed down, looking for any signs that might guide him to his destination – a tiny tributary called Wild Goose Lane. According to the map he'd memorized, it would be about five miles from the turnoff, but the odometer was broken, so his carefully crafted plan was already in jeopardy. Another problem was that the three small roads he'd passed had no markings, and if that held true it would be easy to miss.

Jeffrey slowed even further as he crept toward a sign announcing highway 689 on the right. He closed his eyes for a second and envisioned the map, and saw that his target was four small lanes further north – maybe a mile, at most. Shutting the radio off with a stab of his thumb, he peered at the passing roads and pulled off at the fourth one. A medium-sized two-story house sat fifty yards from the road on the left side, and he rolled by it on a single lane of pavement as he motored to the professor's address – the only home on the cul-de-sac.

A bend curved into the trees, and when he reached the dead end he was confronted with a rusting iron gate held in place with a padlocked chain, barring further progress. He stopped the car and shut off the engine, squinting at a structure in the distance, obscured by a grove of mature trees. A glance at the No Trespassing sign gave him pause, but then he summoned up his resolve and squeezed around the right fence post, a gap in the barbed wire just large enough to accommodate him if he was careful.

Dried twigs crackled underfoot as he trod along the two tire ruts that passed for a drive, and as he neared the ponderous trees he could see a small, simple single-story house in dire need of a coat of paint, its desiccated faded brown wooden shingles peeking through a peeling veneer of mottled white. He was thirty yards from the building when a woman's voice called out to him from a separate building to its left, likely a garage.

"Stop right there."

Jeffrey squinted at the shadows around the building and saw the double barrels of a shotgun pointed in his direction, held by one of the most arresting blond women he'd ever seen. She looked to be a few years younger than Jeffrey and wore jeans and a brown sweater, and even having a firearm trained on him couldn't keep him from noticing that she had a figure that would have made a swimsuit model proud, the perfect complement to an unruly head of long, thick hair. He raised his hands over his head and stopped walking.

"I'm sorry. I tried calling, but the number's disconnected."

"I guess you can't read too well, or did you miss the bright yellow sign at the gate?" she asked, the weapon steady in her hand.

"I saw it. But I really need to find out if Professor Samuel Norton lives here, and I didn't see any other way of doing it."

The shotgun was unwavering. "Who wants to know?"

"Jeffrey Rutherford. I'm an attorney."

"You'd think an attorney would realize that trespassing on property in rural Virginia can get you shot. What do you want?" she asked, and then a male voice called out from the front doorway of the house.

"Kaycee! That's no way to treat a guest, even an uninvited one. Mr. Rutherford, please accept my apologies for my granddaughter's protective impulses. It's nothing personal, I assure you."

The speaker emerged from the entryway, a tall man with a full head of almost white hair, his body thin to the point of fragility, his chocolate corduroy trousers and denim shirt hanging off a bony frame. Kaycee appeared uncertain, and then grudgingly lowered the weapon. Jeffrey took several tentative steps towards him, closing some of the distance, and the old man waved impatiently.

"Come on then. Rutherford, eh? Have you got any identification with you?"

"Of course. Driver's license, credit cards…"

"Let's see the license," the man said, gesturing for Jeffrey to hand it over. Jeffrey reached into his back pocket and removed his wallet, slid a laminated card out, and continued to walk to where the man stood.

"Kaycee. Would you do the honors? I don't have my reading glasses."

She paced to where they stood and took the license, gun now pointed at the ground, and stared intently at his name and photo before handing it back to him.

"Says Jeffrey Rutherford. San Francisco."

"I'm looking for Professor Samuel Norton. I've come a long way and need to talk to him."

The man nodded and slowly stepped forward. "You can call me Sam. We're not big on formalities out here. Kaycee, do you think you could make us a pitcher of that wonderful iced tea you spoil me with?" the professor asked, shaking Jeffrey's hand with a surprisingly firm grip, his eyes clear in spite of his advanced years.

"Sure, Grandpa. It'll only be a few minutes," she said, and then moved past him into the house.

"So you want to talk to me. Here I am. Have a seat and let's talk," Sam said, motioning to a pair of weathered wooden chairs on the porch. Jeffrey did as instructed and took the straight-backed one, reasoning that the rocking chair was probably the old man's.

"I can probably guess, but what brings you out here into God's country?" Sam asked, his eyes studying Jeffrey's profile as they both looked out at the Taurus, which seemed a mile away from there.

"My brother."

The professor nodded. "As I suspected. You look somewhat like him. How is he?"

"He's dead. Killed in the plane crash a couple of weeks ago out of New York," Jeffrey said tonelessly. "He left me a note with your name on it. Said to speak to you. So here I am."

Sam looked visibly shaken, his face ashen, a slight tremor in his hands, which he folded and unfolded nervously. "Good God. I'm sorry. He was such a nice fellow. I know that's inadequate…"

"It's appreciated. But frankly, I'm puzzled as to why he was so insistent that I meet with you."

"Yes, I'm sure you are. It's a puzzling story. And ugly, even if ancient history."

"I think you should know that in the note, he predicted his death. He left it in case he died. Only a week or so before the plane explosion."

They were interrupted by Kaycee, who emerged from the dark interior with a pitcher and two glasses on a rectangular wooden tray. She set it on the small table between the chairs and took Jeffrey's measure, her frank assessment disconcerting for its intensity. Jeffrey tried to avoid staring back, but it was impossible, and he was again struck by her sheer good looks, the lucky recipient of every fortunate gene Jeffrey could imagine.

"Do you need anything else?" she asked Sam, eyes still on Jeffrey.

"No, thank you, sweetheart. I'll let you get back to what you were doing. We're just going to shoot the breeze for a while."

She seemed reluctant to leave, but then turned and bounced down the two wooden steps and returned to the garage.

"Kaycee is a miracle, a true gift. She's been out helping me for the last few months. I fell and hurt my knee pretty badly, and she dropped everything to come tend to me. Like her mother, God rest her soul, in that regard. She'd do anything for you, and never complain."

"I'm sorry for your loss."

"Seems like there's a lot of that going on. Now where was I?"

"You were going to tell me why my brother was so insistent I speak with you."

"Yes. Well, the best way is to start at the beginning, I suppose, as I did with your brother. The beginning in this case is forty years ago, around 1973. It was the end of an era, of the peace and love period of the sixties, with all the turbulence of the Vietnam War winding down and the disco era about to begin. I was a young professor, thirty-six, at Georgetown, happy with my life, married, with a beautiful little girl – Kaycee's mother – eight years old at the time. Anyway, that year a wave of cattle mutilations began in Kansas, and later Nebraska, spreading to New Mexico. To make a long story short, I became interested in them due to what I viewed as an incredibly gullible press parroting all sorts of absurd stories, about alien spaceships or cults, and later, black helicopters. Skepticism came naturally to me, and I'd spent much of my career examining popular delusions and debunking them as a sideline – things like claims of psychic power, telekinesis, spoon bending, that sort of thing."

Sam reached for the pitcher, and Jeffrey beat him to it. He poured them both glasses of tea and handed one to the professor. Sam took a long appreciative swig and then set it down on the table, his eyes staring at a distant point known only to him.

"The cattle mutilations, or more accurately, the livestock mutilations, were like waving a red cape in front of a bull for me. I was zealous about proving that reason triumphed over pseudo-science and superstition, and this was the biggest example of snake oil I'd ever seen. Over the course of three or four years, I became somewhat of a minor authority on the topic, and even went so far as to fly out to some of the locations and do experiments with cattle that had died of natural causes, capturing their decomposition over the course of several days to show that there were perfectly natural explanations for what had developed into a media frenzy."

"So you were the James Randi of the cow world."

"Sort of. But a funny thing happened as I spent more time researching the incidents. Most were pure hokum, incoherent reactions to deaths revealing no nefarious explanations. But there were some that didn't fit my model. That were, in fact, unexplainable based on all available data. I called those the outliers, because while ninety percent could be debunked, ten percent couldn't, and in fact appeared to be something other than what logic predicted. Then, when I began looking into patterns, I noticed that my outliers all had certain similarities – namely that those incidents were closely linked with the nocturnal helicopter reports, and that they all were in clusters grouped in relatively close proximity to suspected or actual military installations."

"The army was mutilating livestock?" Jeffrey asked in disbelief.

"I know. That was my reaction. Why would the military be killing cows, seemingly at random? And only at night? Look, you have to understand where I was coming from. I set out to disprove the whack-job theories, and after two years of it I started sounding like the nut cases. But that's what the facts were telling me. That a percentage, albeit a small one, of the slaughter was deliberate, and most likely being carried out by the government. Once I got comfortable with that idea, I parked it, and addressed the question of why – because simply speculating that it was happening was really no better than the tin foil hat crowd. I also began to suspect that some of the crazy ideas floating around might have been planted with the media to further obfuscate the true facts. Stuff like the alien experimentation. Of course, there were plenty of zealous loons willing to go along for that ride, but it just all seemed too…coordinated."

Sam appeared to falter at the thought, sputtering to a halt as old men sometimes did, and he took another quick sip of his drink, savoring the tea as it coated his throat with its subtle honey and lemon infusion. Jeffrey didn't prod him, waiting for the account to continue at its own pace.

"I eventually developed a comprehensive hypothesis that explained all aspects of the mutilations, discarding those accounts that were clearly natural deaths or predator kills, and focusing on the unexplainable ones. In seventy-six, I published my findings, expecting there to be a public outcry. Instead, it went unnoticed, and in four months I was out of a job for some trumped up reasons – a co-ed who claimed I'd sexually harassed her. Back then I was too naïve to understand what was happening, but in the passing years, it became obvious when I couldn't get a job anywhere else, even though the girl's inventions were eventually disproved: I'd stepped on the wrong toes, and dared to posit an explanation that was dangerous to the powers that be – an explanation that was probably the truth, if an incomplete one."

Jeffrey leaned toward him. "Which was?"

"That the government was conducting experiments on livestock, presumably for its biological weapon program, in spite of assurances that it was doing no such thing. Remember that bio-weapons had been reclassified as weapons of mass destruction, with the U.S. leading the charge to ban them entirely. I believe that even as it talked out of one side of its mouth, it was carrying out a large-scale testing program. Because of the political climate and the anti-war movement, it couldn't very well have thousands of head of cattle and whatnot penned for experiment."

"Why not? Surely the government's capable of keeping a secret that involved bovines?"

"The answer is ominous. It wanted the animals it was experimenting with to be out in the general population. I proposed two possible reasons – to mislead Congress or our adversaries so that it would appear that we had no active testing going on; or perhaps worse, because it wanted to test contagious agents and monitor how they spread in an uncontrolled setting. My guess is that one of those, or perhaps both, were on the money, because you've never seen a paper buried as quickly…and a life ruined. Even now, in the age of the internet, you won't find any mention of my paper. At one point an acquaintance uploaded it to his website, and the site was hacked and everything on the servers wiped clean. Needless to say that freaked him out sufficiently to where he lost his interest in fostering controversy. So it's as though the theory never existed. Revisionist history of the finest order."

"I…Professor, with all due respect, there are protections against that sort of abuse of power. Legal remedies. And the idea that the media would just go dark on something newsworthy…I mean, that was around Watergate, it was a new era of transparency."

"Bullshit, young man. And please. The name's Sam. I haven't held the title of Professor for almost four decades."

Jeffrey waited for Sam to make his point.

"You think the media isn't controlled one hundred percent by special interests that dictate to its owners what story gets told and what doesn't? Don't be childish. Even today, it's the way of the world. Most people are uninformed, which the media relies on, and when there are those who point out that it's all lies, it just pretends that nobody believes the accuser and that they never said anything. How do you think the public stays in the dark? The media doesn't report the truth."

Sam cleared his throat to continue.

"A great example would be the war on drugs. Did you know that most of the politicians who are the staunchest opponents of marijuana legalization own financial interests in companies that directly benefit from it remaining illegal? Drug testing companies, private prison operators, you name it, they own it. And yet you never hear about that from our media. Or how about when Bush and his gang were assuring the world that there were nuclear weapons of mass destruction in Iraq? A bald-faced lie, but the media went along in lockstep. Son, I could go on all day. But hopefully you take my point. The media is nothing more than a propaganda machine for those in power – the rich, the connected, the friends of the handful of men who own the companies that operate the largest networks and papers. And it's always been like that. Trust me, in the early seventies it was the same." Sam paused, catching his breath, his outrage evident.

"I wasn't born yet in the seventies, but I don't disagree about the situation now."

"So you get it? Governments don't like admitting to their populations that they're a bunch of crooks, so the politicians close ranks and their media parrots the party line, and the truth gets buried. That's the world we live in. I doubt you've read one true thing in your entire life if it was in the paper. And TV is even worse."

"Back to the cows. Do you have anything to support your theory?" Jeffrey asked, wanting to steer the subject away from tangents.

"I had, and it went missing when I lost my job. Just disappeared. Of course the university claimed that it was all an administrative SNAFU and that it would be found in time, but that, like so many other promises, was never fulfilled. Years of careful research confiscated, literally overnight, and a career in ruins – all because I took on the wrong people. After I exhausted my savings I found work where I could, and became a pretty fair carpenter, which is honest labor and a real craft, unlike moving integers around in cyber-space or teaching propaganda to students in order to advance in the pecking order. I now live in harmony with nature, nobody bothers me, and the outside world can go to hell as far as I'm concerned. My job isn't to save it."

"Back to your hypothesis…Not that I'm uninterested in how crooked the media is, but my brother thought you had a key piece of information I needed to know–"

"Then you now know it," Sam interrupted. "The military was experimenting on livestock in the early seventies to advance its biological weapons program, in secret, while denying everything and planting red herrings in the press to keep it quiet. I believe they were injecting animals with something ugly, and I mean really ugly, and then going back and pulling organ and blood samples for analysis. If you look at a significant number of the suspect animals I isolated, they had a remarkable incidence of bovine leukemia and unexplainable levels of chemicals that aren't naturally occurring. I speculated that the government was testing viral agents that could be used to infect humans, using cows as hosts. Within weeks of proposing that, I was being accused, baselessly, I might add, of sexual misconduct, and shortly thereafter had been effectively blacklisted from academia."

Sam ran out of steam and shook his head. "That was my claim to fame, and I proved it, and it cost me everything. And nothing about it was ever covered by any news agency. So don't expect anything out of the media. The media is a prostitute, diseased and crooked under its glossy exterior, and it went along with the lies, as it has with most of the big ones during your lifetime. And it worked. To this day, God help us all, it worked."

TWENTY-FOUR

The End of the Story

The afternoon wore on, Sam rambling over the minutiae of his battle against the accusations that had poisoned his promising career, Jeffrey allowing him to talk and recount whatever seemed important to him, much as he was sure his brother had.

Eventually Sam stopped talking, lost in the labyrinth of his memories, fighting unwinnable battles against long-dead adversaries over issues nobody remembered or cared about. Kaycee rounded the garage and came back to the porch, her stride confident and unassuming; a graceful dancer's glide, Jeffrey thought. He watched as she mounted the stairs, brushing a lock of unruly hair from her eyes, and then fixed Jeffrey with a disapproving stare.

"He tires easily. The medications do that. It's time for him to rest now. I hope you got what you came for, because the meeting's over," she said, one hand on her hip, the other clutching a pair of work gloves.

Sam returned from whatever internal neverland he'd retreated to and waved her off with a feeble hand.

"Don't be rude, Kaycee. Our guest was patiently entertaining my stories and asking some questions. This is the brother of the young man I spoke to when you were out buying supplies…what was that, a month and a half ago? I told you I'd had a visitor."

"That was right after the accident, so almost two months," she said.

"We were just talking about the past. Ghosts in the machine. The end of an era," Sam said cryptically, finishing his last glass of tea, the pitcher now drained as the day had drifted past them.

Jeffrey edged forward in his seat. "Is there anything else you can tell me? Anything my brother seemed particularly interested in?" he tried, hoping for more from Sam before he got preempted for good.

Kaycee gave him a dark glare, annoyed that Jeffrey hadn't taken her hint. "Why don't you just ask him and leave my grandfather in peace?" she demanded, her tone still neutral but her eyes flashing with annoyance that he hadn't stood and left yet.

"Be hard to do, Kaycee. He passed on. So have some respect for the dead," Sam chided, his voice low.

She blinked twice, as though not registering the words, and then shook her head. "I'm sorry. Obviously, I didn't know. But I have to insist on you winding this up. He really isn't in any shape for a lengthy interrogation."

"Nonsense. We're sitting on the porch having a drink. There isn't even any booze in it. How much harm can it do?" Sam grumbled.

"The doctor said you weren't to exert yourself."

"I'm seated, not pole dancing," Sam said.

Jeffrey regarded them both. "Sam...Kaycee. I'm sorry, I didn't mean to meddle or disrupt anything here. I'm just looking for answers, and hoping to learn why my brother was so obsessed with the same topic that interested your grandfather years ago. Sam, if you've told me everything, I won't keep you any longer." He pushed back on his seat and rose, regarding the professor with resignation. "Then that's the entirety of what you two discussed? Your theory about the livestock mutilation?"

Kaycee's mouth hardened into a determined line, and she took a step toward him. "That's what you're talking about?" she asked.

"Don't go off half-cocked, Kaycee. I don't mind. It's just a question, only words." Sam turned his attention back to Jeffrey. "I wish I could remember anything more about that afternoon, but it was so soon after the fall, and I was on a lot of meds. I think that's everything we covered. He seemed quite attentive about the detail – he was a very bright young fellow."

"Then he's told you everything," Kaycee said, obviously hoping to end the conversation. "There's nothing more for you here."

Jeffrey nodded, and after a split second of internal battle, extended his hand to Sam, who was still seated, rocking slightly in his chair. "It was a real pleasure meeting you, Sam. Thanks for taking the time with me." His brow furrowed. "Is there any way to get in touch with you if any more questions occur to me?"

Sam scowled. "Don't have a phone. No T.V., either. Don't need 'em. Waste of money, if you ask me. Had a cell phone, but the service expired last month and I haven't gotten around to paying for more. Unnecessary with Kaycee here. But on my to-do list…"

Jeffrey turned to Kaycee, half afraid she was going to slap him. "Would it be possible to get your number?"

She exhaled with exasperation, then turned and hopped from the porch to the ground, ignoring the stairs. "I'll give it to you on the way to the car," she called over her shoulder as she started down the path toward the gate. "You coming?"

Jeffrey gave Sam a parting salute and followed after her. "What did I do that's got you so angry? Whatever it is, I apologize," he said.

"You came here and interrupted an old man's convalescence to stir up a painful past that just about destroyed him, and you want to know why I'm upset? He cries out in the middle of the night sometimes, did you know that? No. How could you? He's had a very rough time of it for as long as I've been alive – my mother told me all about it once I was old enough to understand. He went from being a respected academic to an outcast, an intellectual forced to earn his living with his hands. Everyone he was close to either shunned him, or is dead – my mother, my grandmother, his supposed friends that wanted nothing to do with him once he was no longer the campus golden boy…I'm sorry about your brother, by the way. I never met him. But I'm still sorry."

"I…I didn't realize. I'm sorry too, Kaycee. Really."

They walked along in silence, the treetops quivering from a light breeze, budding with the promise of spring, and Jeffrey tried a different tack.

"What were you doing before you moved out here?"

"I'm a translator. I took a sabbatical to look after him for ninety days, and I've been doing freelance work in the meantime. I'll return to my job in another month, back in New York, and then he'll be alone again, out here in the middle of God's ass crack."

"A translator. That's interesting. What language?"

She stopped and turned to face him.

"Look. Jeffrey, right? I'm sure you're a nice guy, and you mean well, but I'm not in a great mood right now, and I've never been good with chitty chat. Don't take it the wrong way, but we're not going to go get a cup of coffee somewhere while I tell you all about my hopes and dreams. You came, you got what you wanted, and now you're leaving. That's all the contact we'll ever have. So it doesn't really matter what I do or what you do, does it? I'm just the rude chick who almost shot you today – it's probably best if we leave it at that."

He returned her gaze, several responses on the tip of his tongue, then he thought better of it and offered a smile. "Thankfully, almost being shot's like almost being pregnant. That would have seriously ruined my day. I guess I owe you one for not blowing my head off."

Her expression softened, and he noticed that she had tiny flecks of gold in her hazel irises that caught the sun when the light hit them just right. "Around here, I think they actually offer a reward for every lawyer you shoot," she said.

"I knew I liked the place for a reason."

They resumed walking down the path, startling a squirrel that scampered up a nearby tree, and Jeffrey was struck by how idyllic the setting was.

"It's beautiful out here," he said, and she nodded.

"I know. It is. And I'm sorry if I'm wound up. It's just that it's been such a struggle for him to get better, and each one of these episodes takes more out of him than you know. He'll be up for days now, replaying things in his head, and it'll just make things more difficult for us all. He's not a young man, in case you didn't notice, and for all his brave front, he almost died when he fell – he was all alone, and he easily could have. He lay on the floor for hours before he was able to crawl to the phone." She paused as they neared the bend in the drive. "That's why I'm here."

"What are you going to do once you have to go back to work?"

"That's one of my problems. I don't know. He needs someone around, but I'm all he's got. I figure I'll tackle that in another month. Of course he says he's fine, and that he'll do okay by himself, but we've already seen how that turned out. A repeat performance, and he wouldn't be so lucky…"

"No. I can see how he wouldn't be."

They arrived at the gate and Jeffrey offered her his hand. She took it, shaking it with a surprisingly strong grip, her shoulders square beneath the sweater as she studied him.

"I thought you wanted my number."

"I do. Just tell me. I'll remember it."

"You sure you will?"

"I'm good with things like that. I will."

She gave him a 212 area code number and he repeated it back to her.

"There. It's now locked away in my memory banks, never to be forgotten. Kaycee and Sam. Have gun, will travel."

She laughed lightly and spun, leaving him to slip out the same way he had come in. "Take care, lawyer man."

"You too," he said, and for a reason he couldn't have explained, he felt like something important had just happened, something essential to his being that he didn't understand but that was as tangible as a punch to the gut. Then his inner voice came to the rescue, chastising him for having improper thoughts about Kaycee when he was in a hot and heavy relationship with Monica – the new love of his life. That was unlike him. He was usually as ethical as they came. And yet the stirring in him that Kaycee had caused was undeniable.

He watched as she made her way back up the drive, and when she disappeared into the grove of trees he felt unaccountably empty, as though a part of him had been taken with her as she returned to an old man on a rustic porch who was waiting for dusk, as, ultimately, were they all.

TWENTY-FIVE

Suspicions Allayed

Jeffrey flipped the sun visor down as he approached Washington's outskirts, mulling over the professor's disclosures, a dark idea beginning to form. Was there something to his hypothesis that the government had been involved in covert testing of bio-warfare agents forty years ago? And even if so, why would it matter now? That was ancient history – hardly the sort of thing that got planes blown up, even if you were the hardest-boiled conspiracy theorist on Earth.

And yet Keith had chosen to send Jeffrey on a quest to talk to the ex-academic, and had obviously believed that his story was an important enough aspect of whatever he'd been researching to warrant making the trip a priority. He replayed the discussion over and over, but didn't see anything he might have overlooked the first time – and his memory couldn't expunge the image of Kaycee standing in the sun, holding a gun on him, blond mop shimmering like an angry lion's, her eyes radiating an allure that was as undeniable as it was powerful.

No matter how he sliced the professor's account, at the end of the day it was nothing more than a theory about sins of the past that had no bearing on the present that he could see. A tragic tale of abuse of power, no question, and if true, evidence that the government had been dirty, but that was hardly front page news even on a slow day. Try as he might there was no smoking gun, and as he pulled to the curb near Jakes' office, he was no closer to a hoped-for breakthrough than when he'd started in the morning. Although something had shifted in his perspective, and he was no longer thinking his brother had been crazy: Something about the professor's tale had resonated with Jeffrey, and by the end of their discussion he'd been left feeling that his brother had been sane, but pulling at a dangerous thread – and one worth killing over.

He slipped the keys through the mail slot as instructed, forgoing the note since the car was in plain view, and then walked to the corner and flagged down a taxi at the intersection. The driver dropped him off a hundred yards from the storage facility, and he saw with relief that he still had time to rummage through his things so he could bring a box of belongings back with him to the condo, satisfying any prying eyes.

Jeffrey spent a half hour in his locked area and got more clothes, as well as some photographs and personal items, and packed them all into a large carton that would just fit in his trunk. He carefully clasped the padlock and carried his carton past the desk clerk getting ready to shut down and then out to his car. He'd guessed correctly on the box's size, and soon was winding his way back home, glad to be rid of the Taurus and feeling like he'd need to take a long shower to get the vehicle's stink off his skin.

There was a parking space near his building, and after some juggling of keys he manhandled the container to the condo and pushed his way through the front door. His phone rang as he was stepping into the foyer, and he muttered a curse as he dropped the carton in the entry hall and felt for his cell.

"Hey. I tried calling you earlier, but you didn't pick up," Monica said.

"What? Oh, shit. I forgot my phone in the car. No wonder. Where are you?"

He peered into the darkened living room and flipped on the lights. "I just got home."

"Perfect. You hungry?"

"Starving."

"Want to hit Caruzzo's? I could go for their veal…"

"That sounds great. You want to meet me here or at the restaurant?" Jeffrey asked.

"I'll come by. Say, twenty minutes?"

"That will give me just enough time to rinse the dust off and slip into something more comfortable."

"Okay. See you then," she said, and hung up.

He hoisted the box and lugged it into the spare bedroom, then undressed as he moved through the rooms, finishing by hopping on one leg as he wrestled his pants off, narrowly avoiding falling face first on the floor before he threw the bathroom door open and cranked the water on. Ten minutes later he was standing naked in his bedroom, debating which shirt to wear, when the street buzzer echoed through the condo, sounding like the wrong answer on a television game show. He grabbed the green polo shirt directly in front of him and pulled it over his head as he hurried to the intercom, held down the black button for a few moments, and jogged back to the bedroom for pants.

When the knock came at the door he was standing near it, barefoot, brushing his fingers through his damp hair. He twisted it open, and Monica stepped through, moving directly to him and planting a long kiss on his lips.

"Hmm. I missed you," she purred.

"Me too," he said, a twinge of guilt accompanying the words as a vision of Kaycee popped into his consciousness, immediately followed by Jakes' craggy countenance.

"You planning to go out like that? Do the hippie barefoot thing? I'm cool with it if you are, although I think the restaurants generally insist on shoes for service," she teased, looking down at his feet. "You're not in San Francisco anymore."

"I'll be ready in no time. You're early," he said, kissing her forehead.

"Traffic was nonexistent coming here."

"That's lucky," he said, and detached from her and headed back to the bedroom. "Give me two minutes," he called over his shoulder, disappearing through the doorway.

She set her purse on the dining room table and walked to the refrigerator. "We need to go to the grocery store tomorrow. All you have is water, beer, and wine."

Jeffrey reappeared wearing shoes and carrying a jacket. "And water comes out of the tap for free. A waste of valuable beer space, if you ask me," he said with a grin.

"How did it go today?"

"Sort of a disaster, but I expected that. Next time I'll mark the boxes so I know what's in them. This way I had to unpack everything to find what I wanted, then re-pack it all again. Big pain in the ass, but it's over now, and I could eat a horse."

"Which is probably what they make the lasagna with."

"That's fine. You put enough cheese on anything and I'll eat it. Ready?"

"Lead the way. Unless you're feeling frisky first," she said, the offer unmistakable.

The guilty feeling returned, but he shrugged it away. "Can I get a rain check? I hardly ate anything for lunch."

"Poor baby. You need to keep your strength up."

"Exactly. Although beer has calories, so I could always chug one and then…"

"Come on. Let's get you fed. I hate it when my studs fade early from starvation," she said, and took his hand. She smelled great, as always, and any trace of suspicion evaporated. What had Jakes been thinking? And why had Jeffrey let himself be talked out of his money so easily on a snipe hunt? He didn't need the PI to tell him that Monica was exactly what she seemed to be. He'd never been more sure of anything in his life.

TWENTY-SIX

Further Information

"I'd like to get together with you today, if possible. Meet at the same bar at seven?" Jakes asked, his voice emotionless over the pay phone around which the Monday lunch crowd milled like ants.

"Sure, but can't you just give me the high points over the phone?" Jeffrey asked. The connection was terrible, and he strained to make out any nuance over the roar of traffic.

"I'd rather do it in person. See you at seven," Jakes said before disconnecting.

Jeffrey stared at the phone and replaced the handset, a sense of foreboding stewing in his stomach. Then his logical side reminded him that the man was likely going through the motions so that Jeffrey felt like it had been money well spent – the insistence on an in-person meeting to close the case was undoubtedly stylistic, probably so that he could get a check for the final balance at the same time.

He paused as he stared at the pay phone, and considered calling the number Kaycee had given him. There was no reason he could think of for doing so, and after an internal debate he abandoned the idea in favor of returning to work and earning his considerable keep.

Seven rolled around before he knew it, and he begged off with Monica again in favor of doing his own laundry and running errands in preparation for the Switzerland trip, now only two days away. When he entered the darkened pub, he immediately spotted Jakes at the same table as the last time, and after a glance around the place, walked over and sat across from him.

"So? I'm here. What do you have for me?" Jeffrey asked, eyes trailing the bartender as he meandered over to them to take their order. "I'll take a draft ale, please. Jakes?"

"Coke."

The bartender nodded and returned to the bar as Jeffrey studied Jakes' poker face.

"Let's wait for your drink so we aren't interrupted," Jakes said, his voice raspy as a tractor-trailer's exhaust.

"Fair enough. Is it so bad I'm going to need something stronger?" Jeffrey joked, then his smile faded as Jakes' expression didn't change. "What did you find?"

The bartender returned with the drinks, and Jakes leaned back in his chair, which creaked under the bulk of his weight. He fixed Jeffrey with a weary stare and then reached into his jacket pocket and pulled out a small note pad.

"We can start with her living situation. She doesn't live with two roommates. She actually has a very nice apartment about nine blocks away in a high-end building that ain't cheap. So the bit about the roommates isn't true."

"Wait. How do you know that she doesn't have roommates?"

"Only one name on the box, and for a hundred bucks the custodian told us that she's the only one in the place." Jeffrey scowled, and Jakes held up a hand to stop any protest. "I used a female to do it, and trust me, the custodian isn't going to be talking."

"Shit. Are you positive?"

"I do this for a living, remember?"

"Yeah. So I heard. Thanks for the car, by the way."

"There were no new blood stains in it, so I'm glad it came in handy." Jakes didn't crack a smile as he said it.

"Okay, so she misstated her living situation. Why, we don't know."

"Correct. And that's not all."

Jeffrey took a long pull on his beer. "What else?"

"The car was sticking in my craw, so I did some more checking on it. The company is located in Langley, Virginia, but strangely has no storefront, no offices, nothing. It's basically a P.O. box."

"Which tells us nothing other than that perhaps she had an asset protection guy set up something to ensure her anonymity."

"Possibly. But there's the matter of her other car. A white Mercedes convertible, which is in her name. One year old. Nice. About sixty grand, give or take. Paid for. There's no loan on it."

"I've never seen her drive a Benz. Are you sure?"

"Positive. I've got a photo of her behind the wheel – she left for the day about an hour and a half after she took off from your place. Went back to her apartment, changed, and then drove away in her E350. My operative didn't have time to follow her – by the time she'd gotten her car started and pursued her, Monica had disappeared around the corner. Apparently she drives like a maniac."

"I can attest to that."

They both sat in silence.

"That's it?"

"No. She also has a police record, but that will take more digging."

"A police record!" Jeffrey's mouth hung open. This wasn't the conversation he thought he would be having. "For what?"

"I don't know. The record's sealed. The only reason I know is because I pay people with specialized access to a different layer of the database. But I can't see what's been sealed. At least not without a lot more money. So all we know is she was arrested when she was seventeen, and then the records got sealed, which isn't unusual for a juvenile."

"Tell me that's all."

Jakes rubbed a large hand over his tired face and took a sip of his soda, then nodded. "That's it. Which brings you to decision time."

"I'm not sure I follow you."

"You need to figure out what you want to do. I'd advise you to have another day or two of surveillance conducted and throw some resources at discovering what she was charged with. But it's your call, and I don't want to seem like I'm just fishing for a way to do you out of more money. You're into this about three grand now, and what I'm proposing would easily double that. So it's not a choice I'd make lightly."

Jeffrey shook his head. "This is all…I'm really not sure what to make of it."

"Could be nothing. Maybe the lady didn't want you to know she lived alone in case you were some kind of nut job or stalker, so she has a stock line about her roommates, and one thing led to another and she decided it didn't matter or she was too embarrassed to confess. Could be she's rich, and she doesn't want you to know it, which is why she's driving the Alfa. I'm still waiting for bank records. We should have them this week – they take longer."

"How do you do that?"

"We pull a credit report and then mark having done so as an error so it doesn't show up, and then we pretext to get the records."

"That can't be legal."

"Do you really care?"

Jeffrey stiffened. "I'm an officer of the court…"

"Right. But the question stands."

"Officially, of course. Personally, not in the slightest."

"Then it's good this a personal issue. But you still need to decide how to proceed. I'm okay if you want to walk away. Like I said, there could be an easy explanation for it all. On the arrest, she could have been busted for smoking weed, for all I know, or graffiti tagging or whatever the hell kids do these days. It really depends on how sure you want to be. If you want definites, you'll need to go the distance. If not, put your mind at ease with what we have and enjoy her company. I mean, it's not like you're hiring her for a top secret clearance position, right? She's a girlfriend."

Jeffrey mulled over the big man's words. "What would you do?"

"If I was super serious, as in thinking about getting married serious? I'd pay to be sure. If I was hanging out with her, banging around? What do you really need to know besides she's a knockout and she's up for it? Things can't have changed that much since I was young and single…"

Jeffrey drank another large mouthful of beer, which suddenly tasted like motor oil. He wished he could confide in Jakes, but that was off the table. Besides, he was a big boy, and he knew what he needed to do.

"I brought another two thousand. Let's do the full monty. I'm pretty serious about her."

He carefully counted out the cash and slid it across the table to the investigator, who counted it wordlessly before pocketing it and patting his breast pocket.

"Do you want the photo of the car?" Jakes asked.

Jeffrey shrugged. "What's the point? Save it until you have everything and we settle up the final tab."

They agreed that Jakes would begin surveillance on Wednesday – he needed twenty-four hours to arrange for a pro team so they could go round the clock for two days if they needed to. Jeffrey paid the tab and they both left the bar, Jeffrey feeling dizzy from the unexpected turn the investigation had taken. He stopped on the way home and bought a deli sandwich at a corner market and then checked the time – he'd arranged for a locksmith to be at the condo at eight, figuring erroneously that the meeting would take only a few minutes.

When he made it back the locksmith was standing at the front entry, wearing a jacket emblazoned with the company logo on the back, shifting from foot to foot as he checked his watch. Jeffrey apologized for being late and escorted him up to the condo, then showed him into the bedroom so he could check out the safe. After a single glance he turned to Jeffrey and told him it would be two hundred dollars. Jeffrey nodded, and the locksmith knelt and opened the toolbox he'd brought and extracted a stethoscope and some tools. Jeffrey sat on the edge of the bed and watched as he went about his work, and ten minutes later he opened the safe with a metallic clunk and swung the small door open.

Jeffrey waited until the man had left the condo before extracting the safe's contents, which consisted of a steel and gold Rolex Submariner watch, four thousand dollars in hundred dollar bills, five one-ounce gold ingots in protective plastic sleeves, and a sheaf of mortgage documents. There was no hidden message or clue, but he hadn't expected any – if his suspicions about the condo being wired were correct, any intruders would have gone through the safe as well, sanitizing it before anyone could get to it.

Jeffrey donned the watch, trading his Tag for the heavier Rolex, and pocketed the cash and the gold. He'd pack it for his trip – he had no idea what he'd find in Zurich, but having some extra liquidity couldn't hurt.

After memorizing the combination the locksmith had scrawled on the back of his receipt, he returned the mortgage docs and his old watch to the safe and moved to the dining room, where his sandwich was languishing on the table.

As he munched on the tasteless blob of starch and faux-cheese-layered meat, he turned over Jakes' findings in his head, hoping that Monica's subterfuge was all innocent. A coil of anxiety cautioned him that he couldn't assume anything, and to wait to draw any conclusions until he had all the information – hopefully available by the end of the week. A wave of nausea hit him at the possibility that everything Monica and he had shared together had been a lie. After the disequilibrium passed, he stood and balled up the remainder of the sandwich and strode into the kitchen. He tossed it into the trash and retrieved a beer for a liquid dinner, cold comfort against the dread that was inexorably creeping into his soul.

TWENTY-SEVEN

Parting is Such Sweet Sorrow

Tuesday night Monica came over after work, but Jeffrey seemed preoccupied – ostensibly with preparations for his trip the following day. He nearly confronted her a dozen times during their evening together, and it was only through force of will and the awareness that he was playing with his life that he controlled the impulse – a dangerous and foolhardy one, he knew.

Their lovemaking that night was intense, yet for him, lacking, although Monica seemed as passionate as ever. Once she'd drifted off to sleep, helped on her way by a bottle of inky Barolo and a post-dinner Baileys, he slipped soundlessly out of bed to the office, where he watched clips of one of his favorite comedians on YouTube until he was finally drowsy several hours later.

The following morning, he was up earlier than usual and washed some dry, burned toast down with a cup of scalding black coffee before going for a run, Monica still slumbering under the covers as the day's first light glowed behind the blinds. The soles of his Nikes thumped against the moist sidewalk as he developed a rhythm that returned like a chastened friend, abandoned since he'd moved to Washington. Other joggers moved along the same route, a loop that ran for eight blocks square and would take him forty-five minutes if he maintained his pace. His thoughts had been racing distractingly since his eyes opened, and he welcomed the inner calm that came from the exertion, worrying about nothing as he willed his legs to greater speed.

When he got back, Monica was up puttering in the kitchen, wearing one of his dress shirts and nothing else, and she glanced at him as he moved past her and into the bedroom.

"You're sweaty. I didn't know you ran," she commented, whipping some eggs in a bowl with a fork.

"Obviously I don't do it very often. Or ride, anymore, either. You can see that my bike hasn't budged since the movers stuck it in the spare bedroom."

"Feeling guilty about not exercising lately? I mean, not in a structured, outdoorsy kind of way?" she asked, waggling her eyebrows suggestively.

"I'm going to be cooped up in the office all day and then stuck on a flight for eight hours, so it was either now or never. Doubt I'll have motivation, or time, to do much in Switzerland," he said from the bedroom doorway. He peeled off his soaking T-shirt and sweat pants and pitched them into the laundry bin. "Damn, I'm already running later than I'd hoped. Maybe it wasn't such a good idea after all."

"Don't worry. I'm just going to cook up some eggs and I'll be out of here in ten minutes. Then it will be all yours. You want some? Hope so – I'm making more than I can eat."

"That would be awesome, Monica. I'll be finished showering right about the time they're ready."

He emerged from the bathroom in a heavy blue terrycloth robe with its sash cinched around his waist and took his usual seat at the dining room table. The eggs were delicious, lightly seasoned with salt and a dash of chili powder, and he devoured them in thirty seconds.

"You eat like a lumberjack, big boy."

"Guy's gotta keep up his strength, and breakfast is the most important meal of the day."

"Besides lunch and dinner, you mean," she said, finishing her eggs after him and carrying their plates into the kitchen. "So what do you have planned for the day?"

"I was thinking I'll work for about six hours, then take a cab to Dulles."

"You sure you don't want me to drive you?"

He resisted the temptation to ask her whether she was thinking of taking her Mercedes, and instead shook his head as he stood.

"No. Traffic will suck, and I may be able to duck out early and get a head start. I'm going to leave my car at the office and take a cab. But thanks for offering." He hoped he didn't sound distant, although that was how it came out – overly formal. She didn't seem to notice.

"Can I offer you anything else before I leave? Maybe one last round of adult entertainment?" she asked, oozing sex appeal in his oxford button up. "I'm not going to see you for three whole nights. And it gets lonely in the big city…"

He made a show of checking his watch.

"You know there's nothing I'd rather do, but I'm really running late now, honey."

She shrugged and gave him a pout that melted his heart. "Suit yourself. Can't say I didn't offer."

They dressed, and he walked her to the door, her hair still damp from the shower she'd taken while he was out. She stood on her tiptoes and gave him a long, deep kiss, her full lips savoring his in a manner he never grew tired of. When they parted he thought her eyes were moist, but it could have been a trick of the light.

"Safe travels, Jeff. Come back soon."

"To you. You can count on it."

They kissed again, and then she turned and let herself out as Jeffrey watched her go.

He followed her out the door twenty minutes after her departure, his garment bag on his shoulder, a conservative blue suit and red tie his uniform of the day. He let the car warm up for a few minutes while he checked his messages, and seeing nothing pressing, he put the transmission into gear and nosed into traffic, already getting heavy as thousands of workers spilled onto the city streets and jockeyed for advantage in the surging stream, another day in the world's most important capital convincingly underway.

Work was mercifully light, as was the commute heading out of town that afternoon, and the taxi delivered him to the airport almost three hours before his flight. After passing through security and suffering the intrusive search procedures, he made his way to his departure gate, and was relieved to find it near a lounge that boasted hot dogs and cocktails like Mom used to make.

Three beers later he was sitting in the jet awaiting takeoff, his head light from the alcohol, two ill-advised foot longs and too little sleep roiling in his stomach. Shortly after the plane launched into the sky and headed east he was asleep, dreaming about a bank vault in a country he'd never visited and the terrible secrets it might contain.

TWENTY-EIGHT

Zurich

Jeffrey's first impression of Zurich was "clean." The entire city was spotless, as though God's own janitorial crew had worked overtime to keep the buildings and surroundings pristine for the good Swiss people. The airport was a marvel, the hotel efficient and sparkling, and the people glowed with the prosperous sheen of natural superiority.

His room wasn't ready for check-in yet, so he left his bag with the courteous bell staff and headed down to the lower hotel level where the symposium was being held. The first hour or so would be orientation, so he wasn't worried that he'd missed much when he slipped into the panel discussion on the safety of bank deposits in the new fiscal climate of the European Union. The moderator was a renowned German economist well known for his bearish view of the Union's future, and the hour turned into two of parsing the minutiae of the new banking regulations that had been put into place and the likelihood that the next big systemic shock would wipe out depositors, rather than being backstopped by governments.

The next meeting was more of the same, and as the day wore on he developed a splitting headache – a function of stress, dehydration from the flight, sleep deprivation, and jet lag. At a break between sessions at three o'clock, he called Soderbergh Bank on a lobby pay phone and arranged to be admitted after hours, with an appointment scheduled at six-thirty that evening. The vice president he spoke with, a Gunther Rundquist, was extremely accommodating, and assured Jeffrey that at Soderbergh Bank, service to its private clientele was its top priority. With advance notice the safe deposit vault could be accessed up to nine o'clock at night, provided his name was on the account and he could supply proper identification.

The final roundtable discussion of the day was on the changing reporting requirements and the aggressive new information-sharing being rammed down the EU participant countries by their high-tax brethren. It was generally agreed that in a few years it would be almost impossible to have true bank secrecy anymore, which was both positive in criminal cases and negative for anyone engaging in legal asset protection. The revenue authorities routinely overstepped their charters and treated any tax avoidance as being equivalent to tax evasion, leaving the innocent and guilty alike to mount expensive legal battles to defend themselves. For the gathered attorneys it was good news, as their area of specialization would get a huge boost from the deluge of lawsuits the trend would generate.

When the meeting broke up, Jeffrey returned to his room and stripped off his suit. The room's walls and door were mercifully thick, so he wasn't disrupted by his fellow conference-goers returning to their rooms. He lay prone on the comfortable bed and closed his eyes, and in five minutes was drowsing, anticipation over finally discovering what was in the box replaced by the numb embrace of slumber.

Soderbergh Bank at *Bahnhofstrasse* 622 was a staid affair, its conservative, understated façade giving no hint that it was one of the more renowned private banks in Switzerland. Jeffrey surveyed the dark street, noting that the daytime pedestrian traffic had all but disappeared now that normal business hours were over, and then approached the ornate wrought-iron door and pressed a small white button beneath a ten-inch-wide engraved brass plaque with a single word inscribed upon it: Soderbergh.

He shifted from foot to foot, the cold slicing through his casual clothes and jacket. A tall, gray pinstripe-suited man in his fifties opened the inner glass door and peered through the ironwork at him.

"*Ja?*" the man asked.

"Jeffrey Rutherford. I have an appointment with a Herr Rundquist at seven-thirty."

"*Ach*, just so. One moment please," the man replied in slightly accented English, and then swiped a card through a reader at his side. The heavy sound of multiple bolts sliding open was accompanied by the whirring of electric motors, and then the door swung wide. "Mr. Rutherford. Please. Come in. Herr Rundquist is expecting you."

Jeffrey stepped into the large marble-floored foyer, noting the antique tables along each mahogany-paneled wall, oil paintings of pastoral landscapes adorning the space and lending it an aura of formality he would have expected in a castle, not a modest building in the center of Zurich. The door closed behind him. His escort pressed a series of buttons, and the lights increased in intensity as the man beckoned to him, indicating a long hall to his right.

They walked three quarters of the length of the corridor and stopped at the oversized door of one of the offices, where Jeffrey could see a man sitting at a desk in the office beyond the outer reception area. He glanced up from his computer screen and straightened, then rose and called to Jeffrey.

"Mr. Rutherford! How nice to meet you. Come, have a seat."

Jeffrey moved through the empty antechamber and into the office. Rundquist stood and reached across the desk, and shook his hand with polite restraint. Jeffrey sat and studied the banker – perhaps sixty years old, thinning steel hair combed straight back with pomade, ruddy jowls and pudgy hands, a Swiss doughboy who looked like he'd never sullied his life with a day of exercise.

"Before we begin, let's get the formalities over, yes? Do you have your passport and another form of identification?" Rundquist asked, his voice tuned to a pleasant timbre.

Jeffrey slid his papers across the table to him, and watched as he scanned both and then printed a hard copy.

"Please sign here, and here," the banker said, handing him a pen that cost as much as Jeffrey's hotel room.

He dutifully scrawled his name in the indicated spots and then took back his passport and driver's license, pocketing them as he stood.

"Where are the boxes?" he asked as Rundquist stepped out from behind his desk.

"Follow me. In our secondary vault area. At the basement level."

They walked together to the doorway at the end of the hall. The Swiss swiped another card reader with his access card and the door opened inward with a hydraulic hiss. Lights flickered on automatically, and Rundquist led him down an endless flight of stairs to a level two stories below the street. Another door, at least six feet wide, loomed at the far end of the room, and the banker stopped at a screen at the door's edge and stood still while the optical scanner verified his retinal map. A green light blinked twice, and then he pulled the heavy lever. The two-foot-thick solid steel door eased open on massive lubricated hinges, and Rundquist indicated another portal to his right.

"Your box is in there. I hope you remember your code, yes? You'll be unable to open it if you don't have it."

"I have everything I need."

"Very well, then. Take your time. I'll be here waiting for you. When you wish to exit the vault, press 22446 on the keypad and the door will open."

"Should I enter that on this one, too?"

"Yes. We reset the code after each entry, and we don't have many visitors, so that is your code for this evening. 22446. I've taken the liberty of writing it down for you so you don't have difficulty exiting." The banker handed him a business card with the digits printed neatly on the back.

Jeffrey punched in the code and another set of bolts clanked, then the ponderous slab eased open as if of its own volition. Jeffrey pushed by it and found himself in a brightly lit room with row after row of boxes, their red LED displays glowing in futuristic symmetry, a smaller alcove off to his right with a steel table and chair for his use. The door hissed closed behind him, the locking mechanism seated a set of bolts back into place, and he was alone in the room.

He moved along the nearest row, scanning the numbers, and then turned and edged to the far wall, where his brother's box was near the center, at shoulder height. He coded in his secret password; for a moment nothing happened, and then something in the compartment whined almost inaudibly and a latch released.

Jeffrey extracted the long container and carried the metal box to the table, unsure what he was going to find. He lifted the lid, reached in, and removed the contents: a Canadian passport with his brother's photo but the name Richard Muller embossed on the identification page; a glass bottle with an unreadable label; a sheaf of documents bundled together, held with a rubber band, a yellow note visible on the top. He slipped the note from beneath the binding and read it quickly, his brother's familiar script as orderly as ever.

Memorize the contents of the documents and then soak them with the bottle of acid. It will dissolve everything into mush. Your photographic memory is one of the primary reasons I had to get you involved – sorry, bro, but that's not a really common quirk, so you're it.

There are three men you must meet to understand the whole story of what's contained in these pages. I'm not completely sure about the contents myself, but I have a hunch, and if I'm correct it means the end of humanity. But you need to get it to someone who can analyze it and confirm my suspicion. There are only a couple of scientists I've been able to find who aren't compromised, and who have sufficient skill to verify what this is. One is Antonio Carvelli in Rome – a professor. The other is Francois Bertrand, a scientist at the Pasteur Institute in Paris who specializes in virology. The third is a German, but he should be considered hostile: Alfred Schmidt – an ex-Nazi who went to work for the U.S. on bio-weapons after the war. He's now in Frankfurt, living out his last years in a nursing home. I contacted him in February posing as a journalist named Richard Muller, and he agreed to meet. You can pretend to be me and interrogate him. He may be completely senile, but he sounded fairly sharp, even at ninety-four. His address is below, along with Carvelli's and Bertrand's. Jeffrey, find out what this means. You'll have to figure out what to do once you have confirmation. Be very careful – the group behind this will kill anyone who gets in their way. Good luck. Remember – don't take anything from this box.

Jeffrey unwrapped the sheaf of papers and began reading them, taking his time – some kind of printout, page after page of columns of numbers. At the end were a diagram, a row of horizontally oriented bar charts, and a long sequence of seemingly random letters. Jeffrey wished at that moment he'd paid more attention in math and science class, because it was all gibberish to him and might as well have been written in Mongolian. Still, he committed the unintelligible strings of numbers to memory, closing his eyes after each page and verifying that he could instantly recall the whole document as if it were in front of him, the numbers and symbols clear.

Finished, he placed the pages back into the box and opened the bottle, taking care not to splash any of the corrosive liquid on himself, and carefully poured the fluid into the bottom, where it instantly began bubbling the gray paint as it soaked into the paper. An acrid chemical smoke drifted from the container, easily sucked away by the vault's air purification system, and after a few minutes the sodden roll of paper had dissolved into a white, formless goo.

He debated taking the passport, but decided to honor his brother's instructions and replaced it before lowering the lid and returning it to the open compartment. He closed the door, and the LED flashed and displayed the box number again.

Jeffrey punched in the exit code and walked into the outer vault, where Rundquist was sitting patiently. He rose when Jeffrey appeared and faced him with an impassive expression.

"I trust everything was satisfactory?" Rundquist asked.

"Yes, all was in order. Thank you again for agreeing to meet me. I appreciate it."

"My pleasure. We are always available for our customers."

The banker led him through the vault entrance and heaved the door closed, the locks securing with a muted thump after he'd inserted his card in the scanner. They ascended the stairs to the ground floor level, where another card swipe got them back into the administrative area. Rundquist showed him to his office and offered a perfunctory smile.

"So, Mr. Rutherford. Is there anything else we can do for you?"

"No, thank you. Many thanks for accommodating me." Jeffrey extended his hand and shook the banker's, who then motioned for Jeffrey to accompany him to the entrance. The second man was standing there as if frozen in place. No sooner was Jeffrey on the street than the heavy barrier snicked back into place, and then he was alone on the darkened sidewalk, the cold his only companion as he walked to the nearest large intersection.

A shuffling from a doorway behind him startled him; just as he registered a fast-moving form approaching from the shadows of a nearby building, a starburst of pain shot through his head and he crumpled to the sidewalk, his vision already dimming before he hit the concrete, unconscious.

TWENTY-NINE

A Mugging

Jeffrey's first tentative sensation of awareness came in the form of a corpulent man's face only a few feet from his, the steam of his breath carrying with it a vague scent of cabbage and onions. He cracked his eyes open more and the man leaned away from him, yelling something in German. When Jeffrey struggled to push himself to a sitting position, the man returned his attention to him, barking a harsh command.

"*Nein!*"

Jeffrey reached to the back of his head, from which intense pain was radiating, and his fingers came away wet, sticky with blood.

"*Nein,*" the man snapped again, and then everything receded and Jeffrey closed his eyes, reasoning that it wouldn't hurt to get a little rest while all the commotion was going on around him.

The next thing he knew he was being hoisted onto a gurney, a stiff brace around his neck, and he winced as movement caused agony to flare through his skull, which felt as he imagined it would if he stuck it into a car crusher. A burst of static sounded from a nearby radio, and then he was inside an ambulance and bouncing down the road, explosions of suffering greeting every bump and speed change.

It seemed like only a few minutes later that he was being wheeled into a hospital, the smell distinctively medicinal, antiseptic wafting through the air like astringent fog. A physician, Jeffrey guessed from his white exam coat and the stethoscope draped around his neck, young and earnest, appeared in his field of view, and quickly shined a small flashlight into each eye, issuing terse instructions to someone Jeffrey couldn't see.

More movement, and then delicate hands were probing at the back of his head before pulling away.

An hour and a half later he was stitched and had been through his first-ever cranial CT scan, and was waiting for the attending physician to appear and give him the results. The pain had gradually subsided after a nurse gave him an injection, and he was now in a somnambulistic purgatory somewhere between full consciousness and oblivion, barely registering when a figure entered and approached him.

"Can you understand me?" The words seemed to arrive as though from a great distance, and Jeffrey knew that he needed to focus and wake up – this was something important. His eyes flickered and opened, and he saw the same young doctor looking at him with concern.

And speaking English, with a slight German inflection, the particular harshness of that tongue coloring his words.

"Mr. Rutherford. Can you understand me?"

"Yes," Jeffrey croaked, his voice sounding like an old gate creaking open.

"You're in the hospital. You were attacked. Mugged, yes, that is the word? Robbed. You sustained a severe blow to the head, and have a concussion. No intracranial bleeding, but serious, still. I'm admitting you, and you will need to stay for a day or two, yes?" the doctor said, the question more stylistic than interrogative.

"Mugged…"

"Yes. You're very lucky someone found you quickly. You lost a lot of blood. The blow to the head was an ugly one. Only four stitches, but a bleeder."

Jeffrey felt suddenly nauseated, the lights overly bright, his vision fuzzy. "How…how long?"

"How long will you be here, or were you passed out?"

"…Here…"

"That depends on your recovery. All concussions are different. Basically, your brain hit the inside walls of your skull, so it's injured. The question is one of degree. You may be feeling better in a few more hours, or it could take days. We will keep you under observation until you're improved. For now, all you have to do is rest and let your body heal itself."

"What…you said robbed?"

"Yes. The police gathered your things and will be by later to speak with you, but not before I give my approval."

"My…things…"

"I'm afraid your money was stolen, but they left your wallet and passport. And a key card from your hotel. That's all the police told me."

Jeffrey shut his eyes again, too much information hitting him, overwhelming him. "My hotel…"

"The police will notify them so that your room isn't disturbed. Don't worry. In the meantime, I'm going to leave you to rest. Once you're feeling better, I can have one of the nurses make a call for you, if there's someone you'd like to notify about your accident."

"Um…no. I'm alone here…"

"Very well, then. They'll be wheeling you to a room in a little while, and then you're to stay put and sleep. Don't try to get up. Right now, you need to remain immobile. Do you understand?"

"Yes."

The hospital noises drifted away as he closed his eyes, and soon he was back in a stilted dreamland, his last memory before he slipped into complete unconsciousness an image of a diagram and rows of numbers that made no sense to him, as alien as an artifact of an ancient, forgotten civilization.

"I'm telling you, he was clean. There was nothing on him." The caller spoke in soft tones, his voice never rising above the level of a murmur.

"Then what was he doing at a private bank? At that hour? Are you absolutely sure?"

"We searched every inch of him. There was nothing – no notes, no flash drive, nothing. Look – he's an attorney. He specializes in asset protection, right? Is it possible that his visit to the bank pertained to business?"

"Anything's possible, but we aren't paid for speculation. We need to be sure he doesn't know anything that could compromise our effort. We're far too close to implementation."

"Then let me terminate him. Problem solved."

"Not necessarily. If he talked to someone…no, we can't just finish him. We need to continue surveillance and see what he does next. I don't need to remind you how devastating it would be if we were discovered."

"So we maintain our watch," the speaker said resignedly.

"Correct. He likely doesn't know anything, but this makes me nervous."

"Do you have anyone working on getting inside the bank?"

"We're pulling out all the stops. With any luck, we'll know what he was doing there by tomorrow. But that's not a guarantee – if we can't find a point of weakness with the staff, we may never know."

"Well, the good news is that he didn't have anything on him."

"Yes, he may be ignorant of the plan. But we need to be sure."

"It shouldn't be much longer, should it?"

"We're only days away."

"At which point it won't matter. The world will have bigger problems than what one attorney may or may not know."

"But until that point, he's your top priority. That hasn't changed."

"I understand. He's not going anywhere. The hospital is going to hold him for at least twenty-four hours, and probably longer. So for the near term, he's neutralized."

"Report back to me if anything changes."

"As always," the speaker said, and then disconnected. An announcement boomed from the overhead public address system, calling for a crash cart in the emergency room. The man surveyed his surroundings, eyeing the waiting patients, and then moved back into the hospital corridor, his green surgical scrubs making him as anonymous as any of the other staff hurrying to attend to their duties, everyone focused on their preoccupations and uninterested in the young orderly.

At the end of the wing he spied an exit sign over a doorway, and in a minute he was outside, disappearing around a corner, his work at the hospital, at least for the moment, concluded.

THIRTY

Truth Hurts

Jeffrey awoke at one a.m., the squishing sound of a nurse's rubber soles against the hallway vinyl floor tiles as distinctive a sound as a cat yowling in heat. He opened his eyes and gazed around his private room. The chair and rolling table at the far end were illuminated by faint, ghostly moonlight from the window, the bluish-white luminescence leaking through the blinds and coloring everything with a spectral glow.

He groped at the side of the bed and found the control, then raised the back until he was sitting up. His head hurt, but not nearly as profoundly as earlier, which he took as a welcome sign that he was mending. He understood the concept of a concussion, having had a minor one as a child in a fall from a tree – his brain had been bruised, the fluid that surrounded it inadequate to the job of protecting it after a certain amount of force.

Jeffrey squinted in the dark and was relieved to note that his vision wasn't blurry anymore, which was further indication that the trauma was receding. He couldn't be sure, but given his progress, he might be released tomorrow. That heartened him, although he had no intention of trying to catch the last of the conference – while he wanted more than anything to believe that the mugging had been random, his instinct knew better. He had been knocked unconscious literally seconds after leaving the bank. Difficult to believe that was coincidence. Fortunately, he'd heeded his brother's instructions and left everything in the box, so any search would have come up empty. Which was probably the only reason he was still alive. They had no idea what he knew, if anything.

The irony was that he had no idea what he knew, either. The endless columns of numbers meant nothing to him. If someone had threatened him at gunpoint to spill the beans, at best he would have been able to say that he'd seen a nonsensical spreadsheet and an unintelligible diagram.

A lance of pain stabbed through his neck, and he reached up and felt where they'd stitched his head, a tiny shaved area around the wound where stubble prickled his fingertips as he gingerly probed the lump. How the hell was he supposed to save the planet if he didn't know what specifically was going to happen, or who was going to do whatever it was, or how? And how was he supposed to prevail against an adversary that could pick him off on the streets of Zurich at will, and who knew his every move?

Which stopped his racing thoughts dead. How were they tracking him? The obvious method was the cell phone – but he hadn't taken it with him to the bank. Which implied that they'd put him under physical surveillance, further complicating his predicament. So now he'd have to become an expert at ducking a professional surveillance team. *Good luck with that*, he thought morosely.

They'd left his credit cards and identification, which implied they could track the cards whenever he used them. As to his passport, most opportunistic muggers wouldn't have taken it, preferring to do a quick cash grab and then run before they were seen, so his assailants had stuck to that script. That was somewhat of a relief, although he could have easily gotten a replacement passport in a few days through the embassy, so not a meaningful break.

His head swam with the implications of trying to go off the radar so he could track down the contacts his brother had directed him to. Dumping the cell would be easy, but losing a pro team would not, and he hadn't the faintest idea how to go about it.

But he would need to figure it out. And quickly. He couldn't stay in Europe for very long without triggering alarms, and unfortunately all three of his objectives were there.

So now he had to evade detection, interrogate a hostile Nazi, and get to the scientific researchers in France or Italy – all while seeming to be going about his innocent business.

And stay alive.

That last bit would be perhaps the most difficult if he failed in any of his objectives. He had no doubt that he would be earmarked for execution the moment he slipped up – there would come a point where he posed more of a danger to his stalkers than knowing whom he'd talked to would compensate for, and judging by his brother's death, nothing would stop them once they'd decided he needed killing.

He looked at his watch, and an ugly idea occurred to him as he checked the time – the muggers had also neglected to take his Rolex, which struck him as odd, and the suspicion that it could also have a tracking device in it flitted through him. He'd have to do something about it. For now, he assumed they knew where he was, so there was no point.

It was one in the morning, which translated to seven in the evening in Washington. Was it possible Jakes might still be at his office? The man certainly kept odd hours, and Jeffrey debated quietly with himself before deciding to try standing. If that went well, he would attempt to find a telephone – using the room phone was a sucker bet. He carefully unclasped his watch and placed it under his pillow, then swung his legs over the side of the bed. At least he didn't have to contend with unhooking any machines – he'd obviously been stable enough to be relegated to the non-critical ward, which made him feel a little better about his condition.

His feet touched the cool floor and a wave of dizziness passed through him, but after a few seconds everything normalized and he felt stable, if weak. He was wearing an open-back gown, and he tried walking to the small closet and was heartened when he made it without blacking out. His shirt and pants were hanging inside, having been cleaned by a conscientious staff – typical Swiss efficiency.

Two minutes later he was dressed, and he crept to the partially open door, ears straining for any hint of movement in the corridor on the opposite side. Nothing greeted him, and after several moments he eased the door wider and stepped out into an empty, brightly lit hall. Jeffrey checked in both directions and then opted for the right, and found himself in a large main area at the end of the passage, a nurse's station on the far side with a solitary nurse talking on the phone, her back to him. He inched past and then came to a bank of elevators, their oversized doors facing him like silent sentries.

When he arrived at the ground floor there was more activity, and an attendant at the information desk looked up from reading her paperback novel and in response to his one-word question pointed to a bank of pay phones near the bathrooms. He thanked her with a muttered *"Danke"* and shuffled over to them, feeling suddenly worse for wear, the exertion not a great idea so soon after the head injury.

After a few tries he connected to an operator, who put him through to an international operator for the collect call. Jeffrey recited Jakes' number and his last name, then waited as the phone rang, its tone hollow in his ear. When Jakes answered, his unmistakable voice distinctive even thousands of miles away, the operator announced Jeffrey's name and he grudgingly accepted the call.

"Collect from Switzerland? You do lead an interesting life," Jakes growled when the operator had dropped off the line.

"I got mugged. They got my cash, and I haven't had a chance to get back to the hotel and reload. I'm in the hospital. Concussion."

"Are you all right?"

"I'll be okay if I don't stroke out first. Did you get a chance to follow up on Monica?"

A long pause echoed across the chasm, seconds building with tension before the PI cleared his throat.

"Maybe this should wait until you're feeling better," Jakes started, and Jeffrey's heart dropped, dreading what was coming.

"No. I need to know what you learned."

"You sure? Let's just say it's not good."

"I got that from your bedside manner. Just tell me. I can take it."

"You're the boss. The arrest? She was busted for prostitution when she was seventeen. No further collars since then, but generally speaking, you have to have been hooking for a while before you get caught. It's a little like drunk driving – it's never the first time that gets you arrested, you know?"

"Prostitution. You're absolutely sure?" Pained defeat colored Jeffrey's words.

"No doubt. Which brings me to what she's been doing since we picked her up yesterday. I'll spare you all the details. The short version is she had a date. A professional one, judging by the age of her companion. So either she was having dinner with Dad, who she's very, very fond of, or she was making some money while you were out of the picture."

"What do you mean, a date? She went to a restaurant? That's it?"

"No. She went to a restaurant and then to a hotel, where she stayed for two and a half hours before departing just after midnight."

Jeffrey was suddenly reeling, his worst fears coming out of the handset he clutched to his ear. He gripped the small steel counter beneath the phone for support and leaned against the edge of the glass panel separating it from its twin.

"Are you still there?" Jakes asked hesitantly.

"God. I'm such an idiot…"

"No, you aren't. You smelled a rat, and you hired me. So your instincts were good. Look, you aren't the first guy with a few bucks who's gotten involved with a pro who wanted to get out of the biz, and maybe wasn't completely forthcoming about her résumé. Don't beat yourself up. You're not omniscient, and there's no way you could have known, given that she misrepresented everything about herself."

Jeffrey felt like he was choking, and didn't trust himself to speak. He badly wished he could confide in the investigator, but that wasn't an option. Best case he could ask him some questions and get ideas.

The line hummed. In the lobby behind him, a woman coughed. Jeffrey began to regain his composure as he digested the news about Monica – news that he'd feared, but also was better off knowing.

"Jakes, it might not be that simple. Listen, I want to ask you a few professional questions. Hypothetical things I've been playing with…for a book I'm penciling out. Could you help me with them, and not read too much into it?"

"You want to ask me hypothetical questions at ten bucks a minute from Europe, where it's gotta be two in the morning?" Jakes asked tonelessly.

"One a.m., not to put too fine a point on it."

"No better time, then, huh? Hey, it's your dime. Shoot."

Jeffrey spent the next five minutes grilling Jakes on counter-surveillance, how to best evade tracking devices, how to move around without leaving a trail. By the time the investigator finished responding, neither man felt particularly talkative.

"I'll be back in a few days, Jakes. I appreciate this. I'll settle up once I return," Jeffrey assured Jakes, fatigue setting over him like a blanket.

"Yeah. You do that. And some words of advice – the kind of book you're thinking of writing? The heroes usually wind up dead in the real world. So you'll want to keep the protagonist out of too much danger, or it could go badly for him."

"Thanks. I'll keep that in mind."

Jeffrey hung up, Jakes' words clamoring in his skull like an anvil chorus. He turned from the phones and walked slowly to the stairwell, preferring not to wait for the elevator in full view of the lobby, just in case anyone was checking – his whole perspective now changed, on alert for signs he might have missed until talking to Jakes. The man obviously knew his craft, which made Jeffrey feel even worse. What chance did he have against professionals of at least that caliber?

He barely made it to the second floor and staggered to the elevators, winded, his breathing raspy and uneven as he waited for a car to arrive. He'd pushed it too far, and he would be lucky if he didn't collapse while trying to slink back to his wing. It had been a stupid decision, but it was too late now, and when the elevator arrived he stepped in gratefully and leaned against the side wall.

The nurse was away on rounds when he returned to his floor, and moments later he was back in his room and stripping off his clothes, anxious to be asleep when she next came to check on him. He pulled on the thin gown and hung up his pants and shirt, taking care to make them look untouched, and it was all he could do to get to the bed before his knees buckled and he slumped onto the thin mattress, his nocturnal adventure and the realization that he was completely and absolutely alone in the world having drained him of his slim remaining energy.

THIRTY-ONE

An Extension

The following morning a different doctor entered after a perfunctory knock and approached Jeffrey's bedside, a vocational look of concern on his face.

"Good morning, Mr. Rutherford. *Und* how are you feeling today?" he asked, his accent thicker than the other physician, but still understandable, his English serviceable if rough around the edges.

"Better. But my head still hurts."

"Yes, I'm sure it does. That will probably last for several days, but it's all part of the healing process. Nothing to worry about. I'm Dr. Ostenberg, and I'm going to do a little examination on you, make sure you're coming along, yes?"

Jeffrey nodded and immediately regretted it, the stab of pain causing him to wince. The doctor eyed him, and then began a neurological exam that lasted five minutes and involved tapping, prodding, and squeezing. When he was done, he stepped back from the bed and regarded Jeffrey, making notes on his clipboard between glances.

"*Vell*, there is no nerve damage I can detect, so it is just a matter of time. I can keep you in for observation for another day, but honestly at this point you would be just as well served at your hotel, provided you stay in bed. I would caution you not to engage in any strenuous activity for a week, at least, and to avoid flying, alcohol, aspirin, or doing anything that would put strain on your system. Beyond that, there's nothing we can do that time won't do by itself."

"I feel much better."

"Good. You still need to give the police a statement, but that shouldn't take too long. They can be here within an hour of when I alert them. Do you think you'll be up for it a little later? Maybe after breakfast?"

"Fine. I'd just like to get this over with so I can be discharged."

"I'll give them the word, and file the necessary documents so you can be released by noon."

The doctor droned on for a while longer, but Jeffrey was already thinking through his next move and hardly listening. He'd already heard the important part – he would be free of the hospital by lunchtime and could begin taking the steps that would move him out of harm's way.

The police were polite and largely uninterested in his limited recollection, which amounted to seeing and hearing nothing before waking up in the hospital, and obligingly returned his things to him in exchange for his signature in triplicate. Once they left, a hospital bureaucrat stopped in and had him sign a stack of releases and insurance forms, clucking and nodding with each chicken scratch, everything orderly and accounted for, his episode just another income-producing event for the healthcare machine.

By the time he was free to go, he actually felt as though he would be able to make it to the hotel before throwing up. His unsteadiness proved to him that he would definitely need more rest, but he intended to use the downtime to chart out a plan, so when he made his clandestine moves, he could do so efficiently and with complete deniability. That would be the hardest part – he'd need to appear to be taking time to convalesce while in fact traveling to his targets and unraveling the puzzle he'd been stuck with.

The only positives he could see were that his pursuers couldn't possibly know whom he was going to try to see, nor what he had in his head. His miraculous memory wasn't an open secret – he'd only shared his gift with a few people, his brother among them, and anyone who knew or cared was now dead.

That didn't seem like a big edge from where he stood, but it was the way the cards had been dealt, so he had to make the most of whatever he could get.

At noon on the dot his doctor made a final appearance and wished him well. A sternly efficient nurse escorted him to the emergency room entrance in a wheelchair, where a taxi was waiting. He gave the driver the name of his hotel and climbed into the back seat, already feeling stronger than just a few hours earlier. As the car pulled away, Jeffrey watched in the side mirror for any other vehicles moving into traffic behind them, but then gave up when his head protested the strain. He'd have to balance his desire to learn tradecraft with the physical limitations resulting from having his brain batted around like a tennis ball.

Once back in the hotel room he pulled the drapes closed and opened the safe, verifying his gold and cash were still there. Jakes had given him a good idea about how to deal with the watch, and he planned to follow through with it tomorrow, once he was feeling better. Even though he had the sense of a clock relentlessly ticking down on an unknown deadline, there was no point in pushing himself and winding up back in the hospital – or worse yet, further damaging his gray matter, now the sole repository of the information his brother had died to safeguard.

Part of him wanted to go down to the business center and start researching the best way to get out of Switzerland and into the EU; once in, if he picked his crossing points with care, he would be able to travel without any restrictions or having to have his passport logged. He wasn't sure how the scanning system worked, but his guess was that the information was collected in some sort of central archival system, which he intuited could be breached and his whereabouts tracked, pinpointing his location. But much as he yearned to begin fact-checking, he forced himself to climb into bed and close his eyes. There would be plenty of time tomorrow, and he'd be making several difficult calls that evening he wanted to be sharp for.

Monica's betrayal was still fresh, but he couldn't confront her. She was undoubtedly working for the same group that had arranged for his new job – likely told to get as close to him as possible and earn his trust, so that if he knew anything or became alarmed he would confide in her. It was a good strategy. On more than one occasion he'd been sorely tempted to talk to her, but his natural instincts bred from being an attorney had stopped him – as had the recurring vision of his brother plummeting to his death.

But now he knew of Monica's attempted infiltration, and he could use that to his advantage. He'd already begun to concoct a story that would explain his forthcoming travel into France: He wanted a second opinion and had heard that the Parisian hospitals were cutting edge for head injuries. Given that his records would show that he had been both barred from flying for a week and released while still experiencing discomfort and nausea, it would make sense that he would want to ensure that he'd gotten a complete diagnosis. And he would even take it as far as getting a referral for a French neurologist and seeing him while in Paris.

As to the rest – getting into Germany and Italy, figuring how to convince the Nazi to answer his questions, and gaining an audience with the Italian professor – he still hadn't completely fine-tuned a plan. But he would. And it would have to be airtight, with no room for error.

Because if he'd had any doubt that the conflict he was involved in was real, the attack outside the bank had resolved the matter. He was in a deadly game, and the first wrong move would be his last.

Of that, he was convinced.

Jeffrey shut his eyes with a sigh, and after a few seconds drifted into uneasy sleep, his dreams troubling: He was being chased down a dark cobblestone street by several armed figures, and they were gaining on him.

He awoke after what seemed like seconds, his shirt soaked with sweat in spite of the cool room temperature. He struggled to identify where he was, and then remembered – Zurich, the hotel, the assault. His headache returned as if to remind him, and he squinted in the dim light at the luminescent hands of his watch. He'd been out for six hours.

The bedside lamp illuminated with a click, and he waited while his eyes adjusted and then sat up, taking his time, wanting to avoid jarring his head any more than necessary. He slowly stood and shuffled to the bathroom, and after debating the wisdom of doing so and seeing no reason not to, removed his clothes and took a quick shower, avoiding getting his head wet. His stomach protested his having skipped lunch, and as he dried off he considered going downstairs to the restaurant, but opted for room service.

Dinner arrived forty-five minutes later, and he took his time with the excellent steak, savoring each bite as if he'd never tasted meat before. Finished, he pushed the tray away and eyed his cell phone distrustfully, then picked it up and powered it on. He couldn't put off the calls any longer, and dialed his office first.

His secretary answered, and he explained the situation and said he would be following up with an email the next day. None of the partners were available, but she promised to leave a message with them detailing his misadventure and warning that he'd be out for a week. When he hung up he was confident that there had been no suspicion in her voice, and he wondered if she'd already been informed of his incident and was just playing along, then decided it was improbable. Not everyone was likely to be some kind of covert operative spying on him – she was probably what she appeared to be: a harried, overworked woman doing the best she could in a thankless job.

The next call was harder. Monica answered on the second ring, her voice melodious as ever, no trace of guile or subterfuge. For an instant his conviction faltered, and then he forced himself to recall Jakes' disclosure, which snapped him back on track.

"Jeff! How's Switzerland? Did you get my chocolate yet?" she asked, and Jeffrey bit back the angry response that was fighting to get out.

"Switzerland kind of sucks."

"What? Why? Is it that cold?"

"It's not the weather. No, I was at the bank yesterday and I got mugged. I spent the night and most of today in the hospital."

"Mugged? Oh my God…are you okay? Why were you in the hospital? How badly hurt are you?"

"I'm…I'm doing better. I took a hit to the head. Knocked me out, and the doctors said I have a pretty nasty concussion."

"A concussion? Are you sure you're all right? That sounds serious," she said, her voice all frightened concern. Jeffrey made a mental note to never forget what an accomplished actress she was. It was an Academy Award performance, no doubt.

"I'm okay. Not great. But the doctor told me I have to take it easy for a week. No flying, nothing stressful. Basically that I should veg out."

"So you're staying there for a whole week?"

"I don't really have much choice. But I'm…I don't know, I didn't get that great a feeling from the doc. Like I was just one of many he was dealing with, you know? And my head is still splitting."

"I think you should go back in, then. It could be something more serious. Something going wrong after the fact…"

"No, they did a brain scan and there's no subdural hematoma or anything like that. I don't think I'm going to wake up and be paralyzed or anything. But I'm seriously thinking about getting a second opinion."

"Then do it. Don't take any chances with your health, darling."

Darling. Jeffrey controlled his gag response, bitter bile rising in his throat, a pain in his stomach flaring like a wild animal trying to tear its way out.

"I…you're right, of course. Listen, I'm fading pretty fast. I need to hit it. I'll call again when I'm more alert…" he said, the tightness in his voice explained away.

"I miss you, honey. Let me know if you need me to do anything while you're down for the count. I wish I could fly over there and take care of you. Maybe I should try to get a week off and do that?"

That stopped him, and he quickly pulled out of his pity party and grew more alert. He couldn't have her come to Europe. That would ruin everything, and he didn't think he could maintain the farce in person. She might be a complete sociopath with stellar acting skills, but he wasn't, and he'd never be able to make it fly.

"No need. It's only a few days more than I was planning to stay anyway. And if I get a second opinion, I'll be busy with doctors. Besides, I was told to rest, and not to exert myself. I don't think it would be good for my health if you were here – there's no way I would be able to keep away from you."

She seemed to hesitate. "You'll let me know how you're doing? Call me tomorrow, promise? I'm so worried now…"

"I will. I'll call you as soon as I'm up and around."

When he terminated the call, he felt like he needed another shower to wash off the coating of lies and betrayal. Any warmth he'd felt, the last holdout to logic, was gone. She was playing him, and had been, all along. Her concern was purely manufactured, professional, as artificial as a linen rose. Everything they'd had was a charade – it had never existed, and was all an act designed for the gullible consumption of an audience of one. He felt like such an idiot. It was so obvious now, the hollow insincerity in every word as plain to see as a searchlight stabbing through the night.

Jeffrey powered the phone off and cursed silently under his breath.

She'd taken him for a fool. They all had. The bumbling idiot, a peacock, puffed up with self-importance that had been contrived to lure him into a trap, where a black widow with breathtaking eyes and a body crafted by demons lay in wait.

For no reason apparent to Jeffrey, a vision of Kaycee flitted across his mind. She might have threatened him with a shotgun, but at least no one else had put her up to it.

Sleep was a long time coming, his simmering anger fueling his restlessness, and it was several hours before he finally began snoring, his dozing fitful and unsatisfying, the night a poor refuge for him now that he knew the harsh truth.

THIRTY-TWO

Shaking the Tail

Saturday, Jeffrey's first stop was at one of Zurich's many jewelry stores, where he traded his Rolex in a terrible deal for a Hublot on a black rubber strap that cost him his brother's watch plus seven thousand dollars on his American Express card. Which was exactly as he wanted it – a foolish purchase for a bauble; where his surveillance committee would readily believe he'd gotten screwed by the store.

Jeffrey had decided there was a better than good chance that a tracking device had been inserted into the Rolex while it had been ostensibly sitting securely in the condo safe, and he wanted to take no chances. But he couldn't just 'forget' the watch along with his phone, so he needed a bit of theater to explain its disappearance. He'd already set the stage for going to Paris, so now the only thing left was to dump his phone – which he would do once in France, so it didn't look like he was shedding his belongings all at once. For now, he'd left it at the hotel, continuing the pattern of absentmindedness he'd been cultivating.

He found a quiet internet café near the university, logged onto a travel site, and plotted the best way to get to Frankfurt from Paris. There were numerous options, but several mentioned cursory border security in the comments, and those were the ones that drew his interest. His plan was for the trail to end in France, and for any watchers to believe that he was still the clueless young attorney seeking out additional medical attention there.

Which brought him to neurologists. There were any number of prominent ones serving the city, and he selected two, memorizing their numbers and addresses so he could make calls later from his cell. Even with a damaged brain, he was beginning to get the hang of leading a double life – a life that Monica had to have been living for some time.

He brushed aside the rising anger and concentrated on his errands, the last of which was to research the Italian. Within three minutes he'd read the latest article bemoaning the great man's untimely demise – only a day after Keith's plane had gone down. Another thread, another coincidence, another corpse. He sat back, thoughts whirling chaotically, outwardly calm but near panicked inside.

Jeffrey finished his surfing, wiped his browsing history, and restarted the machine before rising and paying the stern woman behind the counter, who took the money and didn't tender any change. When he walked out he was struck by a small bout of nausea and dizziness, and had to lean against the building to steady himself. He took the opportunity to scan the street, but didn't see anything suspicious – which didn't surprise him. Jeffrey wasn't confident that his unskilled eye would detect experienced operatives, but he figured it was never too early to try – that had been one of Jakes' bits of wisdom. Apparently spying was like anything else, and he would only improve with practice. Jakes had also pointed out that if he was a pathological liar it would help, and had joked that being attorney might be close enough to give him a leg up.

Pity he was the wrong kind of lawyer. Another item to store away in the regret locker.

At his hotel he had lunch in the lobby restaurant, his conflicted thoughts revisiting that newspaper account of the professor's suicide, and after chewing a surprisingly tasty sandwich, he retired to his room for a long nap. He wanted to depart soon, but his bouts with concussion-related instability were too severe, and he reluctantly opted for another evening in Switzerland, with a train trip the following morning.

"You don't smell a rat?"

"No – if you look at his behavior, it's consistent. The only question mark is what he was doing at the bank, and we've unfortunately made no inroads there. The damned Swiss take their bank secrecy seriously, and our overtures to the bank officers were rejected out of hand."

"Offer them more."

"That's not the issue. It's an ethical thing with them."

"Offer them a lot more."

The head of the surveillance team shook his head even though he was on the telephone and the other speaker couldn't see him. "I did. It's a non-starter. But there are plenty of reasons he could have been there. Handling something for his old firm being one of the most likely. Or for himself. We have no real idea what he's been doing with his money for the last ten years. Remember that he's an asset specialist. It could certainly follow that he's structured something for himself, too. Do you have any results on the analysis of his bank records?"

"Inconclusive. As you know, if he was smart, nothing would show up. That's kind of the whole point to what he does for a living."

"So far, all he's done is buy an expensive new watch. We tracked that down about an hour ago. Traded in his brother's. Which is completely consistent with a young man on the way up with more money in his pocket than sense."

"The girl said he sounded…distant."

"A concussion can do that. Look, we'll keep an eye on him, but so far everything points to a waste of time. He was clean when he came out of the bank. He hasn't done anything suspicious in weeks of watching him. My money says he doesn't know squat."

"All due respect, analysis isn't your job. It's mine. Just stay on him and report back anything that seems odd. He mentioned he was considering a second opinion."

"We intercepted a call to a French specialist, so again, entirely consistent. He made an appointment for Monday. In Paris. So we know where he's going next."

"Why can't he just stay put? We didn't anticipate that."

"Free will. It's a big pain in the ass. But don't worry. I'm all over it. If he so much as farts, we'll know about it."

THIRTY-THREE

Frankfurt

The early morning direct train from Zurich to Paris took four hours, depositing Jeffrey at the Gare de Lyon at just before noon. The trip was fast and comfortable, the train only half full, and he used the time to doze, saving his energy for the marathon that was to come.

At his hotel, the Novotel Paris Les Halles, he checked in using his credit card and was shown to his room by a grumpy middle-aged man who seemed to disapprove of everything he encountered, starting with Jeffrey. After a cursory tour of the amenities in halting English and a disgusted look at his tip, the bellman left, closing the door behind him a little harder than necessary, his displeasure obvious. Jeffrey quickly unpacked and then ordered lunch in the room, preferring to remain sequestered until his doctor's appointment the following afternoon. The meal was passable, and after finishing it he carried the tray outside his door and placed it in the hallway, using the opportunity to confirm that there were no surveillance cameras. Satisfied, he moved back inside and collected his laptop bag, in which he had packed an extra shirt and a toothbrush, and then ducked back out, taking care to flip the "Do Not Disturb" sign over on the doorknob as he eased the door shut, his phone off and in the room safe.

Jeffrey slipped into the emergency stairwell and descended the four floors at a careful pace, and then left through the service entrance next to the restaurant, paying no attention to the puzzled glances from the hurrying wait staff. Two blocks away he got a taxi to the Gare du Nord, where a train to Frankfurt was departing within the hour. He'd been relieved when he'd bought his train ticket in Zurich – the attendant had barely looked at his passport, as had the immigration officials. Apparently imminent invasion by young Americans wasn't high on the European threat scale, because nobody seemed at all interested in him.

His purchase experience at the Gare du Nord was even more informal, which mirrored what his prior day's research had led him to expect, and when the train pulled into Karlsruhe, the German officials merely glanced at his identification before waving him on, and he easily made his connection to Frankfurt.

Night was falling when he arrived, and he located a small hotel near the nursing home. The clerk on duty seemed happy to have his money and expressed no interest in his papers, which suited Jeffrey perfectly. Dinner was bratwurst at a small family-operated restaurant down the block from the hotel, served by a smiling waitress who looked about sixteen. Jeffrey resisted ordering some of the cold draft beer with a nearly superhuman exercise of willpower, remembering the doctor's final words against drinking any alcohol for a week, and was in bed and asleep by nine p.m., his plan to be at the nursing home at eight.

The following morning he walked past his destination several times to get a feel for it. The retirement home was about what he expected, if a little more upscale, like a smallish three-star hotel filled with geriatrics. After steeling himself for the coming ordeal, he pushed through the entry doors and approached the front desk with a smile, offering his most winning look of sincerity to the middle-aged brunette behind the counter, who returned his greeting with puzzled curiosity.

"*Bitte*. Do you speak English?" Jeffrey asked in German, having looked up the phrase that morning.

"*Ja*. A small," she replied, then repeated it in German while holding her index finger and thumb together, unsure if she'd gotten it right.

"I'm here to see Herr Schmidt. Alfred Schmidt?" he said, taking care to speak slowly.

"*Ach. Ja*. Alfie. *Und* your name?"

"Richard Muller. I spoke with him on the phone a little while ago."

She didn't seem to get the last part, but no matter, she gave him a polite smile and lifted the telephone handset. Her murmured German was incomprehensible to him, but he made out his putative name and Alfie, which was positive. She set the phone down and resumed staring at him, and he continued beaming at her like a dullard.

Several minutes later a man about Jeffrey's age wearing white pants and a long-sleeved white shirt approached and motioned for him to follow into the depths of the building. Jeffrey did so, relieved that nobody had asked him for identification – that was the only part of his plan that he had no solution for, and the best he had was a lost wallet explanation, if pressed.

They arrived at a large common area, where a number of the residents were sitting in easy chairs or at tables, chatting in German or staring at the television, a few of them gazing off into space. His guide walked up to an ancient man in a reclining chair and leaned toward him, speaking loudly so he could hear. The man nodded and gestured for Jeffrey to come nearer and have a seat across from him, and the white-clad orderly then moved to a group of women who were playing cards at the other end of the room. Jeffrey took in the frayed tweed jacket and button-up dress shirt, the clothes obviously expensive at one time. The old German's form now barely filled them out, like a scarecrow that had been outfitted at a haberdashery.

"I was wondering when you would come," Schmidt said in good English, his words somewhat slurred. Jeffrey studied his face and saw the tell-tale drooping of the left side. "Yes, I've had two strokes over the last year. My time is short, which is just as well. Can you imagine being in this hellhole for eternity? Surely death is better than that. Anything is."

"Thank you for seeing me. I appreciate it."

Schmidt waved it off. "I always knew you, or someone like you, would come. I'd just about given up on it, and then you called. In a way, it's a relief. It's about time that the world knew what has been done to it."

Jeffrey was taken aback by his words. "What's been done to it..." he repeated.

"Of course. By me. And people like me. Working for the Nazis, and then the Americans and Russians." Schmidt's voice was little more than a rasp, and he glanced warily to the side as he spoke, his eyes taking on an air of reptilian cunning before settling back on Jeffrey. "Don't worry. The only one of these fossils that speaks English is Helga over at the card table, and she's deaf as a post."

Jeffrey hesitated, unsure of how to proceed. He'd been expecting to have to drag any information out of the old Nazi, and instead found him eager to talk. Jeffrey was wary of a trick, but couldn't see one, other than the man lying – but to what end?

"Where should we begin? Would you prefer if I ask questions, or do you just want to tell me what you have to say at your own pace?" Jeffrey asked.

"You're not much of a reporter, are you?"

"I don't usually do interviews. I'm more of a research journalist. Forensic investigation, that sort of thing," Jeffrey lied.

"If you'd waited much longer, you would have had more use for your forensic talents. I'm old, and I don't have a lot of life left. I think all the doctors are amazed I'm still breathing. Sixty years of smoking, booze, womanizing, and everyone I know is dead, but I'm still here! The devil takes care of his own, they say…"

"The devil. Yes, well, you've certainly lived a long time," Jeffrey echoed, wondering where Schmidt was going with the discussion.

"Too damned long. But I'm not going quietly. I won't sit by and watch my secrets go to the grave with me. I've come too far. Too far…" he said, his last words drifting off as he seemed to turn in on himself.

"Then maybe we should start at the beginning. Or as close to it as you think would be relevant."

"Relevant? *Mein Gott*, it's all relevant. The problem is knowing what to leave out. I could sit here for days with what I know, and barely scratch the surface."

"Well, then, perhaps just the most important parts?" Jeffrey suggested.

"Important. Fine. Maybe we should move back to my room. This is going to take a while," Schmidt said, giving him a sly look from under hooded lids, reminding Jeffrey of the way a fox looks at chickens.

"Certainly. Is that permitted?"

"Of course. This isn't a prison. Don't worry. I haven't fashioned a shank out of a spoon. If I had, I'd have used it on myself long ago."

"Very good. Do you need help?"

"Only to get up. Then take your hands off me. I hate people touching me."

"Haphephobia," Jeffrey recalled, his mind automatically indexing for the disorder.

"No, that's fear of being touched. I'm not afraid. I'm not afraid of anything at this point. I…I just don't like it."

Jeffrey extended his hand. Schmidt gripped it with surprising force and pulled himself to his feet, his body slight, almost nothing but skin and bones.

"That's enough of the shared intimacy. Follow me back to my lavish suite. Come see what you have to look forward to if you outlive your usefulness," Schmidt spat as he shuffled out of the room. Jeffrey trailed him as they moved into another corridor. "I call this 'death row.' Needless to say, my fellow prisoners don't share my sense of humor. Pity. They're all fools. As far as I'm concerned they can't die fast enough. But some, like me, linger on forever, like radioactive waste."

Jeffrey elected not to comment, and struggled to maintain a professional demeanor – as he imagined a seasoned journalist would. At the moment that consisted of following a mildly demonic troll back to his living quarters to hear…what, he didn't know.

"Can you tell me what this is all about, Dr. Schmidt? I mean, I know the broad outline, the cattle mutilations, rumors of experimentation, but not the details…"

Schmidt slowed and then cackled, ending with a wet cough as he moved towards a door on his right. He turned slowly to face Jeffrey, whose blood froze in his veins at the old man's next words.

"The details, eh? Well, my boy, today's your lucky day. I'm about to give you the scoop of the century. In the old days, we called it germ warfare. Now, it's bio-warfare, but it's all the same thing. It's about silently killing millions, using nature to do it. It's all about forbidden fruit, and playing God, and boundless power. It's about the genocide business. And you can call me Alfie. Everyone does."

THIRTY-FOUR

Alfie

Schmidt's room was actually more akin to a tiny apartment, with a separate bedroom and a small living room that barely accommodated a sofa, a faded brown La-Z-Boy lounger, a coffee table, and a small circular dining table with two wooden chairs in the far corner. The German stepped into the room and made straight for the lounge chair, and Jeffrey took a seat on the couch and extracted a notepad from his laptop case – a prop to add to his journalist demeanor. He leaned forward and placed a small recorder on the table that he'd bought at an electronics store adjacent to the station in Paris.

"Do you mind if I record this?" he asked, and Schmidt shook his head.

"Absolutely not. I don't want anyone thinking that you made it up."

Jeffrey switched the tiny device on and then announced the date and Schmidt's name with officious sincerity. Once he was done, he hesitated at how to begin, eyeing the old man as he continued speaking.

"Well, then. Rather than asking questions, I've asked for Alfred Schmidt to tell his story in his own words. The next voice you will hear will be his," Jeffrey said, and then sat back, waiting for the German to begin.

"I originally started working on biological weapons for the Nazis in 1942 after graduating from Justus Liebig University in Giessen. We were weaponizing foot-and-mouth disease, and spent much time on cholera as well. Some of our work was sent to the Japanese, who did widespread testing on the Chinese during the invasion and occupation of China – about half a million dead, but you'll never hear about it. Unfortunately, the research was never able to reach its full potential due to wartime constraints on resources. Those were dark times, with the party coming apart and the

Allies attacking on all fronts. Anyway, that's ancient history, and everyone agrees that the Nazi party was guilty of atrocities that make anything we did on the biological side meaningless."

Schmidt cleared his throat.

"After the war, the U.S. approached me about moving to the United States to continue my work, which I jumped at. I spent the next forty years in its biological weapons program, first working at Camp Detrick, in Maryland, and then later at a number of other facilities, including Plum Island and Pine Bluff, Arkansas, where I was primarily working on lethal viruses, including viruses that could destroy the immune system. Even though–"

"You mean to say…" Jeffrey couldn't help interrupting. "You mean, after all…well, after the Nuremberg trials, our government actually hired you to–"

"Yes, yes, they contacted me. They wanted my expertise. Does that surprise you? The important thing is that, even though your President Nixon officially ended offensive efforts in 1969, the clandestine agencies continued to secretly fund offensive programs that showed promise. So while the programs were supposedly finished, and everyone made a big deal out of signing the Biological Weapons Convention in 1972 banning bio-weapons research, the truth was that select experimentation went on. I continued my work, and perfected a number of different agents before turning to retroviruses."

Jeffrey's ears perked up.

"The cattle mutilation period was when we were testing a variety of pathogens, specifically trying to synthesize a variant of bovine leukemia and splice it with simian immunodeficiency virus. We already knew from experimentation that we could make diseases jump species – that was a major thrust of our research. In 1972, we were able to infect chimps with leukemia and destroy their immune systems by causing bovine leukemia virus to cross to chimps. The subjects died of *Pneumocystis* pneumonia, and there was great excitement at the time because we'd created not one, but two new diseases never before seen in chimps – leukemia and *Pneumocystis*. We did it by having them drink milk from cows with bovine leukemia. Anyway, the findings were later duplicated and written up in 1974 in *Cancer Research*. This was extremely exciting in my circle because it presented a whole new approach to bio-weapons – the ability to create a contagious immuno-suppressive agent that would kill targeted populations."

"Wait a minute. I recognize the second cause of death – the *Pneumocystis* pneumonia. Isn't that one of the primary complications from…" Jeffrey paused.

"Yes. Exactly. It's one of the leading causes of death from AIDS."

Both men were silent for several moments.

"Wait a minute. You're not saying…"

"I will tell you this much: I was working on a contagious bio-weapon that could cause catastrophic damage to the human immune system. Through most of the early and mid-seventies. I was part of a team – one of several teams, as a matter of fact, that had been integrated under the umbrella of the NCI – the National Cancer Institute."

"But…where do the cattle come in?"

"We needed hosts we could use to culture our little germs. And we wanted to see how they would spread in the wild – in populations that were interacting normally, not lab animals in pens."

"Back to *Pneumocystis* pneumonia…and AIDS."

"Yes. And now we get to the real meat – the reason anyone will care about my sordid history. I'm an expert on retroviruses, and as such, I'm one hundred percent convinced that HIV is a lab-created pathogen, an engineered variant of simian immunodeficiency virus, and that AIDS is a man-made disease. I worked on similar pathogens. I should know."

Jeffrey was speechless. In his wildest dreams, he'd never thought the cattle mutilations would lead to…this. His mind raced as he fought to find words.

"But why? Why would a lab-created bio-warfare virus be released into the world?"

"Ah. Finally, a good question. The answer to that, my friend, has nothing whatsoever to do with science, and everything to do with politics and social engineering."

"I'm not sure I understand."

"One of the problems we had should be obvious from the cattle mutilations: We needed real-world data on how our creations would spread, and how lethal they would be in humans. Sure, we had models, and we could extrapolate, but that's not the same – one mistaken assumption and all the models turn out wrong. It's always an issue. A big one. I believe that

HIV was deliberately introduced in Africa in order to obtain data on how a new weaponized retrovirus would mutate and flourish in a general population, and at the same time potentially solve, or at least moderate, the global overpopulation problem."

"In America, it served a dual purpose. It was inserted into a control group that could be easily followed and that was a troublesome minority, so data could be obtained on its spread in that community; a cohort group that didn't seem to be at risk of transmitting it to the general population. Also, though, it was a group that was emerging as a troubling political force based in sexuality – sexuality that was not just dangerous on a political level, but also threatened to undermine the values of conservative America."

"You're saying that HIV was deliberately spread in the U.S. to decimate the gay community? And that Africa was some kind of population control exercise?"

"There's no other explanation for how it was released in both the U.S. and Africa around the same time–"

"Well," corrected Jeffrey, "it started in Africa first, so that–"

"Is that what you think?" Schmidt chuckled slightly. "Well, of course. That's what you've been told so many times you accept it as fact. But actually, it appeared in Africa *after* it did in the U.S." He held up a hand to silence Jeffrey's objections before continuing.

"And there's no question that it was released. The explanations about cross-species jumping from monkeys to humans in Africa via bush meat was always ludicrous, and was first advanced by a scientist who falsely claimed to have discovered the virus, and whose staff were later shown to be perpetrators of fraud. It was a stupid theory that stretched the limits of scientific credulousness to new levels, and relied upon hypothesis on top of speculation on top of guess – never mind that AIDS is a disease of the cities in Africa, and hardly ever occurs in the bush, where bush meat is made and consumed. But it was a convenient bit of theater that took the focus off a lab-created possibility."

The German stared at a faraway spot on the wall for a moment, and then returned to the discussion as though he hadn't missed a beat. "Through repetition, it became the prevailing accepted explanation, which is now trumpeted and repeated as fact – with the original green monkeys now changed to chimps after the Japanese proved that HIV wasn't closely related to the monkey virus. That HIV came from chimps or gorillas, jumping species in the wild, is repeated like gospel, with the weight of fact. Only it isn't fact. It's an invention. A post hoc explanation designed to befuddle and confuse. Because the other explanation is too horrible to contemplate – that factions within the U.S. government singled out whole populations based on race or sexuality, and earmarked them as expendable, part of a big experiment that was both financially and ideologically driven." Schmidt glowered at Jeffrey, and then a tight smile cracked his sagging face.

Jeffrey's eyes drifted over to the recorder, confirming that it was catching everything. His head was swimming with the density of the information the old scientist was reciting as if reading from his notes.

The German coughed and cleared his throat again. "Damned bug is running around here. Be careful, or you might catch a cold."

Jeffrey tried to formulate a response, but words eluded him.

"Back to my role in all this. Remember I told you about infecting chimps with a virus that destroyed their T cells and caused them to die from *Pneumocystis* pneumonia? I was working on creating a virus that would do the same in humans – weaken the immune system and kill the host from opportunistic afflictions. I made great strides in doing so, as the chimp experiments should tell you. Then I was pulled off the project in the mid-seventies and moved to another operation, with no warning. Several years later the first cases of AIDS began to surface out of New York, and then later, in Africa. I didn't have to be a genius to recognize my own handiwork." The German reached to his side and lifted a plastic bottle of water to his lips, drew a few swallows, then set it back down.

"But a bigger question than *whether* it had been released into targeted subsections of the population, was *how*. How had a laboratory-created, contagious bio-weapon made it into the gay population of New York, and into Haiti, and Africa, and even more interestingly to me, how had the perpetrators managed to get the entire scientific community to be comfortable with it being a gay disease on one continent, but a heterosexual one on another? As a scientist, I found it impossible that nobody seemed puzzled by that, and that the possibility of the virus being lab-created was never seriously examined. Maybe because I was familiar with the bio-weapons ability we'd developed that allowed us to target pathogens specifically for different cell types – some for blood, others for mucous membranes. To me it was as plain as day what had happened, and I thought there was no way that the world would blindly go along with the official explanations – that monkey virus had spontaneously jumped species in Africa, and made it to the U.S. as a completely different strain, getting into a time machine in the process."

Schmidt leaned forward and fixed Jeffrey with a hard stare. "Turns out I was wrong."

THIRTY-FIVE

Aftermath

"But this is speculation on your part. You admit it," Jeffrey countered.

"Young man, if I put a cat into a black box and theorize whether it's alive or dead because of a radioactive isotope, that's speculation. If I see one of my lab creations suddenly appear in two populations that are a world apart, that's something else again."

"I just can't believe that the government would experiment on its own population with something as deadly as a bio-warfare agent."

"I'm not saying it's the whole government – I would bet it's a fringe group that has a lot of power within the government. But I don't understand your disbelief. The government has a long, documented history of experimenting on the population, in secret, with deadly diseases and substances. Do you not know this? Haven't you heard of the Tuskegee syphilis experiment? That's where the Public Health Department allowed syphilis to go untreated in hundreds of black men in Tuskegee, Alabama, for four decades, even after a cure for it was discovered in the forties. The 'experiment' went on until 1972, and was only stopped because the *New York Times* broke the story. At no point were the subjects allowed to be treated for the disease, even though it was killing them, and even though their wives and children got it from them – the government, and its hospitals and physicians, stood by and watched for forty years as it ravaged the community, and for twenty-five years after there was a cure, it prevented the subjects from being treated, because it wanted to study the long-term effects on the patient population, which included, obviously, a painful and hideous death."

Jeffrey shook his head. "That was before my time. I mean, I think I heard something about it, but I didn't pay attention. It was ancient history to me."

"And the same group of American researchers injected Guatemalans with syphilis and gonorrhea and other sexually transmitted diseases without their informed consent between 1946 and 1948. They went outside the U.S. to conduct their secret experiments so it would be harder to track any long-term fallout, and because they correctly understood that few Americans know about or care about what happens in third world countries."

Schmidt paused, as if to catch his breath. "Shall I go on? The point is that there are plenty of documented examples of the government doing exactly what I'm saying was done in the late seventies – selecting cohort groups for experimentation based on race or sexual preference. So why is it so hard for you to believe that a faction of that same government would do the identical thing with a different disease? Because the ethic had changed so much between 1972, when it was just fine to do it in Alabama, and 1978, when the first AIDS cases began appearing in New York? Young man, what planet are you from? Ethics – no, *people* – don't change that fast. And certainly, a history of it being acceptable to conduct secret experiments on groups at the margins doesn't change overnight."

Jeffrey rubbed the faint stubble on his chin. "For the record, you believe that HIV was introduced into the gay American and African populations deliberately." He shook his head. "Fine. How was it done?"

"Vaccines. In the U.S., vaccine trials; and in Africa and Brazil, the massive smallpox vaccination program."

Schmidt allowed his words to sink in. "Young man, there are two possibilities. The innocent one is that a number of the vaccines created for the African program, as well as those for the U.S. hepatitis B trials, were somehow accidentally contaminated with a simian virus – and in some unknown way, that enabled it to cross over into humans, simultaneously morphing into HIV. Bear in mind that *how* both the smallpox program and hepatitis B trials could have been accidentally contaminated is a scientific unknown. The other possibility is that HIV was lab-created from simian immunodeficiency virus and then those vaccine programs were contaminated deliberately. I favor the second explanation, largely due to an understanding of statistical probability. There's no doubt in my mind that HIV was made in a bio-warfare lab," Schmidt insisted, his voice steady.

"HIV was introduced into humans via vaccines?" Jeffrey echoed incredulously.

"In the U.S., the first AIDS cases began appearing in New York shortly after the hepatitis B vaccine trials there – which were only administered to young, sexually active, Caucasian homosexual men. Then, a year later, the trials moved to Los Angeles, San Francisco, Chicago, and St. Louis, and again, shortly after the inoculations took place in those cities, AIDS cases began showing up there, as well."

"But how do you know that–"

Schmidt continued as if Jeffrey hadn't attempted a question. "They've tested the stored blood samples in New York from pre-1978, when the vaccination program began, and there was zero HIV in any – zero. But in 1979, HIV is present in over six percent of blood samples taken from the gay men who participated in the hep B trials. By 1982, one year after the official start of the AIDS epidemic, thirty percent of the recipients of the hep B vaccine were HIV positive. That's an incredible, explosive infection rate – far, far higher than Africa, and much higher than anything in the literature since."

His unasked question answered, Jeffrey just sat silently now, both shocked and skeptical.

The old German tried his chilling smile again before dropping his next bomb. "But the most obvious evidence that the vaccine trials introduced HIV into the white, gay U.S. population was the success of the vaccine trial results: Ninety-six percent of the trial participants developed antibodies to hepatitis B!"

Jeffrey scratched his chin. "That's proof? I don't understand. Why is the vaccine trial being a huge success proof of no HIV being present at that time?"

"*Ach*, I keep forgetting you don't know anything about this. It's proof because vaccine efficacy drops off to fifty percent in humans that are immuno-compromised with HIV. If the official theory is that the gay population already had HIV simmering in it, why were the hepatitis B vaccine trials the greatest vaccine success ever recorded? Again, it's impossible that the young men in the trial had HIV before the trials, or *the vaccine wouldn't have worked.*"

Jeffrey digested that piece of simple logic with a dry swallow. An uncomfortable silence stretched between them. "But why target gays?" he asked. "I don't get it."

"Remember that up until the early seventies, homosexuality was listed as a mental illness by the American Psychiatric Association, and the World Health Organization defined it as such until 1990. That's twelve years after AIDS began appearing in the gay population. So to conservative white men, being gay was viewed as a disorder – which perfectly fit the profile of those the government liked to conduct secret experiments on. In the past, prisoners, mental patients, rural black men, retarded children, and its own military were victims of experimentation without their informed consent. Is it such a stretch that homosexuals were lumped into that category back then?"

"But what about earlier patients who died of AIDS? From the fifties or sixties?"

"Most of those have been shown to be either incorrect false positives on tissue samples, or contamination. False positives abound in AIDS research, more than in any other field. Flu shot recipients were testing positive, for Christ's sake. So how definitive do you think those tests actually are?"

Schmidt paused, as if expecting an answer, but Jeffrey couldn't think of a thing to say, and the old man continued.

"Probably the most famous, the 1959 tissue sample from Africa, is now conveniently exhausted after being touted as 'proof' HIV was there for a long time, so can't be retested. You just have to believe that it wasn't yet another false positive, or contamination – something that is also remarkably common in HIV research, and which has affected almost all the American labs. Frankly, I believe the remainder of that handful of cases were carefully manufactured to advance the lie that it's an old disease. Think of the stakes. Do you really believe that those behind this sort of a cover-up wouldn't create conveniently discovered tissue samples to test positive in order to advance their agenda? Were you born yesterday? Come on. I already told you the New York stored blood supplies that were tested from pre-1977 were all negative – you can check that yourself."

"Look, I'm from San Francisco. AIDS is discussed a lot there. There's evidence – at least, I'm pretty sure there is – that it originated in Africa. Now you're trying to tell me–"

"Africa is blamed for being the birthplace of HIV, mainly because 'similar' viruses were found there, and because simian immunodeficiency virus – SIV – is found in African apes and monkeys – but that's proof of nothing. Did you know that originally, Africa was implicated because Kaposi's sarcoma, the cancer that is synonymous with AIDS, is fairly common there? But then, in the mid-eighties, a study found that most of the African Kaposi's victims tested negative for HIV. It concluded that there was no link between the African Kaposi's and the same disease appearing opportunistically in Americans."

"So you're saying the two weren't linked?"

Schmidt shook his head. "Simply put, it was unrelated to AIDS. And of course, there's the massively inconvenient problem of the timeline – Montagnier, the discoverer of the virus, admits that there was no AIDS epidemic in Africa until well after it was well underway in North America – *and* that the African virus is a different strain. But Africa was already the media scapegoat, primarily because of the debunked green monkey theory that was advanced after the Kaposi's theory, and nobody remembers they were both a hundred percent wrong. They just *know* the AIDS epidemic started in Africa, even if it didn't."

"Then you're saying that they're confusing the origin of the simian virus with the origin of HIV."

"Correct. I'm saying that the predecessor virus might be SIV from apes; but the *origin* of the AIDS epidemic isn't some natural cross-species jumping in Africa. It couldn't be. AIDS didn't appear there until after a completely different strain than the African strain appeared in the U.S. and the AIDS epidemic was already well underway."

He leaned forward and fixed Jeffrey with a penetrating stare. "Do you not understand the significance of that? It's like blaming a disease that appears in New York in January on something that appears in Africa in late November of the following year – and is completely different in terms of the tissue type it targets. All it takes to debunk that theory is a working knowledge of a calendar. Look, if HIV causes AIDS, which nobody is disputing, why did the epidemic wait to start in Africa until after it was a wildfire in the U.S.?"

"But I read somewhere that they tested the blood supplies in Africa from older samples, and found HIV."

"Again, false positives. Most of those were retested in Israel and England, and found to have zero HIV. It was malaria and other immune system-destroying diseases that caused the false results. Look, a 1986 study of geriatric Ugandans in nursing homes at the epicenter of the African AIDS epidemic found not one HIV positive, when the general population had a fifteen percent infection rate, so the theory that it had been there for decades or centuries is simply false, predicated on assumptions and tainted lab samples. It couldn't have happened the way the theories say, and yet they're parroted as if undisputed fact."

Jeffrey nodded slowly. "So in Africa, the vaccines were given to everyone, not just one minority."

"Exactly. And the African strain targets mucous membranes, not rectal tissue. So you have supposedly the same virus appearing after widespread vaccination programs, but which amazingly targets different cell types. I never understood why the medical community never questioned *why* it was a gay disease on one continent and heterosexual on another. Even better, nobody wants to explore *how* that happened. It's one of many scientific taboos in a discipline that isn't supposed to have any."

"I always assumed it was lifestyle or something."

"Lifestyle? Humans have been having sex for millions of years. Why within twenty-four months of the first cases being diagnosed in the U.S. did AIDS suddenly explode in Africa and Haiti? Let's see. Big vaccination programs in Africa, including fourteen thousand Haitians there who subsequently went back home, big vaccination trials to only gay white men in the U.S., and then bam, there's an epidemic of a 'new,' and yet paradoxically, if you believe the disinformation, a simultaneously 'old' disease."

Schmidt took a sip from a glass of tepid water on the low coffee table. "Look, the vaccine connection in Africa is so obvious to many that some of the accepted theories grudgingly concede that the smallpox vaccine programs *might* have played a role in the spread... but only because of dirty needles. The only problem there is that there's no evidence of that. It's another convenient invention. With AIDS there are so many flights of fancy touted as official explanations, and when one's debunked, the experts and the media all switch to another, equally absurd theory, absent any evidence."

Jeffrey's headache had returned with a vengeance. "Don't take this the wrong way, but do you…have any proof?"

"Ah. Proof. No, I'm just an old man who helped create viruses that were almost identical. Working for top secret organizations that would deny their very existence. No, I don't have a nice, tidy blueprint with "Top Secret" stamped across it articulating that AIDS is a deliberate experiment, as with my old Nazi bosses, to decimate the 'undesirable' populations of the world."

"Then in the end, while it's compelling on the surface, there's no motive and no proof," Jeffrey said.

"Motive? How about the usual twins, power and money? Think about it this way – in 1970, Nixon declared a war on cancer. A decade later, the retrovirologists who were the great hope of that assault, who had devoured impossible-to-envision resources, were no closer to coming up with a cure than they had been when they started. The whole thing was a failure and their credibility was in shambles. Funding dried up. And then suddenly, this new retrovirus appears, and overnight the stars of medicine and science are the same retrovirologists who failed to accomplish anything with cancer. They went from failures to being on the cover of *Time*.

"And the money? It poured in. Developing treatments, tests, researching. Drug companies made fortunes treating symptoms. Federal money taps were opened and never closed. Here we are, forty-something years after Nixon declared war on cancer, and not one vaccine, not one cure, has resulted from billions and billions of dollars, and two generations of work. Young man, here's a reasonable question: how can scientists who can't develop a cure for even simple viral animal diseases after forty years be expected to cure anything substantial in humans? The money's not in curing. It's in treating and researching."

"Then this was all about money."

"If you look hard enough at most things, you'll find they're about money."

"Genocide. To make money," Jeffrey repeated in a hushed whisper.

"Don't act so shocked. It wouldn't be the first time."

"I don't believe it. More importantly, nobody else will believe it, either. The official position is too entrenched, and people are reluctant to research anything. Whatever the papers say is what most believe, without question."

"So you understand why it's awfully convenient that the establishment's experts all came out of the bio-warfare culture in the sixties and seventies, and that a handful of authorities dictate what will be researched and taken seriously, and what won't? Authorities, like the one who 'mistakenly' claimed he discovered the virus, who apparently couldn't tell them apart for years – or rather, couldn't spot that they were identical – and then concocted increasingly absurd hypotheses about simian virus jumping while making it effectively taboo to acknowledge decades of contamination and species-jumping experiments? Carried out by many of those very same scientists, whose pet meal ticket got shut down only two years before fate smiled upon them and HIV miraculously appeared?" Schmidt looked ready to spit. "Those are your experts."

"They effectively control the dialogue."

"Which is why nobody dares introduce the words 'lab-created' into the discussion. They'd rather conveniently forget they were experimenting in causing simian viruses to species-jump. I don't blame them. Certainly, there's nobody with nearly their money or power to take the opposing view. It's career suicide. So instead, everyone pronounces the origin of the AIDS epidemic 'irrelevant' or 'unknowable,' and prefers to focus on the origin of HIV – the virus – all the while pretending that biological warfare labs weren't experimenting with cross-species virus jumping. No wonder they want it 'unknowable' and can't wait to rush the dialogue along. I would, too."

"Be that as it may, nobody's going to want to hear it, especially absent hard evidence."

"You might be right. In your country it's like everyone has their fingers in their ears rather than simply examining the evidence and calling foul. In that respect it reminds me of prewar Germany – an entire population that so wants to believe in something it will ignore what's obviously happening before its eyes."

"You see my problem, then?" Jeffrey asked. "It's an inflammatory set of allegations, but without proof…"

Schmidt seemed to shrink as the silence stretched between them. Jeffrey decided to change tactics.

"Why haven't you talked about this before now?" Jeffrey probed.

"I was afraid. That simple. I knew the only way I was safe was if I never spoke about the past, and minded my own business."

"Then what changed?"

"I'm dying. I'm old. And I've participated in many evils. But this one, even I am ashamed of. Something I helped create has been used to kill over thirty million people. That makes World War II seem tame. And it will kill hundreds of millions more. I can't go to my grave in silence. It's that simple."

Jeffrey shifted, studying the old German's wizened face, and made a snap decision. He reached over and shut off the recorder.

"I was recently shown a document that made no sense to me. But it might to you. It was a diagram with some kind of a bar chart and a random string of letters beneath it. And pages of numbers. The person who showed it to me was afraid for his life, and felt it might be related to your story somehow. Connected to the animal mutilations. Which you say were experimentation…"

Schmidt's face froze. "A diagram with bar charts and a letter string? What kind of a diagram? Where did the document come from?"

"It was classified, so I presume it was stolen from some government database. As to what kind, if I drew it, do you think you might be able to place it?"

"You can draw it from memory? This thing?"

"I'm sure of it."

"I can look at it. Why not?" said Schmidt, trying to be nonchalant, but failing.

Jeffrey sat in silence, sketching the diagram and charts in detail, and after a few minutes handed the notebook over to the German. Schmidt squinted at what he'd drawn, then retrieved a pair of reading glasses from his breast pocket. An eternity passed, and then he looked over the rims at Jeffrey, his face pale.

"*Lieber Gott*. It's a virus. One of the most lethal in history."

THIRTY-SIX

Revelation

Schmidt's hands were visibly trembling when he lowered the notepad to his lap, lost in thought. Jeffrey waited, wanting to give him time to absorb the drawing's implications.

"It's the Spanish Influenza virus. H1N1. But…different. Modified. I'd need specialized equipment to calculate how much more lethal and contagious this could be, but believe me when I tell you that even with only slight modifications, it would be catastrophic if unleashed on the world. One of the goals of weaponizing this type of virus would be to create something which the current crop of antiviral medications wouldn't work against, and for which there's no natural immunity."

"I…Spanish Influenza?"

"It was a global disaster. In 1918. Killed about fifty million people – more than everyone killed in World War I. What made it particularly lethal was that it hit healthy adults the hardest – the ordinary flu usually is only dangerous to the very young and the very old. The death rate from the average flu season is 0.01 percent. Spanish Flu killed 2.5 percent, and did so within hours of the onset of symptoms."

"How do you know so much about it off the top of your head?"

"It was my line of work. I studied it intensely as a near-perfect example of an incredibly contagious disease that spread like wildfire, and killed faster than just about anything else ever seen. To put it into perspective, it killed four times more people than the Black Death in the Middle Ages. It's one of the true nightmare diseases nature has visited on the planet. It infected nearly forty percent of the world population, and caused the body's immune system to turn against itself. Victims literally drowned in their own lung fluid while their skin turned blue from lack of oxygen. One of the reasons it was so deadly was because those with stronger immune systems had a more powerful response, which translated into it being more severe in the young and healthy. It's incredibly virulent, and a relatively simple protein chain. The full RNA was sequenced in 2005, and I spent considerable effort analyzing it in my spare time. Which believe it or not, I have an abundance of, even with my busy social schedule here."

"And this…is a weaponized form of H1N1?"

"I would say it's definitely lab-created, but I can't tell what the modifications are. The letter string is a description, so I could figure it out in broad strokes given enough time, but the real question would require computing time and a controlled population study."

"The real question?"

"How much more lethal is it, and how much more contagious, than the original eight-gene virus. Whenever you modify something like this, it would be to increase one, or both. But…this is insanity. It could wipe out huge population centers in a matter of days or weeks. I mean, huge, as in a percentage of the total global population. Nobody would want to release this, much less develop it…"

"Unless…" Jeffrey blurted, unable to help himself.

"Unless there was already a vaccine developed that was a hundred percent effective, that could be manufactured in sufficient quantities and rapidly enough to inoculate those you wanted to save from it."

"Wait. Then this could be used for a crude population control?"

"I can't see any other reason to use it. It's akin to releasing the devil onto the planet. If it's been modified substantially enough, it could kill ten, twenty, thirty or more percent of the human race in short order…" Schmidt stopped, a thought obviously occurring to him. "It is madness, but it could make sense to those who released HIV. The big problem there might have been that ultimately, HIV doesn't kill fast enough."

Jeffrey was shocked to his core at the calm speculation, the discussion of exterminating billions of innocent humans with a deadly pathogen.

"…And it incubates for a decade…" he murmured.

"That's another one of the big lies. HIV *can* incubate for a decade – but that assumes that it is transmitted organically, with only a small amount of virus transferring from one person to the other. If there's a heavy dose of virus transmitted, as in a vaccine, it can overwhelm the immune system in a matter of months. That's one of the reasons the official accounts are nonsense. History shows that HIV can take ten years to develop into full-blown AIDS, and yet it became a global outbreak within a matter of a year or two. Like so much in the story, that should be impossible, because the spread would have taken a generation to reach the levels it did within a few years. Of course, the scientists ignore that aspect of it, because it goes into extremely uncomfortable territory."

Schmidt wiped his face with the back of his sleeve, suddenly tired. "Whoever crafted this Spanish Flu variant undoubtedly had a reason to do it. I don't have to tell you how troubling that is. There can't be that many objectives that come to mind."

"Wait. Why would you develop a virus that could annihilate a huge chunk of the population without any selectiveness? I would have thought that if it was for warfare, you'd want something reasonably precise. Isn't this sort of like trying to thread a needle with a backhoe?" Jeffrey asked.

Schmidt sat back and grimaced. "There is a certain line of reasoning among social planners that the current population of the Earth is unsustainable. Seven billion people, all consuming resources and placing a burden, a load, on the planet, and that number growing every day. The prevailing sentiment in that circle is that it would take a reduction to under a billion to have a sustainable load. That would mean six billion would need to die. That's the math. Of course they always avoid stating that in bald terms. They usually simply target an optimum number. But it works out the same. There are far too many people. So a lot of them have to go."

"And this might be a way to decide which ones…"

"Exactly. If you had stockpiles of the vaccine, you could pretend to be working to develop one when the epidemic hit everywhere but at home, do so with amazing speed while immediately quarantining the country to keep the flu from entering the borders, and then blame the death of most of your adversaries, as well as the entire third world, on an inability to manufacture the vaccine fast enough. The survivors would go through a period of crisis, and then bury the dead and move on. And you could allocate the limited vaccine to friendly governments and those in your population you deemed worth keeping, allowing the rest to perish."

"And make a fortune in the process, not to mention emerge as the leaders of the new world. It's…it's pure evil. Diabolical," Jeffrey spat, still trying to get his head around the enormity of the act.

"Yes. Then again, that's the business I was in. Building doomsday bugs. But this eclipses anything I worked on. It's unspeakable. And it makes me relieved I'll be dead soon. Because the world won't be much good to live in after this. It's every megalomaniac's fantasy. A new world order, with the surviving leadership the emperors of whatever civilization is left. Hitler was thinking so small…"

"How would you disseminate it? You'd have a huge logistical problem, wouldn't you?"

"Depends how contagious it is. If highly virulent, you could release it as an aerosol in major travel hubs, like Beijing, Moscow, Paris, Mexico City…or you could do the old vaccine trick. Inject it into the target populations along with something else. It wouldn't be hard. If you're capable of culturing enough to poison the global population, you've probably got the wherewithal to distribute it."

The atmosphere in the room was leaden, the mood hopeless. The German tossed the notepad back to Jeffrey. "It doesn't really matter what you do with the bio-weapons story, you know. There's nothing you could do to stop this. It's a lost cause."

"I could warn people…"

"Warn them? That an old man thinks there's a threat? You have to know you'd be laughed out of the room. And no news network would touch it. Assuming you weren't killed the moment you opened your mouth."

Jeffrey eyed the drawing a final time. "One person already has been."

Schmidt nodded. "Who?"

"The man who gave me the material."

"Then there's your answer. It's not theoretical. Of course they'll kill to keep this quiet. We're talking about wiping out huge swaths of the human race. What's a few more?"

Jeffrey's dour expression was that of a condemned man. He could smell the sour odor of fear seeping from his pores, and hated himself for it. His head had started pounding somewhere in the discussion, and now it felt as if a bear was swatting it like a beehive.

"He also gave me a dozen pages of spreadsheets. But they're just long columns of numbers. Meaningless to me. Would they mean anything to you if I could recreate them?"

"Recreate? What about the copies he gave you?"

"They're gone. Everything was destroyed."

"Then no, I couldn't do anything. Even if you could duplicate them, even one number out of place or one error could significantly alter the thing. And twelve pages of numbers? Forget about it."

"What if I could?"

Schmidt spoke to Jeffrey like he was addressing a none-too-bright student, his voice cracking on the final words. "It still wouldn't necessarily be possible to know what the data was. Although I can guess. It's probably the results of testing. Statistics on mortality expectations, infectiousness, time to death, collateral damage to survivors. But it would take supercomputers to crunch everything and make it meaningful. All of which assumes you could reproduce it, which you can't. So it's like asking how many toys Santa can carry in his sled. The answer's idiocy because so is the question."

Schmidt groaned on the last word and then made a choking noise, and then his chin dropped onto his chest. His breath grew labored, and came in rasps. Jeffrey was shocked by the suddenness of it, and wasn't sure what to do – he didn't know if Schmidt had just nodded off, or was having some kind of event.

He rose and approached the German. "Schmidt. Alfie. Are you all right?"

No response. He listened to the struggling breath, and then one of the German's hands fell from his lap to his side and began clenching spasmodically.

"Shit," Jeffrey exclaimed, and sprinted into the hall, calling out for help. A female orderly came running at the clamor, and Jeffrey pointed her at Schmidt, then stood back as she rushed to him and quickly examined him. Her face was an expressionless mask, but he saw the anxiety in her eyes even as she tried to maintain her composure, and when she raced from the room to get help there was no wasted motion.

Jeffrey retrieved the recorder and his notebook and packed them into his bag, uninterested in hanging around to see how the German did. Schmidt was almost a century old, and keenly aware that his days were numbered. If this was to be how he shed his mortal coil, then Jeffrey would leave him to do so in peace. A flash of guilt hit him, intensifying his already miserable headache, but he shook it off. The conversation and the old scientist's agitation could well have triggered this, but so could a straining bowel movement or the flu he'd been battling. There would be time enough for recriminations on the train back to Paris.

He glanced at his new Hublot and calculated that he could easily get to the station in time to make the ten o'clock train, which would put him back at the Gare du Nord at least two hours before his doctor's appointment.

The nurse returned with an older man in a white exam coat jogging behind her and another orderly in tow, and Jeffrey used the ensuing chaos to slip away, the frigid morning air nipping at his splitting skull as he strode briskly down the long block to find a taxi and be rid of Frankfurt for good.

THIRTY-SEVEN

Return to Paris

Jeffrey tried to sleep on the trip back, but his headache had a different idea, as did his imagination as he cycled back through his amazing discussion with Schmidt and the information he'd gotten about bio-weapons.

It seemed impossible to believe, and yet the German had been compelling and surprisingly lucid, if bitter at his lot in life and dismissive of everyone around him. That he'd actually helped develop an immunosuppressive agent was hugely damaging, as was his matter-of-fact description of how a powerful faction could twist the system to hasten the Apocalypse.

Jeffrey wasn't naïve, but he felt that way as the inside of his eyes pulsed with pain. He'd believed there were checks and balances to keep rogue groups from using their clout to pursue their own agendas, but he'd apparently been badly mistaken. Schmidt had done the forbidden since long before Jeffrey had been born; and judging by the virus diagram, he'd been replaced by others. A part of him wondered how many of those were complicit and understood what they were doing, and how many were cogs in the machine, doing their top secret work and not allowing themselves to know what happened to the fruits of their labor.

His brother's execution didn't bode well for them in the long term. Jeffrey suspected that any individuals who knew about the virus would be eliminated once their usefulness was over.

Then again, maybe not. Perhaps there were psychopaths who could watch billions die and be more interested in what they got out of it than what they had done. As forthcoming as the old man had been in his final hour, as apparently regretful, he'd still participated in a machine that was involved in the death industry, and had helped build better mousetraps that had already been used to kill tens of millions of innocents.

Innocent people. He wondered if that term had any meaning to the group behind this. Did they even think of their victims as humans, or were they just numbers, a morbid crop to be harvested at the appropriate time, expendable resource sponges that had to go for the better of those remaining? Part of him tried to imagine the emotional makeup of someone who was willing to kill billions in order to further some cause, and he couldn't. It was as alien to him as a reptile brain, as incomprehensible as a Hindi phone book.

He cracked open a weary eye and watched the dizzying panorama of countryside whirring past, all green fields and pale stone houses jutting like tombstones up the slight rise of a pregnant hill. Was that all this was to them, were they all integers, interchangeable digits on a screen? The reality of an entire species an irritating inconvenience, the noise of them dying a temporary annoyance, their corpses grist for an insatiable mill?

His senses were overloaded, the knowledge that he now possessed too much for his psyche. It was better to be ignorant of the evil that men could perpetrate; focused on the mundane, plebian day-to-day; scrabbling for a fresher crust of bread and a faster sports car for his commute; agonizing over which leather interior color was more appealing. Perhaps being a dumb animal was better than the evolutionary alternative. The real world sucked, and when he closed his eyes and shut out the light, a small part of him envied the old Nazi, if not now free of the ugliness that was reality, then soon to be.

The rumble of the train lulled him to sleep eventually, and he was startled awake when it changed tracks and began to slow on the outskirts of Paris. He checked the time and saw that he had an hour and a half before his medical appointment, which at the rate he was going, he would actually need. The pain had retreated to a dull throb, the rest having caused it to recede enough that he could move his eyes without a piercing lance of agony splitting his head. It was still a far cry from normal, though, and part of him feared that he had done some real damage with the whirlwind trip. The Swiss doctor had been pretty clear about relaxing, and his journey had been anything but.

The station was bustling, crowds of travelers jostling to make their trains like spawning salmon, intent faces filled with the ennui unique to Paris.

Jeffrey slipped into the stream of humanity and wound his way to the station's huge exit doors, where a line of taxis waited like penitents for confession. The hotel's name elicited a grunt and an eye roll from the swarthy man behind the wheel, and then the Renault launched forward, narrowly missing a VW van that stood on its horn as the driver stoically ignored the commotion and made for the hotel like he was piloting a getaway car.

Jeffrey had the taxi drop him off a block from the hotel, and then repeated his trip through the hotel service entrance. In the room, he noted with satisfaction that his bed hadn't been made, so it appeared his ruse had worked. He figured he would know definitively if someone jabbed an ice pick into his spine in the elevator.

He showered and changed, then opened the room safe and retrieved his cell phone and switched it on. He checked his messages and saw that Monica had called twice, and the office once. Scanning his email, he didn't spot anything that required immediate attention, and forwarded most of it to his subordinates for responses.

He called the office once he was in the elevator, and told them that he wasn't feeling well and was en route to the doctor. With his headache, it didn't take much acting skill for him to sound compromised, and the conversation didn't last long. Jeffrey called Monica once in a taxi on the way to his appointment, which was not coincidentally only a block from the Pasteur Institute, where the French scientist had his offices and lab.

"Jeff! Thank God you called. I've been so worried," she answered, not waiting for him to say anything. "I tried to reach you a few times, but it went straight to voicemail."

The funny thing was that she really did sound concerned, and he marveled again at her powers of duplicity. Unless she really was worried – that he'd disappeared and hadn't told her where he was going.

"I've been vegetating at the hotel. This concussion took more out of me than I thought. I'm in Paris, on the way to the neurologist."

"How do you feel?" she asked.

"Like crap. I'm glad he's going to see me. I really have my doubts about the doc in Zurich."

"Will you call me as soon as you're through with him?"

"Sure. But it kind of hurts to talk. That's why I've been off the radar."

"I understand. I know I wouldn't be chatty if my head had been used as a soccer ball."

"That's about how it feels. Listen, I'm going to go now. Save my energy," Jeffrey said, anxious to get off the line. His voice really did sound terrible, so he didn't have to fake it much.

"All right. Call me later," Monica said, and he hung up, not wanting to hear her say anything more about her supposed feelings for him, which he could sense coming. He wasn't sure how he was going to break off their relationship – or rather, her duty in his bed – but he would come up with a reason when he returned.

Then again, with what he now knew about the virus, the end of the world might wind up being the perfect reason to want some time to himself. All he'd been able to think about since he'd woken up on the train were the German's words and his shocked appearance when he'd seen the drawing of the virus.

The thought that Jeffrey was the only thing standing in the way of the apocalypse was like a crushing weight on his shoulders, and the anxiety that had been nestling in his stomach returned with full force as he slipped the phone into his pocket and leaned back in the seat, the streets of Paris gliding by as the car made its way to the Left Bank.

THIRTY-EIGHT

Check-Up

"Monsieur, the doctor will see you now," the comely young receptionist said in delightfully accented English. Jeffrey stood and followed a second, equally fetching attendant, who led him to a sumptuous office with an en-suite exam room, the furniture high-end recreations of antique French provincial treasures. More than anything, the first impression Jeffrey had upon entering the room was of it being exquisitely tasteful.

Which perfectly matched the stately man in his early sixties who stood in one corner of the room, his conservative Hermès tie loosened, staring out the window. When the doctor turned to face him, Jeffrey was immediately struck by the man's presence, which emanated from him with a glowing aura, like that of a celebrity.

"Monsieur Rutherford. *Bon.* You are here. Welcome. Please sit down, and tell me how I can help you," the physician said, his English perfect, pointing to a chair in front of his desk.

Jeffrey sat and the doctor asked him a series of questions about his symptoms, degree of discomfort, and so on. He told the doctor about his recurring headaches, not needing to exaggerate his discomfort and worry. The older man nodded and motioned for Jeffrey to join him in the exam room.

Jeffrey knew what to expect and slid up onto the examination bed. The doctor approached and began probing his head wound.

"It's healing nicely. I see no complications. Swelling is almost completely gone, and your hair is long enough so it covers the area, so it is not obvious, you know?"

"That's not a huge consideration. I just want to know that there's nothing they missed or that's going wrong. Sometimes the pain is blinding."

"Mmm. Yes, I imagine it can be. Take hold of each of my fingers and squeeze as hard as you can with both hands, please."

Jeffrey complied, and then the doctor did a full neurological workup, taking him through the paces. At the end of the encounter the doctor waved him back to the desk, pausing to study Jeffrey as he made his way back to his seat. He wrote up some quick notes, humming under his breath, and then looked up at Jeffrey as if he'd forgotten he was still there.

"*Bon.* I see no abnormalities, so that is good news. If the scan was normal, then I would say that the headaches are simply a residual effect of the trauma and will fade over the next few days. Have you been resting, avoiding stress and movement?"

Jeffrey didn't say what sprang to mind – that he'd been singled out to save the human race and traversed half of Europe over the last day.

"Yes," he lied.

"Good. Then continue doing so and you'll be fine. If you are still experiencing problems in a week, or if you start to experience any double vision, we will have another appointment, yes? Until then, we must let Mother Nature take her course."

Jeffrey thanked him for his time and left the suite, stopping to pay the receptionist before taking the elevator to the ground level.

Outside, he glanced in both directions down the gray street. Clouds hung over the city, threatening rain. The sidewalk had a few pedestrians making their way towards the main boulevard, and Jeffrey joined them in their pilgrimage, his thoughts elsewhere, on retroviruses and global contagion and death, as well as on a woman who had cheerfully lied to him with the conviction of a Wall Street banker – and on a bitter academic in the Virginia countryside…and his beautiful daughter.

So immersed was he in his inner world that when he stepped off the curb he was almost run down by a truck, its horn blaring as it narrowly missed him. The driver made an obscene gesture as the engine revved and the big vehicle blew past him. He froze in his tracks, and then carefully crossed to the far side and continued on his way, the thin line between life and death again reinforced, in case he'd forgotten the precariousness of his mortal state.

THIRTY-NINE

An Appointment

Jeffrey rose as dawn's first light seeped through the overcast lingering over Paris. His head felt marginally better, fifteen hours of rest having done him good after the prior two-day marathon. After the visit to the doctor, he'd returned to his room and made the obligatory calls to Monica and to his secretary, and after an early meal he'd locked himself away and forced himself to stay in bed so his body could have a needed opportunity to heal.

Sleep hadn't come easily, as he'd worried away at the issue of how to get to François Bertrand, the preeminent virologist in France and a legend in academic and medical circles, one of the top members of the team that had discovered HIV thirty years earlier. Now in the winter of his years, at seventy-two he still worked five days a week in his beloved laboratory, and was considered a national treasure by the French people.

Jeffrey had eventually drifted off into uneasy slumber after taking a pill the Swiss had given him, but his night had been filled with vivid nightmares of himself walking slowly through a hospital ward with the dead abandoned in the halls, covered with stained sheets, anonymous women and children in rusting beds stacked together, gasping for their last breaths as their haunted eyes sought him out, drowning from their bodies' immune responses to a hellish plague from which there was no defense.

When he bolted awake he was shaking, adrenaline flooding through his system, and he cried out, for a moment still in with the sick, sentenced to impossible-to-imagine death. His bearings returned after a few panicked gasps, and his racing heart began to slow as he blinked and groped on the nightstand for his watch.

Jeffrey groaned and pushed himself to a sitting position, and then forced himself to his feet and stumbled half-asleep to the bathroom, where it took seemingly forever for the water to get warm. Once in the shower he dismissed shampooing his hair and instead scrubbed himself vigorously with the provided lavender soap, as if he could wash away the lingering sense of dread that was now his constant companion. Even as he watched the suds swirl down the drain, the clock was ticking, and vials of global death could be on their way for dispersal. He was trying not to allow the size of the responsibility he'd been unwittingly stuck with to paralyze him, but it was hard, given what he now knew.

He deliberately took slow, deep breaths as he toweled dry, regaining control of himself with a pronounced effort that set his head to throbbing again, the pain now as familiar as a favorite song. He needed to focus. How was he going to get to see the scientific equivalent of a rock star? The question nagged at him as he shaved, and then he realized he needed to do more research before he could come up with a coherent plan. Right now he was operating in the dark, and he needed to change that, quickly.

Jeffrey called down to the front desk and asked for housekeeping to make up his room while he was having breakfast. He locked his valuables in the safe and took his phone with him, so his watchers would see normal movement. A table set for two near the hotel restaurant entrance afforded him a good view of the lobby, but either his newly acquired spy skills were dormant before his first cup of coffee or there was nobody watching him.

Service was slow, and it took him an hour to finish up, which gave him more than enough time to plan his day. To anyone paying attention he would appear to be bed-ridden, but as soon as he confirmed that his room had been serviced he'd be slipping out the service entrance and completing the tasks that had been accumulating in his mind like cords of firewood. He stopped at the front desk and told the clerk that he was not to be disturbed and to hold all calls until further notice.

Back in the room he stashed his wallet and phone in the safe and peeled off a thousand euros, folding the notes into a thin wad and slipping them into his trousers. He'd been having second thoughts about the wallet since being mugged – it was conceivable a tracking device had been slipped inside it, although he hadn't been able to find one. But he didn't know everything that was possible, and as with his German trip, he'd decided to err on the side of caution and leave everything that could be compromised in the room while he went about his business on the sly.

The service door was unattended, and Jeffrey had no problem easing it open and stepping out into the alley, heaping garbage containers signaling that it was trash day. Two minutes later he was a block away and making for an internet café, the smell of coffee drawing him as much as the computers. He ordered a cappuccino and bought some time at one of the terminals, and then spent the next hour researching everything he could find on Bertrand, which was plenty. The man seemed to enjoy the reputation he'd built, and there were literally hundreds of articles from the last decade, including a number of YouTube videos of him speaking at scientific gatherings.

Jeffrey watched several as he sipped his brew, and the sense he got was of a charming figure who was somewhat ill at ease with the constant limelight. An academic more at home in the lab than on the stage, but still inexhaustible in his communication with the media.

That made Jeffrey's approach easier. He would again pose as a journalist, this time a freelance investigative reporter doing a series of articles on retroviruses. But unlike the case at the German nursing home, he was pretty sure he wouldn't be able to smile his way past the Pasteur Institute's security, so he would need to get business cards printed up, at minimum, and go in through the front door with his act polished to a mirror gleam.

He jotted down the Frenchman's contact information and created a blind email account using his middle name – Stanley – and once it was active he emailed a brief introductory message to Bertrand, in the hopes that someone on his end checked his correspondence. He chose his words carefully, requesting some time with the scientist as a featured figure in his new article series.

Jeffrey next turned to the job he'd been dreading – recreating the pages of the spreadsheet. He opened Excel and settled in, closing his eyes for a moment while he sorted through his memory and found page one. After a brief pause he began entering headings and numbers, the data as clear as though he was reading from the pages. He stretched another cup of coffee forever, and after several more hours had recreated the entire document.

The woman who ran the little café was obliging and told him how to print his file, and was more than willing to sell him an eight-gigabyte flash drive. He returned to the computer and saved the data to the drive, and sent the document to the printer. Once it was safely in the queue he closed the spreadsheet and wiped the temp file it had created. He then collected the dozen pages the printer spewed forth, shielding them with his body from the watchful eye of the proprietress, and accidentally tripped over the power cord, jerking it free of the wall and hopefully dumping the printer's memory in the process.

Money changed hands and he folded the documents and slipped them into the inside pocket of his jacket. He suspected there was some way an interested party could retrieve the data from the printer if they were motivated, but it would have to be an acceptable risk – he'd covered his tracks as best he could, but he couldn't be a hundred percent on everything.

His next stop was a cell phone store across the street, where he purchased a moderately priced disposable with a hundred minutes of talk time and a local number. Once it had been activated and he confirmed it worked, he moved to a print shop he'd passed the day before that advertised documents created while you waited – at least that's what he'd thought the banners in the display window said. He shouldered his way into the shop and was greeted by a morose young man sporting a sparse goatee, a beatnik-era haircut, and an olive green T-shirt depicting Che Guevara staring into eternity. Jeffrey picked up a business card and pointed to it, and the clerk began rattling off prices and terms in lightning French. Jeffrey turned the sample business card over and wrote a name with his new number below it, along with a title: James Stanley, Investigative Journalist, 46a rue Saint-Guillaume, 75007 Paris.

Jeffrey pantomimed that he wanted some cards made, and after a few minutes of tortured back and forth, the young man snorted and addressed him in English.

"You want these on good, or the best, stock? And how many?"

Jeffrey was taken aback but didn't show it. "The best, and make it a hundred. But I need them as soon as possible."

"Hmm. Yes, I suppose you would."

The clerk tapped keys on the calculator in front of him, paused, took another look at Jeffrey's face and entered more, and then turned the calculator to face Jeffrey so he could read the display. As Jeffrey peered at the tiny screen the clerk moved over a few feet and addressed another customer, an older woman, who had entered the shop after him. The two had a heated exchange with much gesticulation, and then the woman left, slamming the door on her way out. The clerk's long, jaundiced face remained impassive as he returned his attention to Jeffrey.

"Seems very expensive," Jeffrey commented, and the man shrugged.

"You can make your own on a computer and cut them with scissors."

"No, I'll take them. How long until they can be ready?"

The man regarded the clock on the wall, as if making difficult calculations in his head. "One hour."

Jeffrey fished money out of his pocket and handed it to the clerk, who seemed annoyed that the high price and his indifferent treatment hadn't rid him of the American. He counted the bills with studied detachment, then wrote out a ticket and stapled the hand-written card to it before opening a book of sample typefaces.

"Pick one for your name, and the other for the rest of the information. Also, choose a layout."

Jeffrey did, and the man scribbled another few notes on the order and then closed the book.

"*Bon.* In an hour," he said, and then spun and made his way to one of the tables in the rear work area, where an obese woman was typing on a computer. He handed her the order and she glanced at it without comment.

Back out on the street, Jeffrey wandered aimlessly for a few blocks, killing time while trying to avoid jarring his head with any sudden movements. He stopped at a small bakery for a croissant, and then sat at one of the sidewalk tables and watched the Parisian crowd go by. When he tired of the mindless pastime he found another internet café and logged onto his new email, confirming that there were no messages.

With another glance at his watch, he decided to try reaching the scientist on the phone, in the hopes that he could get an interview within the next few days. If that failed, he had no plan B, other than stalking the man and looking for an opportune time to effectively kidnap him.

A woman answered, and when he asked for Bertrand, he was connected to another extension that rang five times before a younger female voice came on the line.

"*Allo?*"

"Hello. *Parlez-vous Anglais?*" Jeffrey asked.

"*Oui.* Yes, I do. How may I help you?"

"I sent an email earlier. My name is James Stanley. I'm an investigative reporter doing a story on retroviruses. I'm in Paris, and I want to interview Dr. Bertrand."

"An email," she said. He heard fingers tapping at keys at blinding speed. "Mm, yes, here it is." She took a moment to read it. "I will need to ask the doctor, Monsieur Stanley. When did you want to try to see him, and how long will you need?"

That was more positive than he'd hoped for – she hadn't just completely shut him down.

"Anytime he can fit me in. And I don't imagine I'll need more than an hour. But he's a central figure in my feature, and it's very important that he has an opportunity to present his perspective."

"One moment, please," she said, and muzak drifted over the line. A man carrying two bags of groceries, one in each arm, nearly collided with him, and Jeffrey stepped out of the way, pressing closer to the building to present a smaller target while he waited. The pedestrians moved with the urgency of gazelles chased by a pride of lions, and Jeffrey was viewed as an undesirable impediment, an obstacle to timely passage. He had just about given up on the receptionist and was going to call back when she returned.

"The doctor can see you today at four, if you can make it. For forty-five minutes."

"That's perfect! At the Institute?"

"Yes, third floor. You will need to ask the guards for an escort. Just use the doctor's name."

"Excellent. Four o'clock. Thank you."

"It is not I you should thank. The doctor always tries to be accommodating for the press," she said, and then the phone went dead in Jeffrey's ear.

Even the truculent look from the print shop attendant upon his return and the additional twenty minutes of waiting for his order to be processed couldn't bring Jeffrey down from his high. He was going to see one of the top virologists in the world in five hours, and hopefully would be able to solve the riddle of his brother's diagram and spreadsheet.

Whether that would be in time to save the planet was a different story, but he'd take the small wins when he got them.

FORTY

Dr. Bertrand

Jeffrey waited nervously in the outer waiting room of the Pasteur Institute's third floor administrative offices, shifting on the leather couch as he inspected his shoes, trying to appear calm while his synapses tingled with adrenaline. He hadn't dared go back to the hotel and risk detection, so he'd spent his afternoon meandering around Paris, with several breaks for coffee, which he was now paying for as the caffeine jangled his frayed nerves.

The room was modern, cold, the lines clean, the furniture contemporary; the few magazines on the table in front of him were French scientific journals, from what he could tell. He'd drawn a new version of the virus diagram and the bar charts, and was satisfied that his newest masterpiece was as detailed as the original. He had the spreadsheets and his handiwork in his jacket pocket. Another notepad and his French cell phone lay in a newly purchased a satchel, along with a recorder and a hundred business cards he would likely never need.

A tall, frosty woman with mannishly cut hair the color of smoke emerged from one of the doorways behind the reception counter, and after a brief, hushed discussion with the secretary, opened the small half door separating the area from where Jeffrey sat and approached him.

"Monsieur Stanley?"

"Yes," Jeffrey said, rising from the sofa, taking her outstretched hand and shaking it. She had the grip of a longshoreman, he thought, and her cobalt eyes scrutinized him with the precision of a laser. For some reason he felt inadequate under her blistering gaze, but he shrugged it off.

"The doctor will see you. Please. Follow me, yes?" she said, the final word not so much a question as an order.

Jeffrey walked behind her, and once through the door found himself in an industrial hallway, sterile and lacking any furniture or art, painted a polar white that the overhead fluorescent lights imbued with an alien quality. She led him to the final door on the right, and paused just before she knocked on it.

"Forty-five minutes," she said, her tone as playful as a marine sergeant's barked drill, and then she rapped on the door three times, each percussive pop echoing in the hall like a firecracker.

A male voice called from inside and the door buzzed, a remote electric security latch presumably triggered by the occupant. She pushed the door open, her eyes never leaving his face as he nodded his thanks and edged by her. He could feel her stare boring holes in his back as he approached the inner office, where a pudgy man with oversized horn-rimmed glasses on his bald head sat behind a desk large enough to house a family of four.

"Dr. Bertrand. Thank you so much for meeting with me," Jeffrey said, his feet sinking into the plush carpet in the scientist's office as he moved toward the desk.

"My pleasure, Mr. Stanley, my pleasure. I'm sorry I have so little time for you, but I'm afraid my days are all like this – many hours of work, and not enough time to get everything I need done..." Bertrand said with a small, apologetic frown. "Your email says you are doing an article about retrovirology?"

"Yes, Doctor. Specifically, on lab-created retroviruses. And the potential for disaster if one of these experiments were ever to make it out of the laboratory and into the general population," Jeffrey explained, pulling his recorder out of his bag and setting it onto the desk. "May I record this?"

"Certainly."

Jeffrey activated the recorder and pushed it between them. "As I was saying, I'm doing a series about retrovirology, recent advances in science, and the possibility that something lab-generated could make it into the real world."

"All facilities doing this sort of research will use level three or four bio-containment protocols, so the odds of anything escaping the lab are so remote as to be incalculable," Bertrand assured him. "Everyone involved in the field is aware of the risks, and it has become standard to have these kinds of systems in order to protect against accidents."

"That's reassuring. Before we get too far into my questions, though, could we go back and touch on your background? You were one of the members of the team that discovered HIV, were you not?"

"Yes. Working with Montagnier in the eighties. I was a young scientist in a cutting-edge field. It was a very exciting time. He was awarded the Nobel Prize for that discovery, you know."

"Yes. And a tremendous honor for you, as well," Jeffrey said.

"It's all part of the job. Most of which involves impossibly long hours in the lab, you know. Nothing glamorous, I'm afraid. Just test tubes and microscopes."

They spent some time going back and forth about the group that Bertrand led, and some of the noteworthy advances he'd pioneered, and then Jeffrey nudged the discussion into the direction he needed it to go.

"As part of my investigations, I've interviewed other scientists, and I've gotten a good picture of some of the dangers involved in certain types of research. Biological warfare programs, for instance," Jeffrey started.

"There are no more biological warfare programs. They were outlawed in 1972, and virtually every country in the world has signed the convention banning them."

"I understand that. But I've also spoken to some who claim that there have been secret programs, in violation of the agreement."

Bertrand's eyes hardened, and his tone went from one of cheerful good nature to unfriendliness. "I wouldn't know anything about that. France has no offensive biological warfare program. That is a matter of public record."

"Yes, I know. But there are other countries with advanced capabilities, and there have been allegations. They're not a secret. The Soviets had aggressive offensive programs that continued until the fall of the Soviet Union, and which continue, some believe, to this day."

"I'm not sure that there is a question in all this. Is there?"

Jeffrey shook his head. "I suppose not. I'm trying to understand the implications of a lab-created virus making its way into the general population."

"That would be most unlikely."

"What would you say if I told you that I have uncovered evidence that there is such a virus, and that it looks as though it's in imminent danger of being released?"

Bertrand drew back, clearly uncomfortable. "Monsieur, this interview is at an end. I am not going to entertain flights of fancy or science fiction. I don't mean to be rude, but this is not what I agreed to participate in," Bertrand said, and lifted his telephone handset from the cradle and prepared to dial.

Jeffrey extracted the diagram from his pocket and wordlessly placed it in front of Bertrand. The Frenchman's finger hovered over the phone keypad, and then he slowly set the phone back down as he squinted at the drawing. He pulled his glasses down from his head and peered at Jeffrey's diagram, his complexion going pale as the minutes slowly ticked by. Eventually he put the paper down and fixed Jeffrey with a shocked gaze.

"Where...where did you get this?"

"It doesn't matter. Do you know what it is?"

"I...I would need to study it more closely to be sure."

"I've been told it is a variant of H1N1. Spanish influenza. But that it has been modified."

Bertrand stared at the diagram again. "How?"

"In one of those offensive bio-warfare laboratories that the Biological Weapons Convention says no longer exists," Jeffrey said.

"I mean how has it been modified? Do you know?"

Jeffrey let him absorb the drawing, and then pulled the spreadsheet from his pocket and placed the pages on the desk next to the diagram. "It's been made more lethal, more infectious, deadlier. The reason I wanted to meet with you is because I suspect you're one of the few people who can tell me just how much more dangerous this new variant is."

Bertrand stared at the spreadsheet like it was toxic. "What is that?"

"I was hoping you could tell me."

Bertrand began paging through the sheaf of paper, then looked at Jeffrey. "These are results. It looks to me like trial results. A data set."

"So they should be able to tell you what it is we're dealing with?"

"Possibly. I would need to enter everything and run some models. I ask you again – where did you get this?"

Jeffrey sighed. This was the moment of truth. The point where he would need to trust the Frenchman with his life. If he called it wrong, or if the scientist was somehow involved in the scheme, Jeffrey would be dead in a matter of hours.

"It started with a plane crash..."

Five minutes later, Jeffrey finished, feeling like he'd run a marathon.

Bertrand was studying the diagram again. "I'll need time. But if this is what it appears to be, then you're correct. This is an unprecedented disaster. I just can't believe that it could have originated in America. It makes no sense."

"The German said that there was a faction in the U.S. government, or that colluded with the government, that's been working on reducing the world population for four decades. That he was part of their scheme, and that the projects he was involved with were approved in the clandestine back rooms. He said that HIV was part of that."

"He said what?" Bertrand demanded incredulously.

Jeffrey took him through the German's claims. His developing an immune-suppressive agent in chimps, and then for humans. The incredibly coincidental timing of the global AIDS epidemic, and his observations of the timing of the AIDS outbreaks and the hepatitis B vaccination trials in the U.S. and the smallpox vaccination programs in Africa.

"These are very dangerous claims, and I would be very, very careful about voicing them. Certainly, there's a case that can be made for HIV being lab-created, but you'll find it's a controversial topic that nobody wishes to debate," Bertrand warned.

"I'm aware of that. It's just one of many things these days that's best not discussed, apparently. Anything that contradicts an official explanation is treated as conspiracy nonsense, even if all the data supports the alternative explanation."

"I'm not going to debate ideology or ethics. But this...this, if it is an actually model of a modified virus, is frightening," Bertrand snapped.

"Can you enter the data and run whatever you need to run in order to better understand it?" Jeffrey asked, finally daring the big question. "You're one of the only scientists in the world equipped to interpret the data. That's what my research has led me to believe..."

A knock at the door interrupted them, and Bertrand hastily gathered up the papers and stuffed them into his desk drawer before pressing the button that opened the remote lock. His assistant stuck her head in.

"Ah, Marianne. We will need a few more minutes. We are just finishing up," Bertrand said, affecting his collegial air.

She eyed Jeffrey disapprovingly and nodded. "*Oui. D'accord,*" she said, and closed the door.

Bertrand returned his focus to Jeffrey. He exhaled noisily, staring at a point somewhere to the left of Jeffrey's face.

"Will you do it?" Jeffrey asked softly.

"What choice do I have? You've dropped a scientific atomic bomb in my lap. How can I not act on this? Of course I have to do it. And it will take many hours of my, and my staff's, time. We'll have to drop everything and work only on this. For which I have you to blame…"

"I'm sorry. There was nobody else I could go to."

"The damage is done. Now I need to characterize this virus and see what the data says. If your story is even half true, we could be facing the biggest threat to our species in history." Bertrand shook his head. "I have long feared something like this, and now that it's here, it doesn't surprise me. Nothing about man's ability to destroy surprises me. As a scientist who has spent his life trying to untangle the riddles nature visits upon us, the greatest mystery I have seen is man's willingness to do the unspeakable to his fellow man."

They agreed that Jeffrey would call him in forty-eight hours for an update and would leave the spreadsheets with him. Jeffrey rooted in his jacket and withdrew the flash drive, and handed it Bertrand as they were walking to the door together.

"That'll save you some time on the data entry, I hope," he said, and Bertrand gave him another surprised look.

"Who are you, really?" Bertrand asked in a low voice.

Jeffrey thought long and hard about how to answer the question.

"Just someone in the wrong place at the right time."

FORTY-ONE

Quiet Contemplation

Reginald Barker watched the waves pound against the shore from the long terrace of his estate home on a secluded bluff in Montauk, New York, at the northeastern tip of Long Island. The area was home to some of the most expensive real estate in the world, and his retreat numbered among the most exclusive, the rambling acreage as far as he could see privately owned – by him – with an almost incalculable value.

The sun had risen a half hour earlier, and the industrialist was enjoying his first cup of coffee of the day, preparing for a walk along the trails that he loved, down the rise and to the beach, which at that hour would be secluded, his only company the unobtrusive security detail that shadowed him to ensure he wasn't accosted.

While some of his neighbors down the island had built gauche, mega-opulent estates that were featured in magazines and whispered about by the locals, Barker had always adhered to the philosophy he'd inherited from his father – that it was better to go unnoticed and not to flaunt the riches with which he'd been blessed. His home, one of eight he owned, was modest by his standards: nine thousand square feet, with none of the garish frills favored by the nouveaux riches; no bowling alleys or movie theaters for him. Simply well-designed, beautifully appointed elegance, boasting Chippendale furniture that would be the envy of half the museums in the world and a collection of art as breathtaking as it was valuable.

His full-time staff at the Hamptons estate included three housekeepers, a butler, a driver, two gardeners, a maintenance man, a chef, and sundry helpers, not counting his bodyguards, which alternated between a core of four to as many as twenty, depending upon which of his abodes he was frequenting. It was the burden of being rich, he mused as he sipped the special Kona blend grown for him at a private farm – he'd bought half the growing land after he'd tasted the roast at a getaway he'd taken there thirty years before, and was the sole consumer of the beans in the U.S.

The accumulation of wealth and power had long since passed from being a passion to a routine, and he didn't bother to track his worth anymore – it was in the hundreds of billions, depending upon the performance of his largest holdings. The number had ceased to be meaningful, and the things money could buy didn't interest him, beyond ensuring that his every need was attended to.

He finished his cup and set it on a small circular marble table by the door, then zipped his coat up tighter, his breath steaming in the chill. With a glance at his rose gold Patek Philippe Sky Moon Tourbillon watch, he stretched his legs and did a series of knee bends, grimacing at the popping as his aged joints protested the exertion. One of the truisms of life, he mused – nothing could stop the inexorable creep of time, not even truckloads of riches. Of course, he had a team of the finest medical practitioners at his beck and call, but even they couldn't sustain him indefinitely. His time was drawing to an end, he knew, but he wouldn't go easily, and he was determined to stay vital until death's cold hand landed on his shoulder. His father had lived to be eighty-four, as mean as a black mamba and twice as lethal, and he had every expectation that the combination of good genes and improved science would keep him drawing breath for as long, if not longer, than his ancestors.

He paced along the terrace, back and forth, three, then five times, before carefully descending the stairs to the path that led through the immaculately tended grounds and into the wooded area, where he could lose himself in the solitude, imagining himself to be the only person in the world – a common dream of his, although he routinely forgot it seconds after waking. The muffled thud of his rubber soles on the well-worn trail was the only sound other than the overhead rustle of the occasional bird and the snap and popping as a gymnastically inclined squirrel leapt from branch to branch on its morning rounds.

Would that the rest of his day be as untroubled as these first hours! As usual, it would be a non-stop series of meetings, his hand firmly in every aspect of the multitude of companies he owned, his habit to stay active in their management as a board member whose calls would always be answered, or in a more silent and deniable fashion through intermediaries and attorneys, of which he employed a phalanx. His accountant had informed him that last year he'd spent eighty million dollars on Washington lobbyists alone, and that had barely scratched the surface of the money he spread around. He knew from experience that there was no point in hoarding his wealth. The cash would only work for him if he put it to use, and he'd bought the very best government he could afford – and he could afford anything.

The amount he'd made during the Vietnam war paled by comparison to what he'd earned from America's undeclared wars in Iraq and Afghanistan, which had paled again compared to what his pharmaceutical companies generated, as well as his partial ownership in a slew of the globe's largest banks – a special club that was by invitation only, and which conferred upon its members unimaginable power.

Barker made kings, decided who ran countries, balanced the fate of nations on his salad fork while debating which wine to enjoy with dinner. He and his clique ran things; which was as it should be, because the planet's people couldn't be trusted to run the place themselves. And now, his most ambitious project was coming to fruition, and he was only days from deploying the virus that would sweep the globe, eradicating the lion's share of the Earth's unproductive and parasitic, leaving a healthier, revitalized planet in its wake.

The brainchild of a group of like-minded thinkers during the Cold War, the latest innovation would transform the future into a better one for the survivors – a sustainable population of only the most productive in each society, selected on the basis of merit rather than emotion. When his company announced that it had isolated the virus after working round the clock, only once the flu had spread far past the tipping point and was ravaging the most problematically populated countries, and then leaked that it had a vaccine that might work, but could only be produced in adequate quantities to protect, at most, half a billion people…at that point, the governments of the world would have to make difficult but necessary choices, for the betterment of all.

Naturally, he and everyone he valued would be inoculated far before the virus could make it to the U.S., and his cronies in the CIA and at the highest circles of government had already put into place plans to effectively seal the borders and shut down air traffic, sequestering all inbound travelers in internment camps until they could be verified as being healthy – which would take a week, even though the effective incubation period was more like twenty-four hours.

The data didn't lie. It would be a plague of unprecedented proportions, and would once and for all reset the clock to an earlier time, when the population was sustainable, given the limited resources of the ecosystem. It was impossible for growth to continue at its present rate, and only the far-thinking and the brave were willing to take the steps necessary for the survival of the species. Left to their own devices, the weak and the liberal would just kick the can down the road, leaving the problem to future generations.

He reached the beach and stood on the sand, breathing in the salt air, the wind crisp, clean and pure, as it must have been hundreds of years before when his predecessors had arrived on these untamed shores. As he had planned, he was the only one on the beach, and try as he might he couldn't see his bodyguards, although he knew they were somewhere in the trees.

There would be civil unrest here at home, he was sure, as only a portion of the population could be saved. Preparations had already been put into effect, the emergency measures that would be enacted for the nation's own good plotted out in secret. He wasn't worried about that – after a few weeks of death, any resistance or argument would have gone out of the survivors, who would just be grateful to have been spared. He expected the same in Europe and the other areas that he would have the vaccine shipped to, and any outcry from the problem areas would quickly go silent as the populations perished.

He stood, face into the breeze for a few minutes, and then he reluctantly turned and made his way back up the hill, revitalized and refreshed by his encounter with nature. He would do what he needed to do. Fifty years of planning would soon come to fruition, and a brave new world would finally see its new dawn – the first of many to come, even if his were numbered.

A thought struck him and he slowed as a grin played across his creased face. *You had to break eggs to make an omelet.* That's what his father had always said when he'd had to consider collateral damage from one of his campaigns. Damned if the old man hadn't been right.

Maybe he'd have Rosa cook up *huevos rancheros* for breakfast.

It was, after all, a beautiful morning.

FORTY-TWO

The Verdict

Jeffrey spent the two days following his meeting with Bertrand on pins and needles, holed up in his hotel room, taking advantage of the time to recuperate and rebuild his resilience. The blow to his head had taken a lot out of him, and the stress from his encounters with the German and Bertrand hadn't helped matters. But even though he knew he needed the down time, every hour seemed to crawl by as if in slow motion.

He'd spoken to Monica once, and begged off after a superficial discussion, mostly her assuring him that she missed him terribly and couldn't wait for him to come home, with him offering anodyne responses. If she detected a cooling from his end she didn't let on, and he didn't really care much whether she did or not – he'd be ending the farce once he got back, beginning with breaking the news that he'd had a lot of time to think, and that things had moved too fast for his taste, and that he'd put off dealing with his feelings about his brother's death by plunging into a relationship and a new job instead of processing the emotions and grieving. It was the kind of psychobabble he heard on television all the time, including when he tuned into one of the forty English channels offered by the hotel.

She would undoubtedly try to weasel her way back into his bed, but he would simply be unavailable, even if it meant taking a long vacation to recover. Which stopped him. Could he return to his job now that he believed that it was all a lie, and that he hadn't been hired because he was a rarity but merely so that unseen watchers could more easily keep their eye on him? And even if he could, was working in an office twelve hours a day, structuring byzantine schemes to help his clients avoid taxes, really how he wanted to spend whatever life he had? He could probably never know for sure that the job was part of the scheme he'd uncovered, but his gut told him it was, and he was learning to trust his instincts.

The events of the last week had changed something fundamental in him: They both depressed and sickened him, but also reinforced how precious his existence was. And his brother's death was always lurking in the background, just out of reach, a reminder that there were no guarantees of a long and prosperous life. It could be over at any moment. And if he couldn't figure out a way to stop the virus, it very well might be sooner than later.

He'd come up with some possible ways to block dissemination of the plague flu, as he thought of it, but none of them was foolproof, and all depended upon him being successful in implementing them before it was released. Once it was, it wouldn't really matter who knew that it was man-made – everyone would be too busy dying. Even as he lay on the bed, watching another mindless show, his mind was racing into the redline, counting the seconds until he could reasonably call Bertrand and find out what he'd learned.

After lunch on the second day, he repeated his sneaking out trick, which had apparently worked like a charm the last time. Whoever was watching him obviously had bought that he was doing little but watching television and running up a big tab while he convalesced. He'd called the neurologist in the morning and made another appointment for the following day, at which point he was planning to give the man a progress report just to keep up appearances, even though he wasn't due to check in for a week.

Jeffrey slipped out of the service door and down the alley, and then paused at the main street, waiting for a lull in the traffic to dart across and melt into the throng. The sidewalks were crowded, and he had no problem blending in with his fellow pedestrians, his dark pants and jacket rendering him as anonymous as you could get in a big city.

Once he was three blocks from the hotel, he sat down at a sidewalk café, ordered coffee, and placed a call on his burner cell to Bertrand. The Frenchman answered on the second ring, and sounded out of breath.

"When can you be here?" the scientist asked.

"In about half an hour, I think."

"I'll tell Marianne. See you then."

Bertrand's voice gave nothing away, but Jeffrey figured that he wouldn't have told him to come to the office if he didn't have big news. Either that or Jeffrey had misjudged him, and there would be an executioner waiting for him with a silenced pistol or a straight razor when he approached the building. There was only one way to know for sure, so he paid for his coffee and scanned the street, hoping to find one of Paris' ubiquitous taxis. It took him five minutes, but eventually one skidded to the curb next to him, and soon the little vehicle was rocketing toward the rue de Vaugirard and the Pasteur Institute.

Jeffrey had the driver drop him off two blocks away, and he approached the main entrance of the six-story tan building from across the street, watching for anyone suspiciously lurking around the front doors. His primitive attempt at tradecraft exhausted after several moments of watching the passers-by, he crossed the boulevard, dodging speeding cars, and entered the lobby. The escort to the third floor was repeated, and Marianne was waiting for him, her face as grim as the last time he'd seen her, not a trace of warmth on it.

"This way," she said in her typically clipped style. Without waiting for a response, she led him down the empty hall to the scientist's office. Three raps, the buzzer sounded, and then Jeffrey was once again with Bertrand, who looked like he hadn't slept since he'd last seen him.

The doctor was sitting behind his desk and started speaking before Jeffrey had a chance to sit.

"It's far worse than we thought. It's H1N1…but it's not. It's something much more devastating. We ran the data, crunched the numbers, examined the modifications that were made. How much do you know about the original H1N1 virus?" the Frenchman asked, obviously frazzled.

"Just what the German told me. Deadly, affected the young and healthy, had up to a five percent mortality rate, typically killed very quickly – within twenty-four hours of the onset of symptoms, in most cases."

"That's probably as much as most know, if not more. This…this makes that look like having the sniffles. The death rates will be off the charts. Literally. The numbers you gave me…it looks like this virus would kill eighty to ninety percent of those infected. And it's extremely contagious. Again, almost immeasurable. If this was released, it would wipe out much of human life. Our rough model says six billion people, possibly more, before it ran its course."

"Good God. Are you serious?"

"I have never been more serious about anything in my life. The main problem is that there would be no resistance – it's been modified enough so that the existing flu strains and the natural resistance that develops over time from exposure to those won't have any positive effect."

"What about a vaccine?"

"By the time we could create one, it would be too late for many. And by the time we could go into full production, it would be over."

"Antiviral meds?"

"Limited to no effect. Again, because we're dealing with a specifically crafted variant that was designed to bypass the two major antiviral drugs, as well as any natural immunity. It's the perfect virus, in that sense – indestructible, highly infectious, and as deadly as just about anything I've seen."

"But you could start working on a vaccine now…" Jeffrey tried.

"Of course, but it would take months. And if your brother was under the impression that it was going to be released soon, we don't have time. I've already checked, and there's a large global flu shot program scheduled to start within a week. That's a likely culprit if you're even half right about your HIV dissemination suspicion. Or it could be as simple as releasing it in a number of popular airports. It wouldn't take much. In fact, if a small group of travelers was exposed, or some security workers, as virulent as this is, tens of thousands would be infected and become carriers before anyone knew it. By the time the first ones started dying, we'd be talking millions exposed, at which point it would be too late. Frankly, this is the worst case scenario of the thousands of nightmare possibilities we've ever contemplated."

Both men sat in silence, and then Jeffrey nodded.

"I have a possible solution. A blocking move. But it will require your help."

"Monsieur, at this point, anything you can suggest would be of interest. The alternative is too horrible to consider."

"The basic idea is to short-circuit the plan so it can't be executed."

"How?"

"I have some ideas…"

FORTY-THREE

Exposure

Jeffrey listened as the phone rang and rang, and then Kaycee's voicemail engaged.

"Hi. This is Kaycee. Leave a message, or breathe heavy, or whatever, but keep it interesting…"

The beep sounded more like a warble on his cheap burner phone, and for a moment his heart caught in his throat at the sound of her voice. He didn't stop to think his reaction through, and instead launched into his message.

"Hi, Kaycee. This is the guy you held the shotgun on last week. I need to speak with your grandfather. It's…" – he checked his watch and quickly calculated the time on the east coast – "…seven o'clock in the morning there, I know, so pretty early. I'll try back in an hour. It's very important that I speak with your grandfather. Hope everything's okay on that end."

Jeffrey found himself wanting to say more, but instead he softly pressed the end call key and stared at the phone. He was back at the hotel, in the stairwell on his floor, so that just in case his U.S. cell was picking up sound in the room it couldn't eavesdrop on his call. He'd read online about how the NSA could activate the microphone in a cell phone anywhere in the world without it appearing to be powered on, and he had to expect that those who were behind the virus had the capability to access it at will.

He'd laid out a plan of attack for Bertrand, who had reluctantly agreed that his proposed course of action was likely to be effective. Short of taking out a full-page ad in the *New York Times* laying out the whole scenario, which they both knew would never be printed, they didn't have any alternatives, and they shared his sense of urgency. Bertrand had already begun making calls as Jeffrey walked out the door, and they'd agreed to follow up with each other the next day.

The hour back in his hotel room crawled by like he was being waterboarded, and he practically sprinted for the stairwell at the end of the empty hallway, scanning to confirm that he wasn't being observed.

This time Kaycee answered on the first ring, and Jeffrey realized when she said hello that he was grinning like a punch-drunk buffoon, in spite of the dire circumstances. He hoped that his voice sounded normal when he began speaking.

"Kaycee. It's me. How's everything on that end?"

"Hello, 'me.' Everything's fine. Is this a social call?"

"Wouldn't that be nice? No, I need to talk to your grandfather. How's he doing?"

"Cranky and troublesome as ever. But I manage. Can I tell him what you want to speak with him about?"

Jeffrey had anticipated this first hurdle, and braced himself for the pushback. "It's about what we discussed when I was there. I have more information for him."

Kaycee didn't say anything, and he could hear the line crackling, as if an occasional electron was veering giddily off course and obliterating itself in a sonic blaze.

"Your last discussion left him agitated for days. I had to deal with the fallout. I'm not sure it's such a good idea to do a repeat performance," she said.

Jeffrey was about to try the response he'd rehearsed to her inevitable protest when he heard Sam's voice booming in the background.

"Kaycee? Are you out there?" he called, and then there was a rustling on the line.

"Look, don't take this wrong, but I can't deal with this right now. He's just now back to normal, and I—"

"Kaycee, it's really important. As in life or death."

"Yeah, I've been hearing that since I was a child. I think I'm going to exercise executive privilege here and just say no. Sorry," she said, and hung up.

Jeffrey swore and took several deep breaths. He'd give her a minute to calm down. He could see her perspective – he was just stirring up troubling history for no reason, and she was her grandfather's protector. Ordinarily he would have agreed with her.

But these weren't ordinary circumstances.

He pressed redial and listened. One ring. Two. Then her voice again, this time decidedly frosty, none of the musicality and slight teasing quality of the first call's opening words.

"Kaycee. Just listen, okay? I have information that I need your grandfather's help with – his advice. I'm in Europe, and I've been attacked. This is serious. I'm not making it up."

"Attacked? What are you talking about?"

He told her about the mugging.

"Please, Kaycee, put your grandfather on. You can listen on the speaker if you want. If you think there's anything he shouldn't hear, you can mute it and tell me there's a problem, okay? But there's a lot in the balance and I don't know who else I can turn to," he pleaded.

"What's in the balance, Jeffrey? Try telling me that, and maybe I'll do as you say."

He sucked in breath between his teeth. "I know it sounds crazy and melodramatic, but the entire human race is at stake, Kaycee. No lie. I'm dead serious."

"Have you been drinking? Did you fall and hit your head?" she asked, her voice disbelieving, but also lighter than when she'd answered again.

"I wish. No…I mean, yes, I hit my head, but no, I haven't been drinking. I got a concussion when I was mugged, but that's the least of my worries."

"Tell me what's going on, Jeffrey. No more games," she said, suddenly all business.

"There's a pathogen that's going to be released at any minute. A flu that will kill almost everyone. It's connected to the cattle mutilations. Your grandfather was completely right – that was medical experimentation and a cover-up. But this is the end result. A global reset."

He could hear her on the other end, her breathing faster, and he knew what she was going through. A man she'd only met at gunpoint was talking like a lunatic, making wild-eyed claims that defied belief.

"What do you expect him to do about it, assuming you aren't out of your mind?"

"That's what I need to talk to him about. I need to pick his brain. See if he has any ideas or contacts. Because otherwise, in a matter of no time, we'll all be dead, Kaycee. That's what I'm trying to tell you. So please, put him on."

She paused, and he sensed it could go either way, and then the line clicked. "You're on speaker. My grandfather's right here."

"Professor. Sam. It's Jeffrey. We spoke recently…"

"Yes, Jeffrey. I remember. I may be old, but I'm not senile yet. Or at least not that far gone that I don't remember a week ago. You're the Vietnamese cleaning woman, right?"

Jeffrey was taken aback, and then Sam continued.

"Little joke, there, Jeffrey. Sorry. But if you're not going to torment the young when you get to my age, what are you going to do to pass the time, right?" Sam said, stifling a chuckle.

"I wish I was calling under different circumstances. It's a good news, bad news situation, but mostly really bad news."

"Lay it on me, Jeffrey. I can handle it. Believe me, nothing would surprise me anymore."

"Well, it all starts back with the cattle mutilations…"

Ten minutes later, he finished. Sam and Kaycee were mute with shock. Sam spoke first.

"These people are psychopaths. Textbook cases. Living, breathing monsters."

"I agree. But the question is, do you have any contacts that I could share this story with? The only way I can see this being stopped is if I can get the information into the hands of other governments – governments that would lose everything if the plan moved forward. I've thought it through, and come at it every way, and that's the only hope. Nothing else makes sense. We can't trust the media, and frankly, I don't think the people behind this would care whether the public knows or not, once it's done. What are they going to do – except die, I mean? Besides, who would the public even blame? The government would just deny it and run its propaganda machine to paint it as conspiracy tripe," Jeffrey said.

"I don't have any viable contacts any more, but you should talk to Kaycee," Sam said.

"Kaycee? What are you talking about?"

The tone of the line changed and suddenly Kaycee was back on the phone, now off speaker mode. "I told you I'm a translator. In New York."

"Right. I remember."

"I never told you where I work."

"Maybe now would be a good time."

"I'm a translator at the United Nations."

The words barely settled before Jeffrey's mind was racing again. "But...so you know people?"

"You could say that. I guess the question is what proof you could get me and how soon. I can't promise anything, but my hunch is I could get it into the hands of the Chinese delegation, and maybe a few others. I know one of their translators extremely well. We had drinks together and went dancing just before I came here."

"I could get you an entire analysis from the Pasteur Institute, as well as a characterization of the virus. It would leave nothing to the imagination," Jeffrey said.

"How soon?"

"Probably by midnight tonight. My time. No more than eight hours, tops. They're already working on a report. Top secret, of course, but not to us."

"I'll give you my email." She held the phone away from her mouth as she spoke to her grandfather. "Grampa, I may need to leave for a day and do this in person. Will you be okay without me?" she asked, her words muffled.

After another few minutes of back and forth, parsing logistics, he terminated the call. Kaycee's network would be invaluable, assuming she could get the documents to the right officials. At this point, he had no better alternative, other than Bertrand's contacts in the French government, but he wasn't convinced they would move quickly – bureaucrats tended to duck conflict or anything problematic, so it was more likely that they would drag their feet rather than take immediate action. Fortunately, Bertrand had intimated that he too had back channels, and would be working those, just as Jeffrey was working his.

Now all Jeffrey needed were the documents.

He placed a final call, and Bertrand answered with a terse, "*Oui?*"

Jeffrey gave him Kaycee's email, and told him to send the report from a blind, newly-created account as soon as he could.

Bertrand didn't comment except to say "*Oui*" again, and the line went dead.

Now it was in the Frenchman's hands. The fate of the world.

Hopefully, not too late.

FORTY-FOUR

Cats Out of Bags

"Mr. President."

"Ambassador Sokolenko," the president said, shaking the Russian ambassador's hand, welcoming him into the Oval Office, his chief of staff standing by one of the book cases. "This is most irregular, but I was able to clear a few minutes from my schedule. How can I help you today? Your emissary said this was the highest priority."

"Yes, it is. Time is of the essence, so if I may speak candidly…"

"Of course. Edgar here is fully briefed to the highest levels. You may speak as though you were in your own home," the president said, the offer a hollow one. Every word would be deconstructed after the meeting. That was one of the reasons Edgar was there.

The ambassador removed a file from his briefcase and handed it to Edgar, knowing that the president wouldn't touch it, on the off chance there was a poison or some contaminant on it.

"This is a top secret document from my government. It details a deadly new virus. A laboratory-created virus, which if released, would destroy the majority of human life on the planet. You can read the document and have your experts review it, but in the interests of time, my prime minister has requested that you be prepared to accept a call from him in twenty minutes. That should be enough time for us to discuss the basics of the file."

The president and Edgar looked puzzled.

"I'm afraid I don't understand," the president said.

"This is a virus that was created in a biological weapons laboratory. In the United States."

"Now see here–" Edgar said, but the president cut him off.

"As you are aware, we do no offensive biological weapons development, Ambassador. Only defensive, and that, very limited. We were one of the first signatories of the 1972 Convention."

"Yes. We also signed that agreement. As I recall, there were some regrettable accidents that indicated that the Soviet regime hadn't completely abided by the Convention. As unbelievable as that may seem…"

"I can state categorically that we have not been developing biological warfare weapons," the president said, an edge to his voice.

"That is good news. Because if this virus was released, it would mean the death of billions and billions of people. Including in my country. And yours, Mr. President. It would be genocide."

"Ambassador, you have me at a disadvantage. I really have no idea what you're talking about," the president countered.

"Perhaps you can take several minutes to digest the report. There are fatality estimates on the last page. An epidemiology nightmare."

Edgar was already paging to the final table, and his eyes widened as he took in the graph and the numbers.

"Are…are these estimates correct? No numbers have been transposed?"

"No. Around six billion casualties. Most of those in the first thirty to sixty days."

Edgar approached the president and pointed out the section to him, and he blinked several times as he scrutinized the data.

"Mr. Ambassador, would you give us a moment?" Edgar asked, watching the president's poker face, which revealed nothing.

"Of course. My prime minister will be calling in fifteen minutes. I trust you will accept the call?"

"We'll be back to you shortly, Ambassador. Please, this way," Edgar said, motioning to the doors.

The old Russian stood slowly, clutching his briefcase, and allowed Edgar to show him out.

Edgar returned seconds later. The president didn't wait for him to begin speaking.

"Get Jaspers at the Center for Disease Control on the line, and distribute that report to him immediately. I want to know what he says before the call comes in. God damn it, Edgar. If this is somebody on our side running a covert op, I want them skinned alive. I'm dead serious. This is insanity."

"Sir. Let's not jump to conclusions. This could be a ruse, or they could have misinterpreted the data."

"That's a Pasteur Institute report. I want someone there to verify it's genuine. Do we have anyone that can?"

"I'll check."

"Do that. Also get Morrell on the line, now. This is the kind of shit that has CIA written all over it. If this is their doing, I will single-handedly flatten Langley and put them out of business. And get DOD representatives on the horn as well. I want to understand what the hell is going on here before I talk to the Russian. Do you read me?" the president snapped.

Edgar nodded, already dialing on his encrypted cell phone.

Thirty seconds after a hushed discussion with an aide, who literally ran to scan the documents and send them off to a list that would be forthcoming from Edgar in moments, the president's line rang. He jabbed the phone on and the CIA director's voice boomed over the speaker.

"Mr. President. Edgar indicated we have a situation?"

"That's putting it mildly. The Russian ambassador just handed me a report from the French, detailing a new virus that they're claiming was developed in an American bio-weapons lab."

"That's impossible. There is no such thing."

"I know that, and I know you're telling me that, but in about five minutes you're going to be getting a document that the Russians are saying leads straight to us."

"It's got to be some kind of a head fake. A plant. Some sort of negotiating ploy. What do they want?"

"Their prime minister is calling in…eight minutes. So we'll see. The ambassador didn't articulate any demands. And he didn't seem like his usual self. I don't get the sense they're bluffing on this. He looks like he saw a ghost."

"I'll look for it and get my top people on it. Is there anything else, sir?"

"I want the full court press. And no bullshit, Morrell. No 'need to know.' On this one, I need to know everything."

The president hung up and then looked at Edgar bleakly. "Cancel everything I have planned for today. Now."

"But, sir. We can't behave rashly. It would send signals, and then we'll be inundated with questions from the press…"

"Then cancel the next two hours. Move things around. Something came up. Whatever you need to tell them. But I want the Joint Chiefs convened within the hour, and a full briefing from CDC and CIA. Get the report to everyone. And, Edgar – give me a minute, and then send the ambassador back in."

Edgar nodded and hurried from the room. The president stood and paced in front of his desk. After a half minute of this, he stopped and extracted a tissue from his pocket and blotted a single bead of sweat that had run from his hairline down his left temple. Ordinarily glacially calm, he was anxious. The most powerful man alive, and he was worried.

When the ambassador and Edgar returned, he was back behind his desk.

"You may tell your prime minister that I will accept his call. In the meanwhile, I need some privacy, please," he said, and the Russian nodded before ducking back into the outer office.

The director of the CDC was on the line by the time the door closed behind him, Edgar standing nearby.

The conversation lasted sixty seconds. By the time it was over, the president's complexion was gray. Edgar and he had a hasty murmured discussion, and then the phone rang again. His assistant announced the Russian leader on line two.

The president pushed the blinking button and the call went live.

"Mr. Prime Minister. Your ambassador just presented me with the most remarkable document. I frankly have no idea what to make of it, but I'm having my top experts look it over now," the president began, affecting a neutral tone.

"Yes, please do that. My experts have had the document for half a day. I have verified with the French that it's genuine. A global calamity in the making."

"I agree. But I need to understand more about it before I can comment further."

"Mr. President, we have our differences, but I must inform you that my country is taking this threat most seriously. So seriously that I am calling to put you on notice. I have been instructed to convey to you that we will consider the first sign that this virus has made it into the world an act of war, as though your country had launched its nuclear arsenal. And the moment we hear of this, we will be forced to retaliate."

The president looked at Edgar and then lifted the handset, shutting off the speakerphone.

"Anatoly. Please. Don't be rash. I have no idea what this is all about."

"Perhaps, Mr. President, but I have said what my government has instructed me to say, so you have our official position. The introduction of this virus will be viewed as a hostile act, to be met with the full weight of the Russian strategic response capability. I've looked at the numbers, and most of my country will be dead within weeks of its appearance anyway. This way, you can rest assured that we will all be in the same boat, as the saying goes."

"I...these are impossible allegations. I can assure you that we are not the creators of this...this abomination. There's been some sort of a mistake."

"If there has, then neither of us has anything to worry about. You are now aware of my country's position. I pray for the future of mankind that you are being forthright with me, Mr. President. This is not a negotiable condition. If the virus appears, it is mutually assured destruction."

"This is an error, Anatoly. I urge you to reconsider. There are some things that can't be undone. The damage from creating a confrontation of this magnitude could be permanent. You're going down an extremely dangerous road."

"I am fully aware of the path I am on, Mr. President. It appears that you are the one in need of a map. I hope that you're able to get to the bottom of this, wherever it has come from, because if not, we're all doomed. Read the report, talk to your experts, as I have spoken to mine. You'll soon understand why our reaction is this...severe. I will keep our communications open, but there is no discussion about our reaction to the virus being released. Please be clear on that, Mr. President, with all respect."

When the president terminated the call, the Oval Office was silent. Edgar's cell rang. He answered, then lowered the phone, looking chagrined.

"The Chinese want an immediate meeting. So does the Indian ambassador."

"Damn it, Edgar. Figure out what the hell is going on here, and quick, or there isn't going to be a tomorrow. Tell the ambassadors that I will see them, but buy me an hour, and convene a crisis meeting immediately. I need answers, and I need them yesterday. I just had the leader of the largest nuclear power besides ourselves tell me he was preparing to launch if this virus makes it into the world. They aren't even asking for anything. Just warning us. I don't think that's ever happened before. Not during my lifetime."

"We need to go onto heightened alert, as well, Mr. President. In response to their elevated status."

The president nodded wearily. "I know the drill. Make it so. And get everyone together. I suspect we're about to discover that India and China are also agitated about the same thing. Let's just hope that by the end of the day we don't have the entire world turned against us. Because that's the way it's starting to look. And for something we didn't even do."

Edgar's phone trilled again. "It's the British, sir. The prime minister wants to speak to you in fifteen minutes."

FORTY-FIVE

Damage Control

Thorn was badly shaken from his round-the-clock meetings in Langley, and it was all he could do to manage a quick flight from Washington to New York to see Barker in person in the wee hours of the morning. As the brains behind the virus effort, Barker was the one who would need to understand the catastrophe that had taken place, and it was he who would have to take immediate action. Anything but a complete cancellation of the scheme was a guarantee of nuclear annihilation, and therefore suicide now. A perfect plan had been destroyed; and the worst part was, he wasn't completely sure how.

Barker agreed to see him at his penthouse in Manhattan, and when Thorn arrived at six a.m. he was shown straight in. Thorn looked like he'd been beaten with a board; whereas Barker, in typical fashion, exuded the healthy glow of the mega-rich, their longevity assured by the best attention money could buy, their sleek, toned, and tucked features those of an elite race, elevated beyond the mere mortals who occupied the lowly gutters of the world. Most of the disparity had to do with the fact Thorn hadn't slept in twenty-four hours, and that he'd fortified himself for the pre-dawn flight with a double brandy that was now making its residual presence known. Acid bile threatened to gag him as he sat across from Barker, who was sipping a glass of fresh-squeezed orange juice and munching on pineapple chunks.

"Tell me what the hell happened," he demanded, his voice low, the cook in the small service room off the kitchen and his housekeeper somewhere in the depths of the cavernous penthouse.

"I gave you as much detail as I had over the phone. It's a disaster. Basically, every country we've spoken with, including our allies, is saying the same thing. If this virus is released, we're going to be a glowing crater. Nobody's buying that it's all a big misunderstanding. The report is pretty clear that only a major technological and financial effort could have produced this virus. And frankly, the attached data sheets are sophisticated as anything anyone's found. I don't think we have any choice but to abort."

Barker sighed, then nodded. "How? How did it leak?"

"Obviously the analyst had gotten hold of the data and made arrangements for the Pasteur scientists to analyze it. Even in death, the bastard managed to screw us."

"Are we sure it was him?"

"There's nobody else. Everyone in the group, in the program, you name it, is a hundred and ten percent loyal and trustworthy. Plus, no one of them had nearly all the data. No, this was a concerted effort, which I suppose we should have foreseen. It's probably by the grace of God that we didn't release the virus and then discover, too late, that every country with a nuke would launch in retaliation. Think about it. One more week and it would have been too late to stop this."

"At great expense, I might add. We'll have to destroy any flu vaccines we manufactured that contain the virus. But that's fine. A sunk cost. We'll invent some pretext to delay the flu shots a couple of weeks," Barker said, thinking out loud.

A thought occurred to him, and he stared hard at Thorn. "You look like hell."

"Thanks. I feel like it, too."

"Could the brother have had anything to do with this?"

"No. We've been all over him. No chance."

"You're sure?"

"Positive. But if you like, we can terminate him. Just for good measure."

Barker cleared his throat, pensive. "Do you want some of my miracle coffee? You know how good it is."

"I was hoping you'd offer."

Barker pressed a small button on a wireless intercom on the table and spoke into it. "Two cups of java. You like cream and sugar?"

"Sure. Two sugars. A dollop of cream."

"You heard him. My usual for me." He released the button and gazed out at the Manhattan skyline, breathtaking from his lofty perch.

"Eliminating the brother is closing the barn door, no? Sort of pointless now, I would think."

"I'm just throwing possibilities out there."

"I'd say it's time to concentrate on salvaging what we can, and focus on the future. We have other options. Perhaps not as elegant or quite ready, but still, options. It will take some work to ready them for deployment and the cost will be significant, but those are details. I won't be denied the culmination of a life's work by one setback. Tomorrow's another day." Barker shifted in his seat. "Run interference, ensure any investigation goes nowhere. You know what to do. If there's a congressional hearing that we can't quash, stonewall. The usual. Since nothing actually happened, I don't think we'll need a fall guy this go-round. In fact, you can probably twist the whole thing to the Agency's advantage."

"I'll think of something."

The coffee arrived, and the cook scuttled away after placing a silver serving tray on the table.

"I'm sure you will. Have no fear. This isn't over. It's just an intermission. A temporary glitch. A resilient man bounces back from his lowest low to hit an even higher high. Which we will," Barker said.

Both men sipped their dark roast, marveling as always at the flavor profile, appreciation on both their faces as they contemplated the next inning, and what they would do differently next time.

Jeffrey waited outside the hotel for the taxi that would take him to the Charles de Gaulle airport. Then home, to Washington. Although he realized that nothing he had back there even resembled a home – his brother's condo, a job that was a sham, a relationship that was a lie.

It had been ten days since Bertrand had sent the report to Kaycee, and Jeffrey had spoken with her a dozen times since then as she'd updated him on her progress. She'd succeeded in getting it to the Chinese and the Indians, and the French had slipped it to the Russians and the British. That had been more than a week ago.

Perhaps the most infuriating part had been the uncertainty – not knowing what the outcome would be, day after long day. Then, that morning, Bertrand had called with a piece of auspicious news. He'd heard from his contacts that the flu shot program scheduled for the following week had been postponed due to some process issues that would delay it for a month. Jeffrey wasn't so sure, but Bertrand had assured him it was a win for them, and that the only conclusion they could reach was that enough pressure had been brought to bear so that those intent on destroying most of mankind had terminated their plan. In the meantime, the Frenchman was working round the clock to create an effective vaccine, putting the full weight of the Institute behind the effort.

If Bertrand was correct about the flu shot program being the dissemination mechanism, its delay was the best news Jeffrey had ever had in his life – and he had no reason to doubt the scientist. But a part of Jeffrey felt empty, hollow, like he'd won a pyrrhic victory.

He couldn't account for the sentiment, but it was there, and very real. Perhaps it was because he was done with his new life and hadn't yet decided what was next. Maybe it was his head injury, which had finally stopped hurting six days ago. Or maybe it was that he'd lost everything, and had nothing to hang onto.

Jeffrey had told the firm that he needed more time due to his injury, and the response had been polite but distant, as if they didn't really care what he did. Which was fine by him – he'd hung around in Paris, ostensibly for the doctor, but in reality because he didn't want to go back and face the shambles of his existence. And it had worked – Monica had seemed less and less interested when he called, which had gone from daily, to every couple, and on the last call she'd seemed as uninterested in talking as he. Maybe she'd finally sensed that he wasn't under her spell anymore; or more likely, she'd been told that her assignment sleeping with Jeffrey was over, so there was no more pay in it. Whatever the case, he was almost positive that her phone wouldn't answer when he got back into town, which was fine. At least he had closure there.

Of a kind.

The taxi rolled to the curb and the bellman held the door open for Jeffrey as he climbed into the car, the sky blue as spring arrived in force. A trio of pretty girls bounced provocatively down the street, chatting with each other, laughing, seemingly without a care in the world, and he watched them with a trace of melancholy, then leaned forward and told the driver in a quiet voice to take him to the airport, away from Paris, to a future that was as uncertain his past.

FORTY-SIX

Home

Monica's phone was disconnected when he got around to returning her latest three-day-old message on his answering machine. He wasn't surprised, and realized as he listened to the automated voice that the only thing he felt was relief at not having to go through a protracted act to wind down their relationship.

When he arrived at the condo he was tired from the flight, and he barely stopped at the refrigerator to retrieve a beer before tossing his bag onto the couch and popping the top. He savored the first icy swallows with relish, then set the bottle down and powered on his phone and called into the office to see what messages he had. His secretary had told him that Fairbanks wanted to speak to him as soon as he was able to come in, and he sensed the other shoe getting ready to drop – again, with a sense of relief. The lie he'd been living, the fantasy world that had been created to keep him under wraps, was disintegrating around him, and he was glad. It meant he was no longer of interest, no longer a target. At least, that was his hope.

His client messages had dwindled to nothing, which he interpreted as another sign. The word had gone out from the partners that he wasn't long for their world, or would be out of the office for the duration as he grappled with his injury. He knew the firm would have to be careful about how it proposed that he leave, so that it didn't seem that he was being let go as a result of the mugging, but he didn't really care how they went about it. He wasn't going to challenge them. He just knew that he didn't want to stay in Washington any longer. There was nothing for him there. It was now just a place his brother had lived – too briefly.

Jeffrey glanced at the beer and realized it had somehow emptied itself while he'd been preoccupied, and he belched as his eyes roved around the room, wondering if all the eavesdropping equipment had been removed in his absence. As his eyes came to rest on his brother's Stratocaster sitting on the stand in the corner, he realized it didn't much matter. At that instant, he knew that he would be calling the realtor and selling the condo, probably early the next day. There was no point in delaying the inevitable, and it would be the first step on the path to a new reality.

Jeffrey picked up the guitar, plugged in the amplifier next to it, and strummed a chord. He fiddled with the volume and tone knobs and then tuned it, plucking the harmonics and listening for the slight dissonance. Satisfied that it was close enough, he reached down and grabbed a pick from the green vinyl amp top, and played a few quick riffs, arpeggios that his rusty fingers struggled with at first, but quickly adapted to, like riding a bike. As the speed increased, he broke into "Little Wing," the soulful wail of the guitar a keening lament, a protestation to an unjust universe that robbed the innocent and rewarded the wicked.

Drums and a bass rift, brooding and roiling, accompanied him in his head, and a tear ran down his face as he played, his heart breaking with every note, a silent prayer to his brother, a final eulogy and farewell, repeating in his mind.

Goodbye, Keith. You will be missed. I'm sorry I never had the time. Maybe someday we will, in a better world than this.

The haunting melody reverberated off the condo walls, the tortured notes painting an auditory landscape of love and loss, a spontaneous requiem for the departed – a man that through his final brave actions had managed to save the world from itself, at least for a time.

Two days later, the condo was listed with Jodie, who was already weaving her spell on potential buyers. He'd packed up his personal effects and put most of them back into storage, to be dealt with at some future time when he was more motivated. The discussion with the firm had gone about as he'd expected, where they mutually agreed that things weren't working out as planned, and that he should take the necessary time off to literally set his head straight. The only pang of regret he felt was when he handed the keys to the BMW back, but it was fleeting – there were millions of cars in the world, and he would soon find another one.

In the interim he negotiated a deal with Jakes to take the Taurus for as long as Jeffrey wanted it, a couple of hundred bucks a month for as long as he maintained it, which as far as Jeffrey could tell amounted to cleaning the ashtray out and topping off the oil every few weeks. He took it in to get it detailed, and the staff at the car wash regarded him as though he'd walked in wearing a clown costume. Still, after four hours of attention, at least the pungent stink and sticky feeling to everything had been purged, and it was without regret that he bundled his bags and the Strat into the creaky trunk and rolled into mid-day traffic, eager to be rid of the city once and for all.

When he arrived at the familiar gate the sun was well past the midpoint, and the trees cast long shadows on the grass, which was taller than the last time he'd been there. The car door closed with a clunk, the hinges squeaking in protest, and he locked it before squeezing past the fence post and onto the ruts leading to the house. As he approached the porch, the front door opened and Kaycee appeared, a look of concern on her face, the shotgun clenched in both hands, and then her expression softened to one of astonishment, and if he wasn't imagining things, pleasure.

She came down the wooden steps, taking measured strides toward him as he loped up the rustic drive.

"This is a surprise. What are you doing here?" she called, her brow furrowed, a scrunching that Jeffrey found instantly endearing.

"Your grandfather didn't tell you?"

"My grandfather doesn't tell me anything."

"I called and spoke with him yesterday for a while. On your phone."

"I leave it inside so if he needs to use it, he can."

"Well, he did. We were talking about the virus, the delay in the flu shot program, and we got to discussing other stuff. He wanted to know what I was planning on doing next, and I told him I didn't know – that I didn't have any immediate ideas."

"What about your job?"

"I quit. It wasn't working. I don't want to be a corporate cog, no matter how well paid."

"So the question still stands. What are you doing here?" she asked again.

"Why is it that every time we meet, you're pointing a gun at me?"

"Just lucky, I guess," she said, waiting for an answer.

Sam's voice boomed from the entryway. "Jeffrey! You're here. Come up to the house. Kaycee. You know Jeffrey. You don't need the shotgun."

"We were just discussing that," Jeffrey said with a small smile.

Kaycee sheepishly realized that she was still pointing the gun at Jeffrey. She lowered the weapon and held it easily at her side. "What's this all about, Grandpa?"

"Jeffrey here is going to be staying for a little bit. That's all. Nothing to worry about," Sam explained, and then turned to go back inside before calling over his shoulder. "Kaycee, go unlock the gate so he can pull his car in. It'll be dusk soon, and I'm sure he's tired after being on the road."

She studied Jeffrey's face for any clues, then shook her head. "I've got to get the gate key. I'll meet you down there. I'm sure there's a story behind this."

"It's pretty simple. You have to go back to New York soon. Your grandfather isn't really in any condition to be here alone, at least not until he's fully recovered. And I'm going through a mid-life crisis before I hit thirty. It just seemed like I could use some time out in the woods to figure things out, you know? Pull a Walden. Get away from it all while I decide what I want to be when I grow up. Your grandfather mentioned that he had a spare bedroom that wasn't being used, and that he could use someone to play chess with that he can beat – apparently he's bitter that you're better than him. So anyway, he offered, I accepted, and here I am."

"Just like that."

"Yup."

"I'll get the key, then," she said, then spun and returned to the house, Jeffrey's admiring gaze following her jeans as she made her way up the stairs. He grinned as he exhaled, then moved back down the drive to the waiting car, a new page turned in the adventure that had become his life; no firm plans, only a heavy fatigue that felt older than his tender years, like he'd been endlessly pushing a boulder up a hill.

A blue jay fluttered overhead with a squawk, and Jeffrey looked up, his eyes shielded from the fading glare, watching as the bird soared and then rode a gust of wind to the far side of the field, intent on some fleeting objective. The car sat like a lonely vagrant, dejected at the side of the road, and he decided that it was the perfect vehicle for him, accurately capturing his mood and sense of…apathy.

Then he heard footsteps trotting down the drive behind him, and felt a lightness in his chest at the thought of Kaycee coming to open the gate, admitting him into her home and her family's life. For the first time in years he had no sense of direction, no real purpose, and he decided that while it would take some getting used to, it felt positive, if alien.

For now, he'd take it one day at a time.

Which was, in the end, the only way he could.

FORTY-SEVEN

Happily Ever After

The sun was baking the work area, summer now rapidly approaching, the trees in full leaf, not a cloud in the sky. Jeffrey had settled into a familiar routine after three months, running errands in the morning, sitting with the professor in the afternoons, playing chess and discussing the wicked ways of the world. Sam had mended and was as strong as could be expected, but he hadn't mentioned anything about Jeffrey moving on, and neither had Jeffrey. Sam seemed to enjoy the younger man's company, and Jeffrey found him a fascinating and erudite companion – a treasure trove of encyclopedic arcania.

True to her word, Jodie had sold the condo in no time, and after paying her commission Jeffrey had wound up with two hundred fifty thousand dollars in his pocket. The estate had settled and he'd liquidated his brother's portfolio, so he now had a tidy half million dollar war chest to tide him over until he figured out what he wanted to do. That part of his sabbatical from the real world had been tougher than he'd thought it would be, and it had only been lately that an idea had begun to gel for his life moving forward.

Living at the house had been an adjustment at first, with no internet or television. Jeffrey had finally convinced Sam to get a phone, and had only shamed him into it by offering to pay for it himself. His offers of rent had been rebuked by the old man, who merely grunted and waved him away when discussions of anything resembling finances came up.

"I never paid much attention to money when I was younger, and I'm not about to start worrying about it now," was Sam's usual response, and Jeffrey had eventually learned not to bother him with it, choosing instead to buy the week's groceries and consistently forget to take the money that rested, like a green stain, on the dining room table. Sam had given up insisting, and they'd reached an uneasy truce, preferring to spend their time in more productive pursuits than bickering over a few dollars.

Besides chess, both men enjoyed a glass of good Scotch in the evenings, and without distractions like computers or TV, they whiled away the hours after dark arguing or trading stories. Sam had learned the hard way about Jeffrey's remarkable memory, and they spent long nights discussing the ramifications of a society that was out of control, where special interests and powerful elites could bring the world as close to the brink as it had so recently been. The fatalistic conclusion they arrived at, time after time, was that they as a species were largely powerless to do anything about it, and that they were on as disastrous a course as if a huge meteor was hurtling toward the Earth — that the inevitable was a matter of timing, not of outcome.

In spite of the depressing talk, Sam was upbeat since he'd learned the truth about his conspiracy suspicions, and the vindication of having been right breathed new life into him, if not new purpose. Jeffrey had even coaxed him into moderate exercise, which he'd eschewed for years before the accident.

Jeffrey was outside, swinging an axe, splitting wood for the fireplace, sweat rolling down his tanned, bare chest, the muscles in his arms now more defined than ever before, the outdoor life agreeing with him. He heard gravel crunching beneath tires down around the bend, and he paused, ears straining for any further signs of visitors. A muffled car door closed, and he moved over to the side of the garage and retrieved the shotgun. Sam insisted that he take it with him whenever he was outside, and Jeffrey had seen enough of the world to take his warning seriously. There probably was no danger any longer, but it was better to be safe...

Kaycee moved into view, her long legs making short work of the track, her thicket of blond locks shimmering like a halo. Jeffrey drew a sharp intake of breath at the sight of her — she'd visited on a few weekends, but it had been a month since her last trip and her sudden appearance took him by surprise. He was constantly unbalanced by the powerful reaction she caused in him, and he always felt self-conscious around her, even though he did his best not to show it. Suddenly aware of his bare chest, he untied the flannel shirt from around his waist and pulled it on as she drew near.

"Howdy, stranger," she said, in an exaggerated drawl.

"Is that your Australian accent? It's very convincing."

251

"Thanks. Nice to see I can impress you."

"That's never been a problem," Jeffrey said easily, and they both smiled. "What are you doing here? Is it the weekend already?"

"What, it has to be the weekend for me to come see my two favorite bachelors?"

Jeffrey noted that her teeth were even whiter than he remembered, and her eyes more captivating. It might have been the angle of the sun, he reasoned, or her tan…

"No. Of course not. It's…it's just nice to see you again. I mean, it's good that you made it up," Jeffrey said, kicking himself for his fumbling words. *Good that you made it up? Really, counselor? That's the best you can do?*

"Do you have the gate key? I want to pull my car in. And I could use a hand with my bags."

"Sure. In my pocket." He patted his jeans.

"Where's Grandpa?"

"Inside. Reading. I bought him a Kindle. He refused to use it for a week, and now I swear he's burning the screen out."

"That was sweet of you." Another beaming smile from her, and a small part of his core quivered.

"Can't believe everything you hear about lawyers. I mean, you can, but not this one."

"I keep forgetting you're an attorney. I keep thinking of you as a ranch hand or something."

"Sounds like way too honest work for me."

They made their way down towards her car, and he saw as he neared that the back seat was filled with bags and boxes.

"Bringing supplies?" he asked.

"No, I moved out. Quit my job."

"Really? I thought you loved it."

"I do. But I can do freelance work and make a good living without the pressure and the rat race. Plus, the whole virus thing got me thinking about what's important. And I realize that my granddad's not getting any younger, and my priority should be to maximize my time with him while he's still here. There are no guarantees, and every moment is precious…"

"So you're moving back in?" Jeffrey said, trying to keep the delight out of his voice.

"If he'll have me. I can help you with him. Assuming you're sticking around for a while. To chop wood and all." Her eyes seemed to dance with amusement at his expression.

"I probably will be, at least through the summer."

"Have you decided what you're going to do? What you're going to be when you grow up?" she asked, rounding her fender and opening her car door.

"I'm toying with the idea of hanging out a shingle in town. Do wills, contracts, that kind of thing. I'm starting to like the rural lifestyle after having grown up a city boy."

"Why, Jeffrey Rutherford! Country attorney? Will you wear overalls and a straw hat?"

"When I wear anything at all."

She popped the lock on the passenger door and rolled down the window. "Hop in, Hoss."

"Yes, ma'am," Jeffrey said, and for a second the tableau froze in his mind, the soft tall grass rippling from a light breeze, Kaycee sitting behind the wheel of her car looking like every fantasy he'd ever had, moving back into the house, where they would be together day and night, only a slim slab of wall between them at night…

For a brief eternity, the ugly reality of a world gone mad receded, and there was only the two of them, the sun warming her toned skin as their eyes met, and she grinned.

And life was good.

Epilogue

Two figures moved out of the level four biosafety laboratory towards the showers and UV light room, their baby-blue ILC Dover Chemturion positive pressure suits rustling as they moved, looking more like astronauts in a science fiction film than research scientists working in one of the only privately owned level four laboratories in the country. The multiple airlocks were electronically controlled, designed to prevent accidental contamination from the lab into the outer world, and the safety procedures to enter and leave were redundant and stringent.

Part of a larger complex in Virginia on the grounds of a major military contractor's facility, the series of reinforced concrete chambers had been built two decades earlier, and were constantly updated with state-of-the-art technology. No expense had been spared in outfitting the secret laboratory, whose personnel were all assigned top security clearances and employed by the Department of Defense, paid out of a dark pool of deniable funds that were administered in conjunction with the CIA.

It was the end of another long day, and the pair had put in seven hours working with pathogens that were being synthetically modified to be resistant to existing antiviral agents. That their work was illegal under international law didn't bother them a bit – they were both old hands, and had long ago lost any moral qualms about doing their jobs.

The lights in the laboratory extinguished once they were in the first containment chambers, where the tedious routine of multiple showers and airlocks were familiar precautions. As they stood in their respective rooms, the glow of dim LED lighting emanated from behind a locked steel door at the far end of the lab, past the row of Class III biological safety cabinets, where the most dangerous of the pathogens were kept – technology that had been perfected in the seventies after furious development activity in the sixties.

Inside the temperature- and humidity-controlled chamber, which had its own airlock entry, sat a row of vials in lab trays, the small canisters surprisingly innocuous, offering no hint of the destructive capacity of the agent stored inside – an agent that had been refined and modified to ravage the immune system in a matter of days, its infective capacity at the extreme end of the spectrum, a virus that had already proved devastating in its first-generation form and was now far more deadly and contagious in its latest iteration.

A tag labeled the tray as well as the tubes, laser-printed in black on a stark white plastic background. Row after row of deadly cargo, waiting, the modifications finally complete, the clandestine testing in the Congo at an end, the corpses burned, the data accumulated and tallied, the limited outbreaks carefully orchestrated and contained before they could go full-blown. And of course, a limited quantity of antidote that would be distributed to the ruling elite safely stored in another facility, ensuring the best minds were spared the ravaging that would destroy civilization, enabling them to create a new, improved order, having learned the lessons of uncontrolled population growth and unrestricted freedom.

In the artificial glow, the script looked like an ancient Roman curse, the innocent combination of letters barely hinting at the nightmare that rested inside, indestructible: a real-life portal to the underworld, the biological equivalent of an eternity in hell. One of the two scientists had just finished painstakingly affixing the decals after creating two dozen with the same name embossed in tiny letters, the name of the pathogen clearly legible through the double-paned glass window in the cool greenish light: *EBOV*.

To be alerted to new releases, sign up here:

RussellBlake.com/contact/mailing-list

Afterword

Upon a Pale Horse is a work of fiction, and the depictions in it are fictitious. There are, however, sections that are based on scientific fact, much of which goes unreported in the U.S. press. Contrary to perception, where science and medicine are the stewards of empirical truth, the reality is that both are fraught with bias, favoring the interests of money, power, and secrecy, and those at the top of the power pyramid in any of the disciplines determine what lines of inquiry are acceptable, and which are effectively taboo. AIDS research is no different, and the fact that so many of the most influential authorities have clear ties to the military-industrial complex has no doubt colored the dialogue, as well as which "facts" are reported as gospel by a credulous media and which are dismissed out of hand, often in favor of theories that have no basis in reality.

What follows is a list of data that was gathered as part of my research for this novel – information that should give any thinking person pause and sponsor further inquiry and, hopefully, a long-overdue public discourse on the possibility of the man-made origins of HIV, be it from accidental vaccine contamination due to preparation of the original vaccines in diseased chimps, or a more damaging hypothesis involving deliberate contamination.

1) HIV occurs in several strains – M, N, and O. M is the most common, and is further divided into eight subtypes. Of these eight, subtype B is the most common subtype in North American and European cases, whereas subtypes A, D, and C are found in Africa and Asia.

2) The subtypes found in Africa are different from the one found in North America. This should raise an obvious question: How could the view that HIV originated in Africa and was brought to America withstand any serious inquiry, when they are completely different subtypes? Would it not be logical that if they were from the same place, they would be the same subtype? If not, why not?

3) AIDS in the U.S. still disproportionately affects gay men and IV drug users. Yet it remains primarily a heterosexual disease in Africa.

4) According to Max Essex, a leading AIDS researcher, HIV subtype B, the predominant strain in the U.S., has a particular affinity for rectal tissue. Subtypes A, D, and C have an affinity for vaginal tissue. See: http://www.avert.org/hiv-types.htm

5) This affinity for different tissue types likely accounts for why AIDS, after thirty years in the U.S., is still not a primarily heterosexually transmitted disease, while in Africa it is.

6) The ability to target specific cell/tissue types has long been a feature of biological weapons research. See:
http://en.wikipedia.org/wiki/Ethnic_bioweapon

7) The AIDS epidemic did not originate in Africa, but was first recognized in 1981 in the U.S. The first few cases of AIDS appeared in Manhattan and were reported to the Center for Disease Control in Atlanta in 1979. The African AIDS epidemic hadn't begun until 1982 *at the earliest*, according to HIV discoverer Luc Montagnier in his book, *Virus*.

A few health professionals have linked the hepatitis B vaccine trials, conducted at the New York Blood Center beginning in the fall of 1978, with the outbreak of AIDS in that city. The experiment used young, healthy, gay and bisexual men in the experiment. For details on these experiments, Google "gay vaccine experiments and the origin of AIDS."

When blood donated by gay men at the New York Blood Center was retrospectively tested for HIV in the mid-1980s, HIV was not present in any of the specimens from 1977 or earlier. HIV was found in 6% of blood samples taken in 1978. By 1979, 30% of blood samples from trial participants tested positive for HIV – an unprecedented infection rate, especially at a time in which the epidemic was unrecognized and at a time when AIDS was unknown in Africa.

8) KSHV (Kaposi's sarcoma-associated Herpesvirus), a close relative to a simian virus that causes cancer in apes (Herpesvirus saimiri), has been identified as the cause of Kaposi's sarcoma in North American AIDS victims. This cancer-causing human virus also spontaneously appeared in 1978 in the New York gay community when HIV did. So not one, but *two* simian viruses "jumped species" at the same time, apparently affecting only homosexual men in New York, followed closely by their brethren in L.A., S.F., Chicago, etc. http://rense.com/general45/cant.htm

9) The New York Blood Center created a chimp virus lab in West Africa in 1974. This lab, VILAB II, was established in Liberia to develop the hepatitis B vaccine in simians. In 1978, this vaccine was injected into gay men at the NY Blood Center in the hepatitis B vaccine trials.

10) Studies conducted during the 1980s and 1990s, analyzing adults infected by HIV, demonstrated responses between 33% and 56% to

recombinant vaccines like the hepatitis B vaccine. The hepatitis B trial saw 96+% demonstrated response, leading me to conclude that HIV could not have been present in the cohort group prior to inoculation.   http://www.jped.com.br/conteudo/06-82-S55/ing_print.htm

11) Here is an excellent summary of the various theories for the origin of the AIDS epidemic in the U.S. and Africa. Of particular note are the unanswered questions in the "official" theory – #1 of the six postulated. I find #5 to be the most plausible, although it is, by definition, unpopular with the scientists who make up the power elite in the U.S. for obvious reasons. #6 also warrants further exploration, given the host of inconsistencies in the official AIDS explanation.
http://www.kckcc.edu/ejournal/archives/october2010/article/The MysteriousOriginofHumanImmunodeficiencyVirus.aspx

12) The U.S. military conducted thousands of radiation experiments on U.S. citizens for a period of over 60 years, without informed consent. This was kept classified until it was revealed in 1993. See: http://www.amazon.com/The-Plutonium-Files-Experiments-ebook/dp/B0046A9JC0   and http://www.counterpunch.org/2013/04/12/inhuman-radiation-experiments/#_cdnrcf1

13) The Tuskegee syphilis trial is well-documented historical fact. For more   information,   see: http://en.wikipedia.org/wiki/Tuskegee_syphilis_experiment

14) Likewise, the Guatemalan venereal disease experimentation is documented fact. Particularly troubling is that this experimentation took place at the same time the Nuremburg trials were in process for Nazi doctors doing experimentation without informed consent. See:

http://en.wikipedia.org/wiki/Syphilis_experiments_in_Guatemala

Skepticism is always the first line of defense against deception in its many forms. I encourage everyone to do their own research using these links as a starting point, and discover the hard facts rather than blindly accepting the spin that has been created to advance a palatable worldview.

Books by Russell Blake

Co-authored with Clive Cussler

THE EYE OF HEAVEN

Thrillers by Russell Blake

FATAL EXCHANGE

THE GERONIMO BREACH

ZERO SUM

THE DELPHI CHRONICLE TRILOGY

THE VOYNICH CYPHER

SILVER JUSTICE

UPON A PALE HORSE

The Assassin Series by Russell Blake

KING OF SWORDS

NIGHT OF THE ASSASSIN

RETURN OF THE ASSASSIN

REVENGE OF THE ASSASSIN

BLOOD OF THE ASSASSIN

The JET Series by Russell Blake

JET

JET II – BETRAYAL

JET III – VENGEANCE

JET IV – RECKONING

JET V – LEGACY

JET VI – JUSTICE

JET VII – SANCTUARY

JET – OPS FILES (PREQUEL)

The BLACK Series by Russell Blake

BLACK

BLACK IS BACK

BLACK IS THE NEW BLACK

BLACK TO REALITY

Non Fiction by Russell Blake

AN ANGEL WITH FUR

HOW TO SELL A GAZILLION EBOOKS

(while drunk, high or incarcerated)

About the Author

A *Wall Street Journal* and *The Times* featured author, Russell Blake lives full time on the Pacific coast of Mexico. He is the acclaimed author of many thrillers, including the Assassin series, the JET series, and the BLACK series. He has also co-authored *The Eye of Heaven* with Clive Cussler for Penguin Books.

Non-fiction novels include the international bestseller *An Angel With Fur* (animal biography) and *How To Sell A Gazillion eBooks (while drunk, high or incarcerated)* – a joyfully vicious parody of all things writing and self-publishing related.

"Capt." Russell enjoys writing, fishing, playing with his dogs, collecting and sampling tequila, and waging an ongoing battle against world domination by clowns.

Sign up for e-mail updates about new Russell Blake releases:

RussellBlake.com/contact/mailing-list

Made in the USA
Columbia, SC
06 July 2024

38199554R00159